Dr Catherine Gavin is one of our most distinguished (and successful) novelists. Born in Aberdeen (and with a First from the University there), she went on into academic life, politics and journalism. In 1944, after the Liberation of Paris, she was sent with eight other women journalists to be tested as war correspondents. Dr Gavin was the only one chosen to be accredited to Supreme Headquarters, Allied Expeditionary Force, and for the next nine months alternated between combat reporting and covering the complex political situation in Paris. She was present at the German surrender at Rheims in May 1945, and was later decorated with the 1939–45 Star and the France and Germany Star. Her experiences at the front intensified her knowledge of war, so convincingly displayed in *A Light Woman*.

Dr Gavin joined the foreign staff of the *Daily Express* after the war, reporting from the Middle East and Paris, where she was married to John Ashcraft in 1948. She also spent two years on *Time* magazine and lectured extensively in America on European politics. Her full-time writing career began in 1955 with an analysis of postwar French politics, *Liberated France*, which was followed by her first historical novel, *Madeleine*, in 1957. She now lives with her husband in California.

By the same author

Fiction

The Sunset Dream

The French Resistance

Traitor's Gate
None Dare Call it Treason
How Sleep the Brave

World War One

The Devil in Harbour
The Snow Mountain
Give Me the Daggers
The House of War

The Second Empire Quartet

The Fortress
The Moon into Blood
The Cactus and the Crown
Madeleine

Biography and Politics

Liberated France
Edward the Seventh
Britain and France
Louis Philippe

CATHERINE GAVIN

A Light Woman

This edition published 1994 by
Diamond Books
77—85 Fulham Palace Road
Hammersmith, London W6 8JB

Published by Grafton Books 1987

First published in Great Britain by
Grafton Books 1986

Printed and bound in Great Britain

Set in Times

To Mary Malcolm

On Saturday morning it seemed as if spring had come again to Paris.

Elisabeth Mercier, a girl known to the artists' fraternity of Montmartre as Babette, smiled as she heard the song of the blackbirds through her open window. The place where she lived was called the Old Farm, new in the seventeenth century, with its barns and stables replaced by a concierge's *loge* and kitchen, and two empty artists' studios on the floor above. Babette's window gave her a northward view over the neglected garden leading to a shuttered house, beside which a vineyard sloped down to the Rue St Vincent.

Her garret contained locked trunks belonging to the landlord, an iron bed and a washstand. The one solid piece of furniture was a mahogany table holding trinkets, toilet articles, a little box of paints and a sketching block. A lustre-ware jug held early daffodils from the garden, and against the jug was propped a letter which had sent Babette running upstairs to take her best dress from a peg behind the door. The letter had changed her day and her

1

mood. Though the war was lost, the Siege of Paris was over, and good times might come again. Babette was humming a tune as she tweaked the artificial flowers under the brim of her bonnet into shape and tied the silk strings in a jaunty bow.

The wall mirror, which showed only her head and shoulders, also showed that the bright flowers above the brown eyes and darker brown chignon were a cruel contrast to cheeks whitened by the near starvation of the Siege. She opened a tin box and took out a hare's foot covered with rouge, a pot of lip salve and a box of pearl powder. The cosmetics hid the ravages of hunger at the price of making Babette look older than her nineteen years, and easy to mistake for a woman of the town.

Madame Verlet, the concierge, who gave the girl food in exchange for help with the housework, was waiting for her at the foot of the stairs.

"Where are you going to, all dressed up?" she asked.

"Out to lunch, and you'll never guess where! Here, read this!" Babette produced the letter from a big wool bag, embroidered by herself with lilies and roses.

"You know I can't read a thing without my glasses What does it say?"

Babette began with a flourish.

" 'Rue des Rosiers, March eleventh, 1871

'Dear Babette, Will you come to lunch in the studio at noon today? David Meade will be there, and he has a fine surprise for you. Sincerely, Edward Carey.' "

"Well!" said Madame Verlet. "How did that get here?"

"A street kid brought it while I was sweeping out the big gate."

"And you're going?"

Before the war that would have been taken for granted. A studio lunch, with wine and laughter and artists' gossip, was the breath of life to a pretty girl who was one of the *grenouilles*, the 'little frogs' who hopped cheerfully from one studio to another, always good company as friends or lovers. Some were models and earned professional fees. Others, if required, would offer a slender wrist, an ankle or a bared breast, to an artist working on the layout of a new picture, and were paid accordingly. They all expected a few sous, or a meal, for such routine tasks as cleaning palettes and paintbrushes or stretching canvases. But the studios had emptied since the painters were called up to fight the Prussians, and "I thought you'd quarrelled with Monsieur Meade," said Madame Verlet.

"We had a nasty little argument on the night of the armistice," said Babette. "Perhaps he wants to kiss and make up."

"And the Englishman? How will you feel about seeing him in Marc Vallon's studio?"

"Perhaps there'll be some news of him."

You poor child, thought the concierge as Babette slipped out by the side door, that's what you hope will be the fine surprise. News of Marc Vallon, who said he loved her, and who had been missing since the end of the war, when the defeated Army of the East was interned in Switzerland.

Babette hurried up the Rue St Jean. It was beginning to look like its Saturday self again, with street vendors, children playing round the knife and scissors grinder, and women gossiping at the fountain. She was resolutely cheerful as she went along the top of the Butte Montmartre, which with its horsepond, windmills and vineyards was more like a village than a part of Paris. But her courage failed when she came out on the Champ

Polonais, and saw over a hundred cannon foolishly abandoned in the artillery parks of the capital by the so-called Government of National Defence, and dragged up the one main road leading to Montmartre by the National Guard. The Guard, enlisted at the beginning of the war with Prussia, had not distinguished itself in the defence of Paris, and during the Siege had been responsible for violence within the Gates. After the French surrender, a newly elected government in session at Bordeaux, with a conservative majority and Adolphe Thiers as Chief Executive, roused the ire of the National Guard by ratifying the calamitous terms of peace dictated by the German Chancellor, Otto von Bismarck. Hence the seizure of the cannon on 28 February; hence, two weeks later, Babette's foreboding as she saw the muzzles of the great guns trained on Paris, shimmering under the golden veil of spring.

The two men waiting for her in the Rue des Rosiers had little in common except their neutrality and their affection for Marc Vallon, whose studio Carey had sublet when the Frenchman was called up on the outbreak of war. They were both good-looking, Carey, fair and well-built: Meade taller, lankier, and at thirty beginning to grow grey. They were not unduly marked by the privations of the Siege. They had eaten some anonymous animals, but had not been reduced to a diet of rats.

David Meade was an attaché at the American Legation, and on arrival had been accommodated, as a single man, with a room in the Legation itself. This let him in for a good many spells of night duty, but before Napoleon III went to war with Prussia the night man had few problems except the stomach upsets and stolen wallets of imprudent American visitors to the City of Light. His horizons had been enlarged after the defeat at Sedan by the upset of the balance of power in Europe, and like a few men in

Washington he was beginning to look beyond the new German Empire to its possible effect on the old and more mysterious empire of Russia. He never discussed such things with Carey, and now they were making conversation about their chance meeting the day before, when goodbyes were being said to the British newspapermen who had scooped the world on combat and Siege reporting and were about to return to London. Meade revealed his real interest when he said abruptly:

"You're taking it for granted Babette'll turn up, I suppose?"

"I told her you'd have a surprise for her, she won't resist that. And did you ever know a *grenouille* refuse an invitation to a party?"

It was a characteristically petulant remark. Ned Carey had come to study art in Paris at his wealthy father's expense in the last brilliant spring of the Second Empire. He had introductions to the British Ambassador from notables in Manchester which he hoped would give him the entrée to the best of French society. He received one invitation to a bachelor dinner from Richard Wallace, a wealthy member of the British community, and the ambassador, Lord Lyons, presented him at an imperial levée. He made his bow to Napoleon III and his beautiful Empress Eugénie at the last ball given at the Tuileries before the gas lamps of the Second Empire faded and the music stopped. To Carey it seemed as if war had been declared to spite him.

"I hate that word *grenouille*. It doesn't suit a sweet kid like Babette," said Meade.

"Babette can be a pretty cheeky kid sometimes."

"That's how she was last time we met."

"When was that?"

"The night the Reds dragged the cannon up to Montmartre, when I bumped into her in the Brasserie des

Martyrs. She was with a rough bunch, all carrying on as if they were celebrating a French triumph, and as an American I wasn't popular with any of them. Babette told me it was disgraceful that the Stars and Stripes was still flying over the Prussian Embassy in the Rue de Lille."

"You explained it was because the United States was the Protecting Power for the whole North German Confederation?"

"Try explaining a point of law to an angry woman! I did worse. I reminded her of how grateful she was when Vallon was cared for so well at the American Ambulance after the defeat at Wörth."

"The American doctors probably saved his life."

"Maybe, but it was a rotten thing to say to the kid. The doctors only patched Vallon up to be ordered back to the front with Bourbaki's Army. Now God knows whether he's in Heaven or interned in Switzerland."

"Jolly decent of you to plan a treat for her after a row like that."

"You know how the French were: the surrender drove them nearly out of their minds, and the Swiss deal was the last straw. Then Babette's had all that extra worry about her sister."

"What's the trouble with the sister? Françoise, is that her name?"

"Fanny Leblanc. Her second child was born in January, three months too soon. The correspondents made a lot out of the starving old folks, Ned, but the Siege took the worst toll of mothers and babies, more's the pity."

"Don't I know it." Both men were silent, thinking of the suffering each had witnessed during the terrible winter. Then Meade went on:

"Babette needs help, she's very young to be all on her own."

"I thought she lived with an aunt, or something."

6

"Madame Verlet's the concierge at the Old Farm. The Mercier girls call her Tante Lise because she was their mother's friend, but she's no relation." He hesitated. "I'm rather sorry you promised her a surprise, because she may fancy it means Vallon's back in Paris."

"Why didn't you write to her yourself, then, with a better choice of words?"

"There wasn't time. I didn't know for sure I could get hold of enough food when I saw you yesterday, until I went out to Versailles with Mr Hoffmann."

Carey jumped at the change of subject. His sympathy for the plight of the French was genuine but abstract; he had no more interest in a little *grenouille* than in one of his father's mill-girls.

"Is it definite then? Is the Legation really leaving Paris?"

"That depends on Monsieur Thiers. As soon as he announced that the Assembly would quit Bordeaux, and reconvene in Versailles on the twentieth, the word came from Washington that Minister Washburne was to stay close to the new Chief Executive."

"I bet you old Washburne's not pleased," said Carey maliciously. "He laid it on pretty thick about how he and his staff never left Paris, while the cowardly Britishers legged it to Bordeaux."

"Bordeaux is over five hundred kilometres from Paris, and Versailles isn't much more than twenty. Mr Washburne isn't going to leave his residence, only move his office."

"He should advise Mr Thiers to close that twenty kilometre gap, and govern France from Paris."

They eyed each other with latent hostility. There were only a few years between the two men, but there was also the breadth of the Atlantic. David Meade, who had fought for the South in the American Civil War, was the senior in experience and also in artistic talent. Sketching was his hobby, and he and Carey had first met in the evening Life Class held at the Atelier Dupuy in Montmartre. Friends by chance rather than by choice, they got into the habit, after class, of strolling down the boulevard for a late drink at the Café Guerbois. In that haunt of artists they met Marc Vallon, who had forfeited a Beaux Arts Scholarship to join the Independents, and he in turn introduced them to Frédéric Bazille, one of the youngest and most charming of the group. Before the war there had been hours of good talk at the Café Guerbois, which Carey with his schoolboy French had tried his best to follow.

Meade, the diplomat, changed the subject again.

"How are you getting on with the Serpent of Old Nile?" he asked.

Vallon's English easel held a vast unfinished canvas, a Number 120, on which Carey had been struggling to depict the meeting of Antony and Cleopatra in a cloud of earth colours and chiaroscuro, the lovers being awkwardly separated by the head of the Roman's charger. When cheeky Babette first saw it she said the animal reminded her of one of the gilded plaster heads which butchers hung above their doors to show they had horseflesh for sale.

"I couldn't settle to serious painting after I began working on the British Charitable Fund with Mr Wallace," said Carey defensively. "My God, how I envy you your facility, David." He knew he must say more, and it came out in a burst of suppressed envy. "I didn't congratulate you half enough on those great sketches you showed us yesterday. Are they all going to be published in America?"

"No, not the victory parade sketches. They're on their way to the *Daily News* in London right now, our friend Labouchere was going to take them over to his editor last night. I was only able to do two Palace of Versailles ones; the Crown Prince and Bismarck at the foundation of the

8

German Empire, and the proclamation of Kaiser Wilhelm as Emperor in the Hall of Mirrors. They've both been bought by *Harper's Weekly* in New York."

"Well, congratulations again," said Carey. "It looks as if you'd found your market. Maybe you're at the start of a whole new career."

"Just a lucky break," said Meade modestly. "After all the strings my tough old Northern grandmamma pulled to get an unreconstructed rebel into the foreign service, I reckon I'd be smart to hold on to the job that pays me a regular salary." He looked at his watch. "I hope mademoiselle isn't going to play the fine lady, and be late. I missed dinner last night, and I bet you're hungry too."

They were all hungry, all the time. Carey stripped off his overcoat and Meade followed his example as if they were going to fight their way to food, while they looked out of the window at the Rue des Rosiers. The studio was on the third floor of a building one storey higher than its neighbours. That part of the Street of the Rosetrees lived up to its name, for the pretty cottages and villas looked more like the follies of prosperous Parisians than the homes of the children of Bohemia. The two foreigners could look down into the grounds of number six, which had belonged to the playwright Scribe and was now a command post of the National Guard.

Ten or a dozen men were hanging about the courtyard, where their rifles were stacked untidily, while three others were sprawling on the steps of the villa, passing a litre of wine from hand to hand. When off duty from guarding the cannon, drinking and smoking were their chief afternoon occupations. After dark they attended meetings of the Red Clubs which had sprung up for propaganda purposes all over the city, or held impromptu concerts of revolutionary song. The two most soldierly in appearance were outside the gate, with tunics buttoned and képis straight, on sentry duty beneath a large red flag.

"What a crew!" said Edward Carey. "That fellow with the ginger beard has stopped me three times and asked to see my papers, though he knows quite well who I am. They think every foreigner's a spy. I suppose they've got to find a scapegoat for what happened to France."

"If that were all," said Meade, "but I'm afraid there's worse to come." He stubbed out his cigarette. "Bad luck — here comes Babette. She's going to walk right into them."

The girl, in a black cloak made for a taller woman, tried to avoid confrontation by crossing the street before she reached 6, Rue des Rosiers. The sentries, seeing a pretty rouged face and a reddened mouth, shouted a lewd invitation as she went by. Babette flung back an insult which made the Guardsmen shout with laughter, and Carey at the window grinned.

"Like a kitten swearing! Come on, David, and let her in."

Babette ran lightly upstairs and on the landing, after a moment's hesitation, held up her face to be kissed. Carey merely touched his lips to her cheek, but the American, after a warm embrace, led her into the studio with his arm round her waist. He saw her eager look at the empty room, the doors open on the empty bedroom and kitchen, and caught her quick breath of disappointment. She hoped Vallon would be here, he thought, the fine surprise. He pointed at the table at the far end of the studio and said too cheerfully, "Well, Babette! What d'you think of that?"

"Oh, Meade, I don't believe it!" she gasped. "I haven't seen so much food for months!"

Part of the heavy oak table was covered with a green baize cloth on which sketching blocks lay next to a japanned box containing two trays of the expensive tubes of Winsor and Newton paints which Carey had brought from Manchester. Coarse white linen on the other part was covered with platters holding a cold roast chicken, a glazed Virginia ham sprinkled with golden breadcrumbs, a cartwheel of Brie cheese and a huge apple tart. Two *baguettes* of crusty bread and an oblong of Isigny butter completed the feast.

"And that's only half the surprise," said Carey. "There's another chicken and a lot of stuff like Liebig's meat extract and cocoa for your sister."

"Oh, my dears, that's just what she needs," said Babette. "You're angels to think of her. She's been so wretchedly unwell since she lost the poor little baby."

"But you look blooming" said Carey insincerely. "Sit down and let's all have a glass of porto."

"Let's have a good look at Babette first," said Meade. He had taken the outsize wrap off her shoulders and untied her bonnet strings when she came in; now he was holding both her hands as he leaned over her chair. Above her close-fitting dress of grey merino Babette wore a garibaldi, a feminine version of the red shirt back in fashion since the hero of Italian independence, General Giuseppe Garibaldi, came to France to join the fight against Prussia. Meade saw the thin cheeks beneath the rouge and the lifeless brown of the once shining hair, and wondered how the child, who had lived through the Siege, would survive what he was certain were evil days to come. She said with a laugh, "How you stare! I can't have changed that much in such a short time, surely?" And lowering her voice while Carey was busy with the porto and the glasses, she added, "I'm sorry for the things I said that night at the Brasserie."

"I'm sorry too," said Meade. "Let's forget about it, shall we?"

So it was to be kiss and make up, as Babette had hoped.

But Meade had something more to say, and he decided to say it bluntly. He asked if she had any word of Marc Vallon.

"I was hoping *you* might have news from Switzerland," she said in a small voice. "You used to get all the foreign newspapers at your Legation."

"We still do, but the Swiss don't publish casualty lists." How can they, was the only possible answer to that. None of the Paris newspapers, even if not given up to political diatribes (which they were) could have published the name, rank and serial number of eighty-eight thousand Frenchmen who had thrown themselves on the mercy of the Swiss, driven like chaff before the wind by the Prussian troops of General Manteuffel.

"But your troops are comfortably interned in Switzerland," said Carey, passing the porto glasses, "a deuced sight better than being prisoners of war in Germany. Drink up, Babette! You'll see, Marc'll be repatriated some day soon, and start painting a masterpiece!"

"You're nice, Carey," she said gratefully, and for once the Englishman did not resent being called by his surname. All the *grenouilles* did it. It was part of their affectation of the camaraderie of a studio to call a painter by his last name instead of his first. Ned Carey had given up expecting to be called monsieur, and at least the little frog didn't call him Edouard.

"We've got to drink to Meade's health now, Babette," he said. "He's sold some of his sketches to the newspapers, and started a new career." Now that he had tried it, he found he liked being generous.

"That's marvellous, Meade," she said, raising her glass. "What were your subjects?"

"Some Paris street scenes," said the American, with a warning glance at Carey.

"It's just what they used to say in the cafés, that you

12

could be a second Daumier," Babette said happily. "What Paris papers will your work appear in?"

"Not in Paris, I'm afraid. In London and New York."

"Oh, *abroad*," said the girl, and David Meade grinned. He knew that only praise from Paris counted: defeated, sick and hungry, Paris was Paris still.

She was still talking politely about his success when they all went into the tiny kitchen to mix a salad. It was a rather pathetic imitation of the impromptu lunches before the war, when artists and models, out-of-work actors and *grenouilles* all joined in the cookery, or ran out to the wineshop for extra supplies. Carey had bought the burgundy. "I hope it's the tip-top thing," he said anxiously. "David brought all the food. They live on the fat of the land at the US Legation."

"We have our sources," said Meade, "and at least now we've got enough to share with our friends."

They drew their chairs up to the table, and three hungry young people made short work of the banquet. The chicken was reduced to a skeleton, the ham had changed its shape, the wine was praised, and they were at the brandy and cigarettes stage – coffee there was none – before they were really aware of the creeping cold in the big bare studio.

"I should have done what the Parisians are doing now," said Meade. "Stolen some of the fencing from the vacant lots next to the Legation. But putting food parcels into a fiacre is all very well; I reckon the cabby would have drawn the line at fences. How are you off for fuel in the Rue St Jean, Babette?"

"Oh, we've a few logs in the cellar," she said with a smile. The chill she felt in the studio did not come from the empty stove, nor the draught beneath the door, but from the absence of Marc Vallon, some of whose canvases, facing inwards, were ranged against the wall – the canvases she had cleaned or primed or stretched in days which now seemed far off. She tried to chatter, but the talk had begun to die away, for the three had so little in common that they could only fall back on 'Do you remember' in a helpless clutch at nostalgia.

Do you remember the balls at the Moulin de la Galette? The trips to Barbizon? The picnics at La Grenouillère, where the little frogs loved to splash in the bathing place while the models posed and Renoir and Manet painted? Carey cut in with his own memories. "Do you remember the marvellous party we had here the night before Marc joined his regiment? With Léonie and Fifine and Doucette and some of the older men from the Atelier? When we sang the *Marseillaise* and shouted 'A Berlin!' till the people downstairs came up and complained?"

David Meade was silent. He recalled the mood of the farewell party, which exactly reflected the mood of Paris in July 1870: the boasting and the belief that the invincible French Army would cross the Rhine and enter Berlin within six weeks. Meade himself, who had been a soldier, and Vallon, who was a realist, were the only two revellers who had been sceptical about the outcome of France's war with Prussia. There had been no party when Corporal Vallon recovered from his wound and was posted to a replacement depot at Rennes.

"I wonder what became of them all?" Carey went on. "Léonie L'Amour lived up to her stage name and went off with a Prussian officer. Belleau was killed at Gravelotte, and Monet and Pissarro went to London. But what about those two painters from the Old Farm, Babette? Is it true they're both abroad?"

"Quite true," said Babette. "They paid their rent and left for Italy, and the studios have been empty since last July. Old Foxy would be raising hell about that" (the landlord's name was Monsieur Renard) "but he rented the

14

Vine House furnished to some Russians, only last week."

"Where's the Vine House?"

"Don't you know? It's the big house at the foot of our garden, and it's supposed to be as old as the Old Farm. People say the masters of the vineyard lived there before the Revolution."

"So the Russians are arriving in Paris when most other neutrals are leaving," said Carey. "What d'you bet the National Guard runs them in for Czarist spies?"

"No takers," said Meade. "Russians travelling abroad are just as likely to be anarchists, and the Reds will welcome them with open arms. How many Russians came to the Vine House, Babette? What are their names?"

"A lady and a gentleman, called Igorov or Egorov, with their manservant, and they had 'London' on their luggage when it came through the big gate. But I've hardly seen any of them, because they use the stone stair at the back of the house, and walk round the vineyard to the Rue St Vincent."

"Highly inconvenient, I should have thought."

"Not if they want to use the new road at Caulaincourt. Anyway, does it matter?"

"Everything matters in times like these. I wish you lived in a safer place, child."

"What could be safer than *La Vieille Ferme*, now the Siege is over?"

"Right on top of the National Guard and the guns of Montmartre?" said Meade.

Babette remembered her misgivings of the morning. "The Guards are French like us," she said stoutly. "Why should they want to harm French women and children?"

"Because they're unemployed and hungry and defeated, and when that happens to men they do crazy things."

"Don't you worry about me," said Babette with her teasing smile. "I'll get through all right. I always do. And

2

The National Guards had tired of sentry go outside their command post by the time David Meade and Babette left the studio. The sunny morning had turned into a grey afternoon, and the red flag drooping above the gate of number six was the one spot of colour in the narrow street. Only the uncurtained mansard windows of the house that once was Scribe's were visible from street level, and there were no heads at these windows, nor sounds of activity from inside the villa. Babette was encouraged to say,

"I can't believe the Guard wants to fight. Did you really mean all you said upstairs?"

"Come on, don't stand staring at the place. – Yes, I did. I think they have the leaders, and the will, to start a civil war in France."

"I can't imagine Frenchmen fighting Frenchmen, after all we've been through since last July."

"Americans were fighting Americans, half a dozen years ago."

"And you were one of them. You've never let any of us

17

forget you were a soldier, since the war with Prussia began."

"I was right about the war with Prussia, wasn't I?"

"Yes, you were." Babette put her hand on the man's proffered right arm, as he shifted the big parcel for her sister to the left. "Which way are we going?"

"The nearest way to find a fiacre," said Meade.

"There's not much chance of finding a fiacre in Montmartre. Why don't we walk down to the boulevard and get an omnibus? They started running again today."

"I saw exactly *one* omnibus between here and the Etoile this morning. My driver said there's a cab stand at the Reine Margot restaurant."

"Where on earth's that?"

"It used to be the Restaurant Magenta. They changed the name."

"Oh, of course." Magenta had been a victory in the Italian war waged by Napoleon III, and anything that glorified the Emperor was anathema in the new Republic.

"We'd better take the *raccourci* to the boulevard, then," said Babette, indicating on their right a walled lane, narrower and shabbier than the Rue des Rosiers. There was only one highway from the centre of Paris to Montmartre – the highway up which the National Guards had dragged the cannon – but the Butte was seamed with *raccourcis*, or short cuts, some leading across the waste land called the *maquis*, where vagrants and gipsies were encamped in shacks or broken-down waggons. This particular lane was uninhabited, but there were houses on the slopes above, and heavy buttresses had been built against the walls of the lane to keep them from collapsing. It was a dirty byway, where after dark elderly prostitutes plied their trade with slobbering mouths and skirts pulled up, for a few sous and a gulp of absinthe. It stank of corruption.

18

Meade stopped before they had gone far into the alley.

"If I had any sense," he said, "I'd escort you back to the Old Farm, and take this stuff to Madame Leblanc myself."

"Oh no!" she protested, and her pretty vivid face, with colour in it after the food and wine, was mutinous. "You couldn't do that, Meade!"

"Why not? You only need to tell me where your sister lives."

"But she doesn't know you! You're a stranger to her – a foreigner – and she'd think of your kindness as charity –"

"All right then. Let's go down to the Reine Margot as fast as we can, and get into a fiacre."

"Not the two of us together."

"Why not?"

He was hurrying her on all the time as they talked, and Babette was almost running to keep pace with his long strides. "I hate to say this," she gasped, "since you've thought of Fanny, and brought these wonderful things to give to her, but you can't come to her house with me –"

"Why not? Are you ashamed of me?"

"Don't be silly!"

"What is it, then?"

"It's Fanny who'd be ashamed to have you see her home, because she lives in a Belleville slum."

"You think I don't know Belleville?" asked David Meade. "I've been there often enough since the Emperor went to war."

"Looking after your poor dear destitute Germans?" she said scornfully, and Meade resisted the temptation to shake her.

"I thought we agreed to forget all that," he said.

"I'm sorry! I'm sorry, truly! I know it was part of your job, and something to do with international law, forgive me! But it's poor Fanny who's ashamed of the slum where they have to live. And then there's Didier, her husband,

19

he's in the National Guard. Well, since he joined, he's got in with a bunch of what you call Reds, and he's begun to hate all foreigners—"

"Especially Americans?"

"Perhaps."

"He'll eat the Virginia ham, won't he?"

"He will if he can get his clutches on it. But my God, I'm going to see that Fanny gets her fair share first." She spoke with an angry resolution that made David think of Carey's expression 'like a kitten swearing' and he laughed.

"All right," he said. "I shan't butt in. Just let me pay for the fiacre, and tell the driver to wait to bring you home."

"Wait in the Impasse du Drapeau? The cab would be stoned and the driver too. And if the neighbours saw Madame Leblanc's sister getting out of a fiacre, they'd never let her hear the last of it."

"Very democratic, are they, in the Impasse du Drapeau?"

"You think the boys in the Rue des Rosiers are Reds? You should hear them at the Buttes Chaumont! *Voilà*! There's an idea! I'll take a fiacre, if we can find one, to the park gates, and have the man stop there. I can walk the rest in five minutes."

The end of the sinister alley was in sight, and Babette was taking two steps to Meade's one.

"You're not very easy to look after, darling," he said.

The '*chérie*' never spoken before made her look up at him in surprise.

"Fanny and I have been looking after ourselves since *maman* died when Fanny was only eighteen. Not that poor Fanny has done very well at it."

They were almost at the boulevard. There were no lights in any of the shops which had been open earlier in the day, but there was a bustle of movement, and the jingle of harness. The short cut petered out into a patch of scrub and stones, and Meade drew Babette into the shadow of a clump of bushes.

"Forgive me, darling," he said, "but tell me how you're off for money."

"Oh, I'm rich," she said sturdily. "I've still got some of my earnings left from sewing the balloons."

"Yes, I remember you were doing that." A number of Montmartre girls had been drafted into a makeshift factory opened in the Elysée-Montmartre restaurant, to sew the material for the balloons which had been a spectacular feature of the Siege of Paris. Republican leaders, couriers, journalists, aeronauts had been lifted pell-mell out of the beleaguered city, some to escape and join the Government of National Defence at Bordeaux; others to crash. Meade wondered what Babette's earnings had amounted to. Before the war a skilled workman had earned no more than three francs a day. He doubted if the sempstresses, even in a national emergency, had earned more than two. And since the French sued for an armistice at the end of January that source of revenue had certainly dried up.

As if she read his mind, Babette continued, "I had a message from Morisot the other day. She's coming back to Paris soon, and then she'll pay me for looking after her studio, as she did before."

He tried to conceal his distaste for hearing a lady like Madame Berthe Morisot (and a fine painter too) spoken of by her surname, like one of the men at the Café Guerbois.

"Morisot's awfully generous to me," said Babette. "She gave me this warm cloak before she went away."

Meade set the food parcel on the ground, took Babette in his arms, and kissed her. She gave a little sigh, and nestled close to him as if she were willing, after all, to be taken care of.

"*Chérie*," he said, "you've been so brave all the way

21

through. Are you brave enough to admit that poor Vallon may never be coming back?"

"Carey seemed to think he was interned in Switzerland."

"Carey knows nothing about it. Dear, what I want to know is, will there be any hope for me?"

"What do you mean?" But she knew very well, from the pressure of his tense body against her own, and the heat of his lips against her mouth and cheeks.

"I've fallen in love with you, Babette."

"But monsieur!" Like *chérie*, it was a word never spoken between them before. "Monsieur, you hardly know me!"

"I know you're lovely, and lovable, and sweet, *chérie*. Who needs to know more? Listen to me. When I was at Versailles yesterday, looking for a house for the Legation, I saw half a dozen pretty cottages standing empty. The owners had got out of France, and left them to be let furnished. Will you allow me to take one for you? Don't say no at once. Remember I want to look after you, and get you away from Paris before the worst happens—"

She pulled away from him and set her bonnet straight. "What worst? Oh yes, the civil war. Would you fly the Stars and Stripes above the cottage?"

"The Stars—now, that's just silly."

"But you'd be the Protecting Power, like at the German Embassy?"

"You'd be under my protection, yes."

"No."

"For heaven's sake, why not? Bring your sister, if you think you need a chaperone!"

"You feel no *grenouille* ought to need a chaperone? You're right, of course, but that you could say such a thing proves that love in a cottage was never meant for you and me. And speaking of my sister, I ought to get on

22

to Belleville as quickly as I can."

He couldn't deny it, for the early twilight was beginning to fall. He protested, "You're angry with me."

"No, not angry. Surprised, perhaps."

"I realise I spoke too soon. Will you let me come to the Old Farm and give me a chance to show how much I care for you? I refuse to take my dismissal on the boulevard."

She gave him an enchanting, even a provocative smile, and said, "I didn't mean to 'dismiss' you, as you call it. I'll be glad to see you whenever you like."

So there was the shadow of hope at least. He kissed her again, picked up the parcel and led her down to the street, one in the long string of boulevards which the Second Empire's great town planner, Baron Haussmann, had constructed as part of the rebuilding of Paris. It connected the new *arrondissements* of Montmartre and Belleville. There were three fiacres outside the Reine Margot, ex-Magenta, where well-dressed men and women were emerging satisfied from luncheon and throwing small coins to the beggar children whom the flunkeys were hustling away from the gilt-encrusted door. Little did the sympathetic English think, as they subscribed to the British War Relief Fund, or the Lord Mayor's Fund for French War Victims, and other funds intended to ease the sufferings of France, that the food money would be diverted, in part, to restaurants which had never needed to modify their menus during the Siege. To David the spectacle was sickening. He knew that two million dollars' worth of food had been sent to Paris by American sympathisers as soon as the Siege was lifted, and had been allowed to rot on the piers of Le Havre when nobody had been found to unload the ships. He had witnessed the ugly scenes at Les Halles, the great Paris market, when the French themselves had begun rioting to snatch and steal the victuals which arrived from Britain. At the moment he was almost ashamed of the eatables he had appropriated as a means of getting in touch with Babette Mercier.

"*Holà, cocher!*" he shouted to the next driver in line, "this lady wants to go to the Parc des Buttes Chaumont, what's your price?" He helped Babette into the fiacre, to make sure of it while the haggling was going on, and set her bag and parcel at her feet. Then, when she leaned out of the window to say goodbye, he put a heavy envelope into her hand. "For the fare there and back," he said. "Do try and make the fellow wait. And if you have to take the omnibus, don't go through that short cut after dark."

"Gas lighting is supposed to come on tonight," she smiled, and Meade told her not to count on it. Nothing worked in the Paris of the *après-Siege*.

Babette blew him a kiss, and the cabby clicked his tongue to an animal too old and scrawny to have been sold to the butchers with the gilded horse heads above their doors. Meade bowed, and stood with his hat in his hand until the fiacre drove off, when he walked away in the opposite direction.

Babette might have been surprised and piqued if she had known that her suitor had mastered his disappointment fast enough to take the long way round to the Rue St Vincent, there to examine from the street a shuttered house with a stone stair and a path leading round the vineyard, which had just been rented to a Russian called Igorov or Egorov.

The girl was more concerned with the envelope Meade had made her take. She knew by the weight that it held far more than the fiacre fare, even for a double journey, and sitting well back in the shabby vehicle, where she could not be seen from the pavement, she opened one corner with her thumb. It contained five gold napoleons – still legal tender – worth one hundred francs, a small fortune to a girl accustomed to count in sous. Her first thought was of the medical care it would provide for Fanny; her second, that Fanny would be soft enough to let Didier get his hands on it and spend it all in the cabarets frequented by the National Guard. Her third, and most important, reaction was the realisation that David Meade had had the money ready before they met that day. This was not a cab fare produced on the spur of the moment: the envelope had been sealed and addressed to Mademoiselle Mercier, and bore the printed address at 95, Rue de Chaillot of the Legation of the United States. "The Protecting Power," she thought scornfully. "Does he think he can buy me?"

She reckoned up the very small amount of money in the purse at the bottom of her embroidered wool bag along with a few good things to eat for Madame Verlet, and then, glad of the gathering dusk, she pulled up her skirt (no longer the cumbrous crinoline of the Second Empire) and slipped Meade's envelope into the pocket of her white cotton petticoat. The Impasse du Drapeau was no place to be carrying gold coins.

She had asked to be put down at the west gate of the Parc des Buttes Chaumont, and as the weary horse stumbled on down Haussmann's boulevards, where all the trees had been cut down for fuel, she thought of the spring of 1869, when she came there first. She had been a work-girl of eighteen, avid for pleasure and the admiration in the eyes of men. In the year of the Great Exhibition, 1867, their mother was dying, and she and Fanny had made only one trip down from Montmartre to the Champ de Mars. They rode in a public omnibus called an *impériale*, with a few other girls like themselves who worked at the cruel trade of making artificial flowers. They criticised the magnificent toilettes of the ladies, and stared at the foreign princes who came to Paris to bow before Napoleon III and the beautiful Eugénie, but Babette still remembered what had pleased her best: it was the *bâteaux-mouches*, the excursion steamers then plying on the Seine for the first time. Babette Mercier had spent all she had on trips up and down the river from the Pont Neuf to the Place de la Concorde, feeling a dreamy ecstasy in watching the play of light on the water and the refracted sunlight on the palaces which told the story of her country's past. The love of light remained with her and kindled an ambition which nobody suspected until she went for the first time to the Parc des Buttes Chaumont.

It had been a place of execution in the Middle Ages, when the gibbet of Montfaucon stood on the highest hillock, later the site of gypsum quarries worked out over a long period, and finally an enormous midden where the refuse of the two communes of Belleville and Ménilmontant was dumped. When Napoleon III incorporated them into his Greater Paris like Montmartre, he planned the area as a people's park for the two new *arrondissements*. The refuse dump was cleaned up and a reservoir created for the ornamental waters which included a waterfall and a lake where swans preened themselves. The Buttes Chaumont became a green place of shrubs and flowers, where in new restaurants and outdoor cafés the same tunes from popular operettas were played as in the fashionable Bois de Boulogne. The quarries, recently the lair of cut-throats, drunks and deserters, became charming alcoves for lovers' assignations, and on the highest *butte* of all stood a copy of the Temple of the Sybil at Tivoli. It was in this setting, in the summer of 1869, that the lives of Fanny and Babette Mercier took a new turn.

Fanny, by then twenty, had been growing restless. She was tired of the Old Farm and the workroom, tired of sharing a bed with her younger sister, and beginning to worry about her health. The making of artificial flowers involved the steady pressure of a heavy metal tool against the worker's chest, and Madame Mercier, a flower maker herself, had died of breast cancer. Fanny wanted ladylike employment like serving behind the counter in one of the new department stores, but they had no money to grease the palms of the floor supervisors at the Bon Marché or Au Bonheur des Dames. They knew nobody with the money or the influence to get them an apprenticeship in one of the great dressmaking houses, then at the height of their glory. Fanny, eager for a more glamorous life, agreed to join a group of working girls who were planning a gala night in the new Parc des Buttes Chaumont.

For this outing the girls clubbed together to hire a *char-à-bancs* drawn by two spanking bays with bunches of flowers on their bridles, and they looked like a bunch of flowers themselves in their bell-shaped crinolines and bonnets tied with ribbons in all the colours of the rainbow. It was evening, and fairy lanterns strung through the new shrubberies were already lighting up the park when the girls got out and started larking and joking as they set off arm in arm among the crowds. Babette was separated from her friends almost at once, but she knew when and where they were to meet again, and went off unconcernedly on a voyage of exploration. There was a brief display of fireworks, which she watched from a bridge over the ornamental lake. Babette had changed her place more than once, to avoid the touches on her elbow and the insinuating voices of strange men, when a voice which was not insinuating but warm and interested, said above her head:

"Why aren't you looking at the fireworks, mademoiselle?"

"I am looking at them, monsieur."

"No, you're not. You're looking down, not up. What are you seeing in the lake?"

"The reflection of the fireworks in the water."

"I'd like to hear more about that. Are you all alone?"

"My older sister and her friends are somewhere in the park, monsieur."

"Do you think your older sister would object if I asked you to drink a glass of wine with me?"

"Oh, I don't know—"

"Over there in the *guinguette*, as publicly as possible?"

Well, why not? the man was tall and thin, well-dressed and good-looking in his way. He had a light brown beard and a humorous face with laughter lines in it, and the table for two to which he led her was certainly public enough, right at the entrance of the little open-air café and underneath a loop of brilliant lamps. He bought and paid for a bottle of sparkling Asti, just right for an adolescent palate, and when he had filled her glass said, "Now tell me about the reflections in the water."

Babette found herself telling the stranger about the sunlight on the Seine from the deck of a *bâteau-mouche*, and this new experience of seeing the crude greens and reds and yellows of the fireworks transmuted into different hues on the dark waters of the lake and the white breasts of the swans. He listened attentively and then asked her name.

"Elisabeth Mercier, monsieur, they call me Babette. What's yours?"

"Just call me Frédéric. I think you have a painter's eye, Babette. Come and meet my friends."

Over her protests he got up, seized the bottle of Asti by the neck, and with his arm round Babette's shoulders hurried her to a big table in the middle of the café, where half a dozen men and as many girls were eating and drinking.

"*Allez, les gars!*" cried Babette's companion. "I've found a new one for La Grenouillère."

She was made welcome at once, asked her name, and given a seat among those free and easy people. After Frédéric had poured more of the sparkling wine into a clean glass for her, he plunged into an argument about refracted light with the other men, while Babette smiled shyly at the girls. She was afraid they might be grand ladies, but clearly they were not, and there was a camaraderie among them she had never encountered before. The young man on her other side was friendly too, asking 'where Bazille had picked her up', and if she wanted anything to eat.

"No thank you, I'm not hungry," said Babette. "Please tell me about the gentleman who brought me here. Is that his name, Monsieur Bazille?"

"Jean-Frédéric Bazille. I don't suppose you ever heard of him."

"No. Is he a painter?"

"A very good one."

"He said I had a painter's eye."

"Did he indeed? We'll have to find out about that."

"Are you a painter too? What's *your* name?"

"Marc Vallon."

"Should I have heard of you?"

"Not yet, but you will some day."

Babette sipped her wine and studied him. He was somewhere in his early twenties, not as old as Bazille, and his face hadn't that humorous, lived-in look, but he was handsomer, with a firm clean-shaven chin and dark eyes. From his intonation she guessed that he was *Parisien de Paris* – Paris-born. And a wave of delight engulfed her, at being here in this lively company of artists and laughing girls, in her native city when Paris was at the apex of her power and brilliance, with the warm spring night and the fireworks adding enchantment to the scene. Marc Vallon was smiling at her confidently.

"Please, what's La Grenouillère?" she asked. Frédéric Bazille overheard her and turned to her again.

"That's where we're going to test your painter's eye," he said.

"But I can't paint."

"Did you ever try?"

"La Grenouillère's only a restaurant," Vallon cut in. "Don't tease the kid, Bazille."

"It's where little froggies learn to swim in their very own pond," said another man, with the owlish solemnity of the slightly drunk.

"Have you ever been to Bougival?" Vallon tried again. "The Frog Pond's at Chatou, not far from there. It's on an island in the Seine where we go on fine Sundays, and we paint, or swim and go boating, and picnic. Come with us next Sunday, if you like, Babette. It's no distance at all on the St Germain railway."

That was how it all began, casually, impersonally, as Elisabeth Mercier was absorbed into, was accepted by, a group of men who had the simplicity of genius, and became one of the girls who were as independent as the men's conception of their art. Bazille repeated the invitation to join them on Sunday, but it was Vallon who walked back with her at midnight to the gate where the *char-à-bancs* was waiting and the coachman grumbling and shouting to the dallying girls to hurry up.

It was Vallon who kissed her lightly on both cheeks when they parted, and told her to be ready in good time on Sunday when he came to take her to the train. She said goodbye hurriedly, expecting a scolding if Fanny had seen that quick embrace. But Fanny, like every other girl in their party, had found an *ami* of her own in the park, and was saying a languishing *au revoir* to a short, slim young man in a fashionable light grey suit, a tall silk hat and lavender gloves. He was introduced as Monsieur Didier

30

Leblanc, who soon made his appearance at the Old Farm. He described himself as a skilled sheet metal operative (and when the lavender gloves were off his hands were seen to be a manual worker's) and the son of a civil servant. It was later discovered that he worked in a *fumisterie-tôlerie*, repairing broken-down kitchen stoves in his master's yard, while the 'civil servant' was a jailer in the prison of La Roquette. Didier earned very little, but with what he had he speculated on the Bourse like everybody else in that great boom time, the close of the Second Empire, and put every sou he got into fine clothing and the barbering of his silky blond hair, moustache and imperial. The lies he told about himself could have been exposed by another man in a week; it took the Mercier girls much longer to see through him, and when they did it was too late for Fanny. Didier was sulky and evasive, Fanny tearful, coaxing and three months' pregnant when they were married at the *mairie* of Montmartre by the newly elected mayor, Dr Georges Clemenceau.

"When are you going to let me take you out to Barbizon, *petite* Babette?" It seemed to the girl sighing over the ruin of the Parc des Buttes Chaumont, that she could almost hear Bazille's voice in that entreaty so many times repeated. He wasn't the only one; in the free and easy life of the studios the girls were always being invited to weekends at Barbizon, Marlotte, Moret-sur-Loing, Fontainebleau itself, and most of them accepted cheerfully. The Babette of nearly two years later wondered how she had resisted Bazille so long, for she was romantically in love with him – she thought now that Fanny's weakness had stiffened her own pride. In the beautiful spring of 1870 she yielded, but not in any of the beauty spots of the Forest of Fontainebleau. It was in Bazille's studio that he became her lover, and they were both by nature so

31

secretive that although there was much ribald speculation among their friends, nobody ever knew the truth. Within a few weeks the affair was over when Bazille went south to paint; within a few months he was killed in action, and Babette turned from her private memory of a light love to a graver feeling for Marc Vallon, who had never hidden what he felt about her.

Every time she had come to Belleville during Fanny's illness Babette had seen the steady degradation of the neighbourhood round the park, where the lake had returned to its former function of kitchen midden. The shops of quality encouraged to open in 1869 had closed since the outbreak of war, and their doors and windows were covered by iron shutters. All the trees in the park had been cut down for fuel, and the empty flower-beds held the strange bloom of cannon. Like Montmartre, the Buttes Chaumont was a National Guard artillery park, and even the Temple of the Sybil had been replaced by a confiscated cannon. That Babette had seen before. What was new on this livid March afternoon was the platform erected in the grounds of the little café where the painters had met for a jolly party, and the torches and red flags which had taken the place of the fairy lamps.

From a sheltered doorway she could see a man addressing a crowd of other men – could even hear him, for his voice was clear and practised, and there were no interruptions except grunts of satisfaction. He was denouncing one of the first laws passed by the Thiers government before the Assembly left Bordeaux. It enacted that the payment of rents and the interest on debts, suspended during the war, should be resumed within two days, which in a time of almost total unemployment was completely impossible. The Law of Maturities, as it was called, was a tremendous grievance to working people without work, and nothing the speaker said to condemn it would have been too bad, but he lost his audience when he launched into a eulogy of Karl Marx, and urged them to follow the resolutions of the Second Congress of the International Working Men's Association. Men desperate for food and shelter were not prepared, in the shadow of the new German Empire, to hear a lecture on German Socialism, and as they began to drift away Babette picked up her heavy parcel and was about to start for the Impasse du Drapeau when a woman's voice cut through the gloom.

Babette knew who the second speaker was, the woman who had taken the place of Karl Marx's champion on the makeshift platform. She was a well-known figure in the streets of Montmartre, where she was one of the Vigilance Committee of Women, and frequently appeared in paramilitary uniform. She was a self-styled feminist, and when the term was explained to Babette she had asked why a champion of women's rights should go about dressed as a man. Her name was Louise Michel, and in January, when a demonstration by the National Guard turned into armed conflict with government troops, she fought with such frenzy that she was given the nickname of the Red Virgin, which in all respects she deserved.

She was in uniform now. Although Babette in her doorway could not see red trousers, she saw the blue cutaway coat and the red képi aslant on the Red Virgin's lank dark hair. By torchlight the gleam of steel revealed the bayonet which was her trademark. From the first word of her speech, impassioned, pell-mell, she was revealed as a genuine rabble-rouser, passing over Marx for the home-grown variety of Socialist, and evoking the names of those who had suffered in the Emperor's prisons. Blanqui! Flourens! Delescluze! Rochefort! What will their fate be at the hands of a tyrant like Thiers! Free the prisoners! Bring home the exiles! Kill the tyrants!

"Comrades!" she cried. "We, the People, were cheated of our glorious Revolution by the Corsican usurper Bonaparte! Whose nephew led us to defeat at Sedan and now sits in a German palace while we starve! Cheated of liberty in 1830, cheated once more in 1848, shall we be cheated of our Socialist republic again in 1871? I say no! I say man the barricades! I say fight fire with fire! Kill, burn, destroy in the sacred name of Revolution!"

Babette regained her breath three streets away. The roar of the crowd was still audible; the echoes of the applause and the singing of the Carmagnole were the more terrifying by contrast with the silent alleys and kennels of the slum into which she had plunged. The unknown man, whose arrogant detachment seemed somehow to be enhanced by his pince-nez and jutting beard, had frozen the crowd with his statistics, but the Red Virgin had kindled them to flame. The two of them had done more than all David Meade's solemn predictions to convince Babette Mercier of worse times to come. Worse than the huge war indemnity, the Occupation troops and the loss of Alsace-Lorraine to Germany: a civil war.

3

The Impasse du Drapeau (to which some wit had added in red paint the word *Rouge*) was a dead-end street dating from the previous century. There were six hovels on each side, with a narrow pavement and a broad sluggish gutter in the middle, originally built to house workers from the gypsum quarries. The Impasse lived up to its name by ending in a red-tiled outbuilding used as a communal washhouse and privy, with a partition between the wooden washtubs and the two earth closets. Whose turn it was to use the tubs or empty the reeking pails was a constant source of friction between the women of the wretched alley.

When Didier Leblanc and Françoise Mercier were first married, they had rented a decent room in a respectable street, and got together some solid furniture. Fanny took the mahogany fourposter from the garret at the Old Farm, leaving the table to Babette, these two pieces representing the whole estate of their parents. Babette made white cotton curtains for the bed, and Madame Verlet added a patchwork quilt as her wedding present. They bought some good second-hand stuff, including a mahogany dresser to hold glasses, china plates and bowls. The mahogany furniture was sold after they moved to the Impasse du Drapeau, and the glass and china, like the Leblancs' clothes, had been to the pawnshop and back a score of times after Didier's ignorant plunges into the stock market bankrupted him, and his master turned him away for persistent tippling and absenteeism. It was not true to say, as he always said later, that the Emperor's defeat and the resultant panic on the Bourse had ruined him. The war had saved him by giving him the National Guard instead of unemployment, a uniform, regular meals at his barracks, and an allowance of one franc fifty a day with half as much again for his wife.

The little alley of one-room houses had never been thought worth gas lighting, and on this Saturday when gas was to be restored to the streets of Paris only a guttering oil lamp hung in the arched entrance to the Impasse. Aware of the gold coins in her pocket, Babette was glad of the light, although there was nobody to be seen but three ragged children playing in the gutter near the second door on the left of the alley, at which she knocked.

"*Entrez*!" A man's voice called. "Come in! The door's not locked!" It was swollen with the damp of the snowy winter and opened outward with difficulty. Babette had to give it such a vigorous tug that she lost her balance, stumbled on the doorstep and heard her brother-in-law laugh.

"Not a very grand entrance for *madame la marquise*, come to visit her poor relations," he mocked.

Didier Leblanc was half propped against the white-washed wall and half lying on the pallet on which the family slept, wearing the unbuttoned tunic and breeches of the National Guard and with his booted feet on the bed cover. The patchwork quilt, now tattered and dis-

36

coloured, was twisted into a nest for a little weeping boy, sucking his fingers and still unable, at one year old, to sit up without support. A tallow candle on the table and a smouldering fire of green wood gave the only light to the room.

"Bonjour, Didier," said Babette. "Where's Fanny? And what's Louis crying for?"

"God knows, he's always whining: getting another tooth, his mother says. Here, you miserable brat, go to your aunt." The man got to his feet and put the baby into Babette's arms. The child moved feebly in protest. At birth Louis had been a healthy, vigorous infant. Now he was a typical Siege child, retarded in speech and movement.

"Don't cry, darling! Don't you know your *tante* Babette? Where's *maman*? Where is she, Didier?"

"Went out to try to get some bread and milk."

"But it's dark already."

"I don't know what your aristo friends do on the Champs Elysées, but the Belleville bakers don't open till four o'clock. And if you don't get there ahead of time there's no bread left."

"That means standing in line for an hour, maybe. Couldn't you have gone instead of Fanny?"

"It's a woman's job."

"Not when a woman's been as sick as Fanny was."

"She's getting better fast," said Didier defensively. "I had the kid to look after, hadn't I? Better give him to me, Babette. He's scared of the fine lady in her fancy bonnet. I know what'll shut him up."

There was a knotted handkerchief on the wooden table which held the remains of a meal. Didier untied it, put a crust inside and sprinkled the roll of cotton and stale bread from a bottle of cheap brandy. Then he gave it to the child, who began to mumble and suck on the sodden pacifier.

"You shouldn't give him brandy, Didier. I've brought some meat extract for Fanny and Louis too, it'll do them both good." She saw that the man had been at the brandy before she came in.

"Where'd you get meat extract in Montmartre?"

"It was given me by an American friend."

"Then you can tell your American friend we don't want his damned charity." It was an automatic retort, quite meaningless, and Didier showed no interest in the parcel she had pushed beneath the table. "Have a drink yourself. Warm you up. Do you good."

Babette sat down and let him pour some of the raw spirit into a glass with a cracked stem. She tried to be friends with him for poor Fanny's sake, and she told him what a fine liqueur it was before she said cautiously:

"Didier, did Fanny ever go to see the doctor?"

"She went to the hospital and got a bottle of tonic from some *croquemort* or other, that's all I know."

"I thought she meant to go to that woman's doctor on the Boulevard de la Villette."

"He charges five francs for one visit."

"I gave her three francs myself last time I was here."

"All right, so we couldn't afford the rest, and you know why. What are you doing?"

Babette had taken the child from his father and laid him back in his quilt-nest with the brandy-soaked rag still in his tiny hand. He was dropping off to sleep. Babette picked up an iron kettle from the embers of the fire, and shook it.

"Is this water fresh, Didier?"

"Fanny brought it in from the outside tap at noon. Why?"

"She'll need a hot drink, some of the stuff I brought, when she comes in from the shops."

38

"She'll be like the rest of us, ready for a glass of brandy. Damn the girl, I wish she'd hurry up. She's already made me miss Rigault's rally in the park."

"Rigault. Was that the man speaking with Louise Michel?"

"Were *you* there?"

"I came down that way. I heard a bit of Monsieur Rigault, but more of Madame Michel."

"Comrade Michel," Didier corrected her. "The women's champion."

"Thank you, I'd rather not be championed by her. 'Kill, burn, destroy' – what a hope for the future!"

"Girls like you don't understand politics," said the man loftily. "You, a victimised worker's daughter, whose own father was killed working on the railway – neither you nor Fanny ever lifted up your voices to demand compensation for his death –"

"I was only six when poor father was killed."

"Even if you'd been sixteen you should have had a man like Rigault to take your case to court and get you justice." Didier took another mouthful of brandy. "You mark my words, Comrade Michel may be a brilliant speaker – for a woman – but Raoul Rigault has the brains. He knows unemployment is the real enemy. Look at me, I've no job, and we'd starve without my pay from the National Guard. And now the government has stopped the wives' allowance and the rent moratorium, so we must pay back rent for this pigsty or be thrown into the street. That's what we've got to fight for now, justice for the people! Full employment and a living wage, and State support for wives and children! We'll never get it from Thiers and his traitors. You're not listening."

"I've heard it all before. Save it for the Red Clubs, Didier."

He lurched to his feet, exasperated by her mocking

39

look. "You're laughing at me," he said. "You think it's a great joke to come here – you, an artist's model – and patronise Fanny and me. Good advice! Money for the doctor! Charity from your American friend! I bet you gave him plenty in return. What's left over for me?"

He pulled her towards him and crushed one breast between his fingers. It was not the first time, in his wife's absence, that Didier Leblanc had tried to fondle and maul Babette, but this time she had the poker in her hand and raised it threateningly.

"Get away from me, you drunken brute!" Coaxing him for Fanny's sake was quite forgotten, but as Didier instinctively retreated there was the grinding sound of the stiff front door, and Fanny herself came in.

She was an older version of Babette – much older, for at twenty-two she looked like forty, with her pinched face and brown hair limp beneath a summer bonnet of black straw. Her shawl was torn, and on one arm she had a willow basket containing the thin loaf of bread called a *ficelle* and a litre bottle of skim milk.

"Why, Babette, whatever are you doing with the poker?" she said.

"Trying to get your sulky fire to burn, and boil some water."

"You won't do it that way." She adjusted the kettle on a chain above the green wood, and laid a few pieces of kindling on the reluctant flame. "Has Loulou been good, Didi?"

"He's asleep now, at any rate." Didier looked inside the basket. "One *ficelle*! Was that all you could get?"

"They had nothing but *ficelles* in the afternoon baking."

"I told you to go in the morning, you stupid cow."

"I don't suppose either of you thought to change him," said Fanny, absorbed in her child.

His wife's arrival seemed to have sobered up Didier

Leblanc. "No nursemaid work for me," he said with an oath, and as the child's dress and soaking undergarments were removed Babette saw the limp limbs and pot belly of malnutrition, and wondered with a pang if another sorrow were in store for his mother. Didier, without looking at his son, was buttoning his tunic and buckling on his bandolier, and with his képi in his hand told the women he was on duty at the barracks until nine. "Then I'm going on to the Red Club meeting, so I'll be late," he said. "*Au 'voir*, you two, be good."

Fanny put the child down on the pallet bed and laid her shawl over him. As she sat on the edge of the bed, mechanically stroking his hair, she used the other hand to untie her bonnet and the candle light fell full on her face.

"What on earth have you done to yourself?" Babette exclaimed. An ugly bruise spread over her sister's left cheek.

"That wretched door sticks. I pulled too hard trying to get it open, and it banged into my face."

It was possible, for Babette had found the door stiff herself, but the bruise could as easily have been made by a man's fist. Without giving Babette time for more questions, Fanny asked what brought her there that day, and cried out in delight when she took the American food parcel from under the table. They opened it together.

"A roast chicken! What a lovely Sunday dinner for Didi!"

"Didier" — Fanny's pet name for her husband always set Babette's teeth on edge — "is going to have a good supper in barracks and as much wine as he can lap up at his Red Club. You're the one who needs a good chicken dinner tonight."

"Oh, I couldn't cut into it, just for myself. Didi wouldn't be pleased. We'll have some tomorrow with a slice of ham, and thank you for bringing it, Babette. I didn't know

41

you were still seeing Monsieur Meade."

"You know how it is with the artists, they come and they go."

"I daresay." There was a faint criticism in Fanny's voice, and nothing would make her taste the chicken. They made a jug of cocoa with water at last boiling and some of the skim milk, of which Louis seemed to enjoy some spoonfuls. Fanny sopped bread in her own bowl of cocoa, but declared she had no appetite and was too tired to eat.

"Didier said you went to a hospital this week and got a tonic." Babette introduced the subject diffidently. "Where exactly did you go?"

"To what's called the Belleville Ambulance, in that new school they built on the Rue Montfaucon. I always thought an ambulance was a waggon with horses, didn't you?"

"I think they say ambulance now when they mean a field hospital, or a temporary hospital in some building they've taken over. But I thought they were only for wounded soldiers."

"This one was. Oh, Babette, it was a horrible place! Think of it, two months since the armistice, and even the halls and corridors were full of men lying on stretchers or creeping about on crutches. The Sister I spoke to said some were so feeble they've contracted fevers even after they were admitted to hospital. I felt like running away, I was so scared."

"Poor Fanny! Was it a Sister of Charity you talked to?"

"No, it was a Red Cross lady. Soeur Emilie, the nuns called her. I think she was English, though she spoke good French."

"What did she say about yourself?"

"She said the Belleville Ambulance wasn't a hospital for women, and I ought to consult a woman's doctor, because the constant bleeding sounded as if my poor baby's birth had been mismanaged, and something had gone wrong

42

inside."

Babette remembered the grimy harridan, a resident of the Impasse du Drapeau (Rouge), who had delivered Fanny of her dead daughter, and thought mismanagement was probably an understatement. She said, "Fanny, you *must* see a proper doctor. Yes, I know it costs money, but wouldn't Didier's father do something to help you? He can't have many expenses where he works, and doesn't he live in the prison?"

"You like to throw the prison of La Roquette in my teeth, don't you? That old miser takes bribes from the prisoners, I'm sure he does, but he wouldn't spend a sou on us."

Babette was miserably conscious of the envelope with five gold napoleons in the pocket of her petticoat. Should she share the money with her sister, or was she a miser like old Leblanc? Common sense told her that two gold napoleons, like the three francs of her last gift, would find their way to Didier's pocket, and from there to the nearest wineshop. She came to an impulsive but far more difficult decision, and began:

"The best thing for you would be to get out of Paris, to somewhere clean and quiet with country air."

"Have you gone crazy? There's no place clean and quiet, because the Germans are everywhere. Don't you know half a million soldiers are staying on in France until the war indemnity is paid? Didier explained it all to me, and he says the rich left Paris long ago for their châteaux in the country, or to live abroad. People of our class have got to stay and put up with it."

"The Prussians aren't everywhere," said Babette. "They're not at Versailles any more, and there's good air and plenty of food there. A friend of mine will lend us a cottage at Versailles for – for as long as we like, if you'll come with me, and bring Louis."

"What friend?"

"We were just talking about him. David Meade."

"The American? Is he your lover now?"

"No."

"I don't believe you. Not make love to you – a man who can afford to set you up in a country cottage? You go to Versailles if you want to, but don't expect me to leave Didier."

"You'd rather stay and let him knock you about?"

Fanny's hand flew to her bruised cheek, and in her misery she taunted her sister, "I don't interfere in your way of life. Don't you try to interfere in mine!"

"What do you mean, my way of life?"

"*Grenouille*, they call you, hopping round the studios, at any rotten painter's beck and call –"

"There's been hardly any work in the Montmartre studios since the Siege. But when I did do it, it was useful work and – and inspiring, to work with real artists –"

"Inspiring, I like that! What's so special about cleaning palettes and stretching canvases? You might as well be a maid of all work, washing dishes and scrubbing floors and being grateful for your mistress's cast-off clothing, as you were grateful for Berthe Morisot's old cloak!"

"Madame Berthe didn't only give me her cloak. When she had time she gave me drawing lessons."

"*You* take drawing lessons! You'll be posing as one of the Independents next! I suppose you think that gives you the right to come here and lecture us, and try to break up my marriage to Didi!"

"Break up your marriage?" said Babette. "I wish I'd broken it up before it ever took place."

"Yes," said Fanny, crying violently, "why didn't you? Because you weren't interested in me, you were never in the house, all those months when I knew Didi first you were running with those artists, studio to studio, ball to

44

ball, picnics in the forest: all the gaieties you never asked me to share in—"

"You were infatuated with Didier."

"As you were infatuated with Monsieur Bazille. And when he sheered off you took up with Marc Vallon. And now it's the American, who seems willing to keep you. I don't think you need worry about a way to earn your living."

4

As soon as the door of the studio in the Rue des Rosiers closed behind David Meade and Babette, Edward Carey looked at his heavy gold watch. The timing had been perfect: cheeky Babette had snubbed Meade in the middle of his prophecies of doom, and now Carey was free to make his leisurely way back to the Hôtel St Honoré, even if he had to walk the whole way. He could go to his room and change into a silk shirt, a silk cravat, and be with Elvire at half past five.

There was even time for a last cigarette before the concierge, Madame Camille, came upstairs as arranged to clear away the dishes and take the left-overs down to her *loge*. He had to give her money and some instructions, since he didn't know when he would be seeing Madame Camille again. He had faced the fact that his days as an art student in Montmartre were over.

When he first began to badger his father for the means to study art in Paris, the shrewd Manchester businessman told him he was the living proof of the old saying, 'Clogs to clogs in three generations'. "My old dad was a

Lancashire weaver," said Mr Carey, "and though I say it myself, I'm a successful manufacturer. But you never seemed to take to textiles. From the first day you came into the counting-house you've had highfalutin' ideas about what you call the aesthetic side of life, whatever that may mean. First it was the Drama, now it's Art. Well, ain't there plenty of daubers in England to give you lessons here? That fellow Millais now, or Rossetti, who both sound foreign enough to please you – don't they take pupils?"

Ned expressed his dislike of the Pre-Raphaelite Brotherhood.

Many arguments later, the manufacturer gave in. "Can't stand you sulking about the place," he said. "Go and get it out of your system. I'll put enough funds to your credit in the Banque de France to keep you for a year. But you must promise me one thing, Ned. If it doesn't work out, you're to come back to England a year from May, and give an office stool another try. I still have a fancy to see the name of Carey and Son above the mills."

Ned Carey had been out of his depth in Montmartre from the word go. In the Atelier Dupuy it hadn't been too bad, because in the Life class he had certainly improved his drawing, and the Old Masters Maître Dupuy set him to copy at the Louvre at least made sense. You knew where you were with Aeneas and Dido, Hector and Achilles, and painters like David and Delacroix. But the Independents were another matter. What could you make of Manet's *Déjeuner sur l'Herbe* or Renoir's *La Grenouillère*? What could you make of their talk? This Manet had a wide circle of friends, including Dr Georges Clemenceau, who had just come back from America and was the new mayor of Montmartre, and a writer called Emile Zola, whose portrait Manet had painted. They often joined the artists at the Café Guerbois, where everybody was raving about

47

Zola's new novel, *Thérèse Raquin*, and the influence it had had on their painting. Carey had tried to read it, and got far enough to discover that it was the story of two murderers — not classical murderers like Nero or Herodias, but two grubby little people in a Paris back street, types such as the Independents seemed to enjoy putting on their canvases. Then after Zola the artists wanted to talk about photography, which they said had given light a new dimension, or Japanese prints, a new enthusiasm since their original composition and brilliant colours had first been revealed in the Pavillon Japonais at the Great Exhibition of 1867. It was beyond Carey's power to understand how a novel, a camera, and the work of an Oriental dead three hundred years ago could have anything to do with painting.

After the defeat at Sedan, when the Prussian armies with their Bavarian and Hessian allies were advancing on Paris, all the letters the Carey family were able to get through from Manchester to the young man in Montmartre were appeals that he should come back to England. But he had a good reason for staying: he had been asked to assist Richard Wallace and Edward Blount, the British Chargé d'Affaires, in administering the British Charitable Fund which Wallace set up in aid of the four thousand British subjects remaining in Paris during the Siege; then the £100,000 Wallace gave to the French; then the donations of food sent from England. Ned Carey discovered that he had a talent for organisation, as if the years in the counting-house had not been wasted, and he had an unexpected reward. It was Mr Wallace who had introduced him to Elvire.

He could hear Madame Camille panting her way upstairs. She was talking to someone, and he wondered if Meade had come back for another lamentation about the likelihood of civil war in France. Meade was an alarmist

48

and also a hypocrite. Instead of that elaborately staged lunch and the pretended concern for her ailing sister, he should have taken the little *grenouille* to a *cabinet particulier* in one of the dives on the Place Clichy – there was no need to be careful of her reputation. But instead of Meade's voice he heard a low murmur of extreme fatigue, and then Madame Camille's high-pitched shrieks:

"Oh Monsieur Carey! Oh monsieur! Here's Monsieur Marc come back!"

Carey was at the door in an instant, and there they were, the concierge with her apron to her eyes, and a tall man in army blue leaning on the baluster. A man who seemed hardly able to carry the weight of the pack on his shoulders, with his uniform almost in rags and the uppers of his boots gaping from the soles, a man recognisable only by his smile. Carey grasped him by both hands.

"Good God, Vallon, is it really you? We thought you were in Switzerland. How are you, and how the devil did you get here?"

"Walked most of the way," said the apparition. "– No thanks, Madame Camille, I don't need to use you as a crutch. Just let me come in, Carey, there's a good fellow. I'd like to sit down."

He might have rejected an elderly woman's shoulder as a crutch, but Vallon – Sergeant Vallon, for Carey saw the new and already dirty chevrons on his sleeve – was glad enough of the Englishman's strong arm to help him inside the studio. He pulled off his pack with a final effort, and threw it with his red képi into a corner of the room before he sank down on a sofa in the window, clearly at the end of his tether. Carey seized a clean glass, splashed it full of brandy, and handed it without speaking to Vallon. He swallowed half in one gulp and choked.

"My God, that's good," he said.

"Have you been" – Ned fumbled for the word *rapatrié*.

"None of the internees have been repatriated yet. Or so they told me at the *mairie*."

"What *mairie*?"

"The *mairie* of Montparnasse, where I was called up last July, and where I turned my rifle in and got my discharge today. There's a little hotel next door where they sold me soup and bread and a glass of wine, but they couldn't give me a bed."

"You walked here from Montparnasse?"

"I got an omnibus as far as the Trinité."

"Even from the Trinité!" cried Madame Camille, listening to every word. "Even that! What a walk for a tired man!"

Marc smiled, "It was the last lap, madame, and easier than most. Carey, I'm sorry to burst in on you like this—"

"If only you'd come sooner! But there's plenty of food and drink left, what would you like?"

The soldier became aware of the remains of a meal on the table. "Been having a party?" he asked drily.

"Babette Mercier and David Meade were here for lunch and we were all talking about you. They left less than half an hour ago."

"Babette and David — is that something new?"

"No, no, I mean David brought some food for Babette's sister, she's been sick. And they went off together to find a fiacre—" He was stumbling over his explanation, but Vallon, intent on his own explaining, said he had written to Babette from Lyon, had she got his letter? Madame Camille, interrupting again, said there was no mail service between Paris and Lyon.

"Because the Red Flag flies over Lyon, I suppose," said Marc. "Then it's ten to one my mother won't have got my letter in Biarritz."

"At least the poor lady is safe in Biarritz," Madame Camille got in. "Monsieur Carey, shall I clear away the

50

luncheon dishes now?"

"Not until Monsieur Marc has had something to eat. But you might light the lamp." It was on the green baize half of the table, a student-style petrol lamp with a clear glass shade. By its yellow light Ned saw the soldier better, with the strong planes of his face blurred by stubble but the friendly smile unaltered, as in the good days at the Café Guerbois.

"Don't trouble about food for me," he said, "I've got to go easy on the rations for a bit." After the first gulp he had not touched the brandy. "I really only came here to get clean, if I can, and put on some decent clothes. But I'm afraid, *monsieur mon locataire*, that I must appeal to your kindness and ask to sleep on the sofa tonight. I don't think I can go any further."

"No need for the sofa, your own bed's waiting for you here."

"But what about yourself?"

"I've been coming here to paint occasionally" (Ned had noted that after one glance in the direction of the easel, Marc had averted his eyes from Antony, Cleopatra and the Horse) "but I haven't used the bedroom for the past month."

"Why the devil not?"

Impossible to tell the truth, and say it was too cold, to a man who had been on the freezing winter campaign in the mountains of the Jura. Carey ignored the question, and asked Madame Camille if she couldn't find any fuel, somewhere, somehow, to warm the place up a bit for Monsieur Marc.

"Well now," said the concierge demurely, "I *have* got a little bit of a fire going in the *loge*. I could bring up some hot ashes in my warming pan, and with a bit of kindling and a log or two, you might be able to take the chill off, mightn't you?"

Carey agreed enthusiastically. He waited until the door shut behind the woman, and then he told Marc that he had been working for British War Relief for France, and had moved down to the Hôtel St Honoré where the committee had its headquarters.

"British War Relief for France!" echoed Marc Vallon. "Is that something we're supposed to be grateful for?"

"That's entirely up to you."

"Two British infantry divisions sent across the Channel at the right moment might have done more good than war relief."

"The Prime Minister thought our intervention would turn the French war with Prussia into a European conflict. I think myself Mr Gladstone was right," said Carey.

"Oh probably, if you take the short view. But things have changed since last July. There's a German Empire in the world now, and Bismarck's the master of Europe. You English will have to fight the Germans sooner or later, and you might as well have taken them on last summer as ten or twenty years from now. However, it's none of my business; I'm through with war." He drained his glass of brandy, and Ned rose to refill it, with his own.

"I wish you'd tell me what happened," he said. "How did you get back? Were you wounded again and sent home? Or did you escape from the internment camp, or what?"

"I did my escaping before we asked for Swiss hospitality, though I didn't plan it that way. No, I wasn't wounded, and I warn you it's not in the least a romantic story."

"Why can't you begin at the beginning?"

"You know how it all started. Last December Marshal Bourbaki went south with one hundred thousand men, with orders to cut the Prussian communications lines as General Faidherbe cut them at Amiens. But Bourbaki was

52

no Faidherbe. He said himself he was too old for the job. But Garibaldi's an old man too, and Garibaldi, with those two wildcat sons of his, gave us all a lesson in guerrilla warfare. We took Dijon (you heard about that, of course?) but we couldn't hold the city. We beat General von Werder, but Manteuffel was too much for us, and so was the snow and the shortage of everything from food to ammunition. Bourbaki tried to commit suicide, but he made a botch of that too, and General Clinchant took command. We didn't even know that the Government of National Defence, so-called, had surrendered, and the war was over. If Manteuffel knew, he kept it to himself, and carried on chasing us across the Jura into Switzerland.

"That was about the time I came down with dysentery. I told you it wasn't going to be a romantic story, but in fact that bout of dysentery saved my life. By that time most of us had either dysentery or typhoid, and the boys in our field hospitals hadn't much chance of survival. I was one of three lucky fellows who got as far as an old priest's house in a hamlet about ten kilometres east of Pontarlier. He nursed us in that presbytery till we recovered, on the same day as Clinchant was shaking hands with the Swiss general outside an inn at Les Verrières, and the Swiss peasants of the Val de Travers were wondering how they were going to feed over eighty thousand Frenchmen, and for how long. I heard the story of the surrender from two fellows who *did* escape across the border, and joined the three of us in Pontarlier."

"The surrender, or the internment, whatever you like to call it, was reported in Paris," said Carey. "But what did you do after Pontarlier?"

"Went off on my own, while the other boys made for Besançon. They had plans for living off the country, otherwise looting, which didn't suit me, so I headed for Lyon, where I spent a while dodging the National Guard's recruiters. I told them I thought I'd done my bit for France."

"But the Prussians, man?" said Carey. "Half the country's still under the Occupying Power."

"The Prussians were all right. They gave me food sometimes, and even a lift in their waggons. It was the French who had their knives out for me. A defeated man's never popular in France."

Marc's voice, which had been growing faint and unsteady as he told his story, suddenly grew louder again, and a feverish flush on his thin face alarmed Ned Carey.

"Steady on, old man," he said, "you need to rest. Bed's the place for you."

"That's what I told those leather-bottoms at the *mairie*," ex-Sergeant Vallon said. " 'Don't bother calling me up again, for I won't be there. I'm a painter, and from now on I'm going to paint.' My grandfather died in the snow in the retreat from Moscow. I was hunted through the snow like a sick wolf in the Jura, and now I – I'm through. . ."

His voice tailed off, his head fell forwards on his breast. With relief Carey heard Madame Camille's footsteps on the stairs. He went out silently, leaving the studio door ajar, and found the good woman on the landing, struggling with a wicker hamper containing logs and kindling.

"Here, give me that," he said. "Where's your warming-pan?"

"I couldn't carry everything at once, monsieur."

"Of course not. But get it now – I'll light the fire with newspaper – and put it straight into Monsieur Vallon's bed. Sleep is what he needs the most."

The concierge nodded, and Carey carried the hamper into the studio. A change in the position of Vallon's body on the sofa made him set his burden down in alarm. The

54

man had slumped forward with his head buried in the cushion and his long legs sprawling, with one hand trailing on the floor. But he was breathing, and Carey, that unappreciated painter, was artist enough to be aware of the symbolism of his faded uniform. The dark blue of the cutaway coat, once-white of the gaiters, scarlet of the baggy breeches, were a ghastly copy of the colours of France. If David Meade's powerful charcoal could have drawn that unconscious figure there would only be one caption for it:

Defeat.

The street lighting which came on while Edward Carey was hurrying back to his hotel was a great deal more impressive in the Place Vendôme than the oil lamp which created sinister shadows in the Impasse du Drapeau. A dozen gas globes illuminated the headquarters of the National Guard, the façade of the Ministry of Justice, and the bronze column erected to the glory of Napoleon I.

Carey had eyes only for the Justice Ministry on the west side of the square and for the lamplight which burned behind every shuttered window, particularly the light behind three windows which he knew belonged to one of the most powerful men in France. Baron Hubert de Grimont stood high in the councils of Adolphe Thiers, the newly elected chief executive, and it was predicted that from being under-minister of Justice he would be the Minister in the new cabinet when the Assembly reconvened at Versailles. His father had been plain Henri Grimont – the 'de' came with the title – whose financial expertise had helped to make life more comfortable for Louis Philippe when the old king fled to England in 1848.

Grimont had followed the maxim of the old king's minister, Guizot, which was '*Enrichissez-vous*', so well that his son was now a peer, a cabinet minister, the owner of a house in Paris and a château in the Sologne. He was also the husband of a beautiful woman twenty years his junior, who had taken Edward Carey for her lover.

His enemies, who were many, acknowledged de Grimont's immense powers of work. He was at his desk at nine o'clock and whether he lunched with his wife or some other man's wife, he was always back at the ministry by three o'clock, and never left it until half past seven. This was the fact that Carey was verifying by looking first at Baron de Grimont's lighted windows and then at his watch: it was still short of five o'clock, and Elvire would be with him in half an hour.

Sunday was the only day of rest observed by the devoted public servant, and even then he resumed the burdens of his office in the evening. Monsieur and Madame de Grimont's Sunday soirées were famous. No foreign envoy, no foreign correspondent could afford to miss one of these occasions, if only to hear his own rivals castigated by their host's sarcastic tongue. The American Minister, Elihu B. Washburne, had refused to return to the de Grimont house on the Rue St Florentin after being told:

"We expected nothing from the Americans, Monsieur le Ministre. Your country is too far from France to come to our aid with troops in time of war. But money, arms, support for our cause in your Congress and your press, these I think we did deserve. After all, did we not send you Lafayette and Rochambeau to lead your Revolution to victory against perfidious Albion?"

"I'm not goin' back there to be insulted," said the sturdy old Minister to his staff. "You young fellows can take it in turns to show the flag at Mr and Mrs Grimont's. I want to know what Britishers go there, and what they say."

A few sneers at the 'cowardice' of the British Ambassador and his staff in moving to Bordeaux was as far as Hubert de Grimont ever went in reviling perfidious Albion, and the Britisher who was the most honoured at his soirées was the munificent Richard Wallace. This was not only because of his great generosity to French sufferers from the war, but because Mr Wallace was the illegitimate relative of another Paris resident, the late Marquess of Hertford. The usual view was that Hertford, though only eighteen years older, was Richard Wallace's father, but specialists in English gossip held that Wallace was the bastard son of Hertford's mother. However it was, Hubert de Grimont, a parvenu baron of the Orleans monarchy, was not the man to sneer at a bar sinister when it lay across the coat of arms of an English marquisate. As for the young English painter whom Wallace brought once or twice to the Rue St Florentin, he was not worth wasting a mordant wit upon. He seemed to amuse Elvire.

"That poor child," said Paris society in the days when Elvire de Grimont was a bride of fifteen, "would never have had his offer of marriage if she hadn't been born the Princesse de la Treille, and she might never have accepted it if her bankrupt old father hadn't forced her into it for the money."

"De Grimont is good to her mother, give him his due," society was saying in the year of the Great Exhibition, when Elvire was no longer an ingénue. "It can't be easy to have old Marie de la Treille bedridden in your house year in and year out."

"That's why Elvire hasn't thrown her cap over the windmill long ago. She's just the sort to bolt with a stableboy, or her husband's secretary, or the second

57

footman —"

Or an art student.

The society of the Second Empire, piqued by Elvire de Grimont's steady refusal to yield to the seductions of the emperor, who laid siege to the young beauty as a matter of course, was wrong in its estimate of her character. She was not the woman to throw her cap over the windmill for a servant. Her affairs were conducted with great discretion, and in the satisfaction of her own intense sexuality she was avenging herself on the man to whom her father had sold her, and perhaps on her dead father himself. When her fancy fell on Ned Carey, with his English good looks and his frank admiration of herself, she began the liaison with a delightful sense of the risks she ran. His room at the Hôtel St Honoré was midway between her home and the Ministry of Justice. On the way to his arms it was always possible to meet her husband, but the place of their rendezvous was so well hidden that she felt safe from prying eyes.

The Hôtel St Honoré, which was highly respectable, stood next to the Hôtel de Bruxelles, which was not. The top floors of the two hotels were divided by a door to which a key could be had by bribing the head porter of the Bruxelles, and when Ned Carey got the key and opened the door he entered a different world. He took a second room there, an attic room which he called for form's sake a studio, and to which he transferred all the canvases, except Antony and Cleopatra, painted since he arrived in Paris. It also contained a divan bed with freshly laundered sheets which never lost their smell of patchouli, and a bidet on an iron stand behind a screen.

Madame la baronne de Grimont approached the place of assignation by another route. On the St Florentin side of the Hôtel de Bruxelles was a hat shop which had never run down its shutters during the Siege, with the words

'Delphine – Modes' in gilt curlicues on a window in which only two ultra-fashionable bonnets were ever on show. Some of Madame Delphine's customers went through the shop and upstairs to a salon where the most exclusive creations could be tried on in privacy. A few more went up higher, and used Madame Delphine's own key to enter the attic corridor of the Hôtel de Bruxelles. Madame Delphine's charge for this service was exorbitant.

At the same time as Babette Mercier and her sister were squabbling and crying and making up in the Impasse du Drapeau, Elvire and Ned Carey were in each other's arms in the Rue St Honoré. That pleased the young man: his mistress never put him off with chatter or endearments, nor, in their secret room, did the brilliant political hostess of the Sunday soirées waste time in discussing the political situation. She was there for primitive physical satisfaction, and when he unfastened her garments she flung herself on her young lover with an avidity which matched his own. This time, however, he was startled and dismayed when, after he had unwound her veil and kissed the blond curls at the nape of her neck, Elvire burst out:

"Hubert wants me to go to Hyères!"

"Hyères! But that's an impossible journey!"

"The trains are running to Marseille next week, and Hubert can get me a *laissez-passer* and a private coupé. He collaborates very well with the Occupying Power."

Carey almost asked her why Hyères? Then he remembered that her child was there, and had been in the care of her brother and his wife since the fall of the Empire. Elvire admitted she was 'not maternal', much as she loved her son. "I was only sixteen when I had him," she would say pathetically, "just a baby myself! He's far better off with his cousins at the Château de la Treille than in Paris, and for a delicate child the climate of the Riviera is *so* beneficial. . ." In fact Alain de Grimont was a sturdy boy

59

of ten, who had never had a day's illness in his life.

"But why Hyères now, when everything is settling down?" said Carey stupidly. He knew their affair would have to end some day, but not yet! He pushed her dress off her shoulders and kissed them in a frenzy of possessiveness.

"That's just it," said Elvire, trembling in his arms. "Hubert doesn't think anything is settled yet. He thinks there'll be big trouble with the Reds when Monsieur Thiers comes to Paris next week. He wants me out of the way."

The Reds and Monsieur Thiers. Carey was as sick of the sound of their names as he was of Bismarck, Trochu, Gambetta, Favre and all the adversaries who had bedevilled France almost since the day of his arrival. Heard from Elvire's lips after listening to Meade's sanctimonious pessimism about the National Guard, and Vallon's tragic account of broken men hounded across the frontier into an unwilling Switzerland, it was too much of a good thing. If his sister had been talking he would have told her to shut up, or at the very least snapped, "Now don't *you* begin!" It was impossible to say that to his mistress. He was deeply conscious of her noble birth, and sometimes at the height of their passion his unworthy thought would be, "I'm in bed with a princess whose blood is older than the blood of the Bourbons! If Meade and his little *grenouille* knew about this!" At that moment he took his cue and whispered,

"But *I* don't want you out of the way, my darling! I don't believe there's any danger now the war's over. I won't let you go."

He stopped her words with kisses, and Elvire had the assurance of her power over the young man whose splendid body, now bare, took her own with the brutality she craved. As they fell writhing on the divan, she would

60

have only known a more intense pleasure if Ned Carey
had beaten her.

5

The Rue St Jean was narrow, and the houses opposite threw their shadow on the Old Farm, but an unusually wide window on the ground floor gave light to the kitchen and to that part of it, divided by a wooden partition, which was officially the concierge's *loge*. It contained an empty rack for letters, an empty board for keys, and a bell rung by those who came to the little postern gate beside the big barred one to request admittance. There had been no callers for weeks now, but Madame Verlet insisted that there must always be someone in the kitchen, if not in the *loge* itself, to attend to the postman or to visitors. That was why Babette was sitting at the well-scoured wooden table on Sunday morning, while Madame Verlet attended eleven o'clock mass at St Pierre de Montmartre, two streets away. She had been zealous in the practice of her religion since the Siege days.

It was not uncomfortable in the kitchen. There was a curtain of crimson plush along the back wall, forming another partition behind which the concierge had her bed and a stand holding the night bell which before the war had often roused her to the cry of "*Cordon, s'il vous plait!*" There were two easy chairs in front of the stove, with a rag rug between them, there was also a small wood fire in the stove. Pushed to the back of it was a coffee pot containing the *petit noir* which was the wartime substitute for the real thing. It was a concoction made from coffee grounds which had done duty over and over again, as much sugar as could be spared, and boiling water mixed with the lees of brandy. It had been popular with the defenders of the Sixteen Forts.

Babette herelf was the uncomfortable element in the cosy kitchen. Neatly dressed in the grey merino and red garibaldi, with her hair brushed out of the fashionable chignon and falling in its natural wave to her shoulders, she was pale and drawn after a sleepless night, and sipping a *petit noir* without enjoyment. The miserable scene with Fanny, like all quarrels between young women, had gone on far too long, and covered other and older grievances than Babette's suggestion of a stay at Versailles. It ended, of course, in tears and kisses, and the gift of two more francs 'for the doctor' from Babette's own slender purse. The knowledge of how little money she had left made her think, inevitably, of the five gold napoleons in the American Legation envelope, now hidden under her mattress.

What am I going to do?

In spite of herself she had been impressed by what she had heard the speakers in the park and Didier Leblanc himself say about the new government's financial measures, so much more real to the workers than the unimaginable indemnity to be paid to the new German Empire. Babette realised that she herself would now be liable for eight months of back rent, and though she told herself "Old Foxy can't be hard on me, my attic's really his own storeroom!" she knew better than to rely on Monsieur Renard's generosity. I must find work, she thought. Perhaps I'd better make up my mind to be what Fanny called me, a *bonne à tout faire*, scrubbing floors and washing dishes for some bourgeoise down yonder in the Rue Caulaincourt.

At this moment the bell rang imperatively.

Startled, Babette opened the door in the partition and went into the *loge*. Standing in the Rue St Jean, with a girl by her side, was the woman she had least expected to see in all Montmartre: Louise Michel, the Red Virgin, whom she had heard inciting the crowd to arson and assassination in the Parc des Buttes Chaumont. She looked equal to any or all of these activities as she stood in the Sunday street, hatless, with dark hair brushed back from the broad brow which failed to compensate for a receding chin. The chin was not a weakness in the Red Virgin at forty. Her burning eyes, prominent nose and wide, compressed mouth all expressed her long grudge against society. She was out of uniform today, wearing a shabby black dress with a wide red sash, but still carried her rifle and bayonet, the blade rusted as though by blood.

Babette reluctantly opened the window, and asked, "*Vous désirez, mesdames?*"

"We desire to see the Citizeness Egorova," said the Red Virgin. "She lives here?"

"She lives in the Vine House, madame."

"Will you show us the way?" As she released the spring of the postern door Babette, with still greater reluctance, made for the back door of the Old Farm, and joined the two visitors in the green space where the daffodils grew and the path to the Vine House began. The younger of the two was a pretty girl in a pretty dress, who smiled in a friendly way at Babette.

Louise Michel, on the contrary, was surveying her

sternly from head to foot.

"You're too young to be the concierge, surely?" she said.

"The concierge is at mass, madame. I just live here."

"Don't say madame, say citizeness. What's your name?"

"Elisabeth Mercier, mad – *citoyenne*."

"How old are you?"

"Twenty next July."

"How do you earn your living?"

"I worked in the studios before the war."

"As a model?"

"Sometimes."

"You look strong and healthy. Why don't you join the Women's Battalion of the National Guard, and share in the fight against tyranny?"

"What fight?" said Babette. She felt a wave of fury at the catechism. "When France was at war I was a sempstress in the balloon factory in the Elysée-Montmartre. I thought that was a more useful job than parading through the streets with a rifle."

The other girl, silent until now, intervened with a laugh, and said, "Don't tease the child, comrade! She's wearing the right colour, isn't she?" She had an attractive foreign accent. "Come along now! I want to see Irene Egorova."

"You're right, Elisaveta. There's no time to lose," said the Red Virgin, and Babette, pulling the red garibaldi tightly round her shoulders, led them silently down the narrow path between the lilac bushes to the Vine House.

The shutters were all closed, but their approach must have been spied through a slat or a crack, because before they reached the door it was flung open, and a young woman appeared with outstretched hands.

"Louise! Elisaveta Karlovna!" There were kisses, and Babette, as she turned away, thought how ridiculous it was to see a bayonet involved in an embrace. She had time to notice that Madame Egorova had cropped auburn hair, and wore a dress strange to Parisian eyes. The black wool jersey, short pleated skirt and broad belt of pale leather was, if Babette had known it, the costume beginning to be worn by the young anarchist intelligentsia of St Petersburg, and a necessary prop was the yellow-paper cigarette in Irene Egorova's nicotine-stained fingers. All this she saw before the door shut, and she began to run up the path to the Old Farm. The concierge had come back from church, and was ready with the bad-tempered query:

"Where were you?"

When Babette, breathless, gave an account of the visitors, the concierge sniffed.

"I wonder if Monsieur Renard understood that his new tenants were mixed up with the Michel woman," she said. "She's hardly a good reference."

"I think she's horrible," said Babette. "She wanted me to join her awful Women's Battalion!" and Madame Verlet laughed.

"The only good thing I ever heard about Louise Michel is that she's devoted to her mother," she said. "She was a servant in some squire's house and the usual happened. I suppose that's why the Red Virgin, as they call her, hates all men ... Well, at least you remembered to put on the soup."

Their lunch consisted of thin potato soup and stewed apples (in no French time of crisis was there ever a shortage of apples) and was soon eaten. Babette was unusually silent, and broke into her friend's chatter about the church service only to remark that Madame Egorova's name appeared to be Irene, what was her husband's? The concierge must have a note of it somewhere, it was the law.

"It's Nicolas, I think," said Madame Verlet vaguely.

"And what does he do?" pursued Babette.

"Monsieur Renard said he was a correspondent for a Russian newspaper."

"Oh."

A new brew of *petit noir* was prepared, over which the older woman smacked her lips. Seeing Babette still pensive, she said tentatively:

"Are you going dancing this afternoon, my dear?"

"I'm not in a dancing mood today."

"You're upset about Fanny, aren't you?" The whole story of the Impasse du Drapeau had been told after Babette came in exhausted from her long tramp up the boulevards. "You didn't take the things she said seriously, did you?"

"Not really. I know it was just because she's ill and frightened about Louis, but oh! to see her in such awful poverty, at the mercy of that horrible man!"

"Maybe it would do you good to go dancing. You enjoyed yourself at the Moulin de la Galette last Sunday."

"I'm sick to death of that Malaval crowd."

And then, since 'Jo-Jo' Malaval and his brothers, formerly deserters and presently hard men, were those in whose company she had quarrelled with David Meade at the Brasserie des Martyrs, the whole story of Meade and his proposition of yesterday came tumbling out – every detail except the money he had forced on her. She waited for Madame Verlet's reaction to the love nest at Versailles, and was amazed to hear her old friend say,

"Really, child, you might do worse."

"Worse than set up house with a foreigner, just because he fancies me, when I've never even pretended to care for him?"

"Foreigner? He's an American, and all Americans are enormously rich. He'll treat you well, and who knows? If you pretend a little, you might even get him to marry you."

"The same way as Fanny got Didier to marry her? No thanks."

"Fanny was a fool, and missed her market, but you're not Fanny, Babette."

"Indeed I'm not."

"I only met Monsieur Meade once, but I knew he was a gentleman, *un vrai monsieur*, and if he'll give you a cottage and money in your purse it would be more than worth your while—"

Babette flushed scarlet. "Oh, Tante Lise, I'm sorry I ever told you. Don't let's talk about it any more."

Madame Verlet smiled. To Babette's excited imagination it was not the friendly smile of everyday but a death's head grin, the smile of a procuress. She jumped to her feet, and with unnecessary clatter began to wash up the luncheon plates in the stone sink. Madame Verlet rose too, and sank her portly body in the easy chair by the stove. Her next move, normally, would be to her feather bed behind the plush curtain for her Sunday afternoon siesta, with the *cordon* to her hand.

Babette cast one or two furtive glances at her counsellor over her shoulder. The concierge had been 'Tante Lise' to the Mercier girls since their father died, their mother's good friend; further than that they knew only that she was now sixty, and had been a dancer. No more details. For the first time Babette wondered what devious ways had brought a slim pretty girl of twenty, dancing in front of the lamplights of the Palais Royal in the July Days of 1830 when the Bourbons fled from France and Louis Philippe came to the throne, to a workmen's tenement in Montmartre and eventually to the security of a concierge's *loge*. What bargains, what compromises had she made with life? Tante Lise cleared her throat and said in a conciliatory voice:

"I was thinking, if you're staying in, I might walk round to the Place du Tertre and spend an hour or so with poor Madame Jaloux."

Madame Jaloux, a qualified midwife, was the widow of a minor official at the *mairie*, and her son was one of 400,000 Frenchmen prisoners of war in Germany.

She's going out because she went too far with me, and she wants to give us time to settle down, thought Babette, and said, "You do that. I'm sure she'll be glad to see you, poor soul." It was how house-mates kept the peace with one another, but when Babette was alone she had never felt more forlorn in her life. All her natural gaiety seemed to have frozen in twenty-four hours. Meade's purchase money, Fanny's ugly accusations, and now Tante Lise's cynical advice added up to a miserable fear of the future.

But there was one consolation which never failed her, and it was close at hand. Babette went up to her garret. It was too cold to paint there, even if she had dared to leave the *loge* (the Red Virgin might appear again, in uniform, with side-arms) and a thin veil of rain was falling between her window and the Vine House. She collected her sketching block, her box of watercolour paints and brushes, and the lacquer jar of daffodils. Back at the kitchen table, she filled an empty crock with water and began to paint.

Now she was back in the world she first entered when the fairy lamps shone over the lake in the Parc des Buttes Chaumont. The yellows, the blues and browns of her subject began to come alive, the daffodil petals seemed ready to stir. Babette had painted at this table when the cannon of the defenders belched death from the Sixteen Forts, and the Old Farm shook; she had painted flowers as an antidote to hunger in the Siege days; she was aware that she had more command of her paintbrush now. She worked until the first twilight came into the room, and then she sat back, flexed her shoulders, and drew a long breath. It was quite silent in the Rue St Jean.

When she heard the footsteps Babette's heart seemed to miss a beat. Only one man she knew ever walked like that, with a quick light tread which not even the army cadence had destroyed, and when her breath came back she pulled the cord which released the postern (there was no need of a summons), ran out of the back door into the grassy yard and straight into the arms of Marc Vallon.

He was so much taller than she that in earlier days he had caught her up in those strong arms, off the ground, bringing her mouth to the level of his mouth and laughing as he kissed her. Now there were tears on both their faces, and Marc seemed to stoop over her, leaning all his weight on her sholders, while she felt with dismay how thin he was under a familiar jacket of brown corduroy. She smelt rather than saw that he was no longer in uniform, for his clothing had the Marc-smell of male flesh, turpentine and cigarettes, and as he kissed her with dry lips their first words were nothing but childish repetitions, You're back, you're back; darling, darling; I'm here, I'm here, Babette.

The rain was falling, and the yard disengaged the scent of crushed grass and opening flowers. All Babette's joy was in the unspoken recognition, now at last it's spring.

It was Marc who drew the girl towards the open door and into the kitchen; it was Babette who said, "You're so wet, Marc! Would you like a *petit noir*?"

"Just you."

He sat down in Madame Verlet's big chair and pulled her into his arms, dropping his beret on the floor and opening his jacket to keep the damp away from her dress. She lay against his long thin body, feeling the uneven beating of his heart and the feverish heat in the hands

70

stroking her breasts. She captured one of those trembling hands and whispered that he must tell her how he made his way to freedom, so insistently that Marc began to talk, not in a whisper but audibly, lucidly describing the long road from the Swiss frontier to the Rue des Rosiers.

"And that's where you spent last night?" the girl said, raising her head.

"That's where I slept like" (he was going to say 'like the dead' but changed it to 'like a log') "from four yesterday afternoon to eleven this morning."

"What happened to Carey?"

"Carey was very good. He helped me to bed and then cleared out, I suppose to his hotel."

"His *hotel*?"

"Yes, he's had a room at the Hôtel St Honoré since he started working for some relief fund or other. Didn't you know?"

"Meade and I were there for lunch yesterday and he never so much as mentioned it."

For some reason Marc looked satisfied, but he only said, "Carey's a strange man."

"He's an *Englishman*," said Babette, as if that explained everything.

But the spell was broken. The mere .nention of their friends brought the thought of other friends, other problems, and destroyed the bubble of happiness which had enclosed their reunion.

Babette slipped out of Marc's arms and lit the tallow candle which stood on a shelf beside the stove. He opened his eyes and said, "What are you doing that for?"

"It's growing dark. Besides, I want to see you. You don't look very well, dear." In spite of her inexperience she knew he had some fever.

"I look a devil of a lot better than I did this time yesterday. A shave makes a big difference." But when he stood up he swayed and nearly lost his balance. Babette caught him by the arm and asked him when he ate last.

"I'm not hungry, darling. Madame Camille brought me some broth about one o'clock."

"Will you drink a glass of burgundy and eat a slice of bread?"

"Please." Marc sat down at the table while Babette drew the plush curtains across the window, fetched the best bottle they had in the cupboard and drew the cork expertly before he could offer to help her. She was the archetypal Siege girl, thinking first of food and drink, and Marc, raising his glass and saying "*Salut*!", thought how the conventional situation had been reversed. In a man's image of himself he was always the hero – even if not a conquering hero – coming back to the girl he left behind. Who would receive him as lovingly as Babette had done, listen to his story as worshipfully, but who had no story of her own. In the Siege of Paris the women had suffered as much from enemy action as the warriors in the field. He took Babette's hand as she sat down beside him and kissed it almost humbly, as he said, "You've lost your pink cheeks, my life. But there's something in your face now that 'takes the light', as Renoir used to say."

"Dear Renoir!"

"Have you any idea where he is now? Have you seen him?"

"No, I haven't seen him. I haven't seen any of the painters I first met in the Parc des Buttes Chaumont. But I do know where Renoir is – at Louveciennes with his parents."

"At Louveciennes! But that's no distance away! He got his discharge then, like me?"

"I suppose so. But he didn't have a war like yours. After the call-up he was with his regiment at Bordeaux, then he was posted to Tarbes, but never to any fighting front."

"Well, good for him. That's one of the great ones saved for posterity."

In a low voice Babette said, with her hand in his, "You knew about Bazille?"

"Of course I did." His voice was matter of fact. "Bazille was killed in action at Beaune-la-Rolande while I was at the Rennes depot, don't you remember?"

"There was so much killing, then and after."

"But he was the big loss. After he painted *Réunion de Famille* it looked as if he'd be the greatest of us all. And he was only twenty-nine when he fell. It must have hit you hard, Babette?"

With an attempt at lightness, she said, "He introduced me to a new world, darling. You could say he was my first love."

"And your first lover?" His calloused hand clenched on hers.

"Why didn't you ask him?"

"Oh, I did."

"And he said no."

"He said no."

"Suppose we leave it at that?"

The plush-hung walls of the kitchen seemed to be closing in on Babette. What's happening to us? she thought. Ten minutes ago *we* were lovers, in all but the final act, and now he talks as if he hates me! That harsh voice . . .

"Well, go ahead. Bazille's dead, Renoir's safe, what do you know about the others?"

"Not very much," said Babette. He had released her hand, finished his wine and accepted more. Ten minutes ago we were in each other's arms, and now we sit passing the bottle from one to the other like two friends at the Café Guerbois. "I don't see any of the old crowd now," she explained. "They're all scattered. Cézanne's still in Provence. Monet and Pissarro are still in London. Degas

73

and Manet both joined the National Guard, but I don't think they're in Paris. I'll tell you who *is* in Paris, and making a great to-do about revolution: Courbet." Even 'Jo-Jo' Malaval had heard of Courbet, Independent painter turned National Guard.

"Drunken old fool," said Marc. His feverish restlessness made him rise and prowl round the kitchen. "A revolutionary, you say? Not bad at fifty-two." He stopped short. For the first time, so deep was the shadow outside the ring of light cast by the candle, he had seen the jug of flowers, the painting materials and the half-finished picture on the sketching block. "Is *this* what you've been doing? Bring the light."

Babette took the candle from its shelf and set it on the table beside the flower painting. "I was working by daylight," she said needlessly. "Do – do you think it's any good?"

"Very – good – indeed. Far better than any of the little things you used to do." He studied the water-colour judiciously. "Darling, you ought to be working in oils."

"Oh, M-Marc!" Stammering with pleasure, but pretending it was a joke, she said, "But I haven't got any oils."

"There's a whole box of Winsor and Newton tubes waiting for you at my place. Carey made his collection over to me before he left."

"Does that mean he's giving up painting?"

Carey would have recognised cheeky Babette in the tone of the question, which Marc ignored. In another swift change of mood he seized her once again in his arms, and asked "Do you love me, Babette?"

"Don't you know I do?"

"Then come home with me now."

"Oh, Marc, you know I can't do that!"

"Not this very minute, but after the old girl comes back from wherever she is. Tell her you're moving out. Pack what you need and come back with me to the Rue des Rosiers. I can't do without you, my sweet. I need you to share my life."

"Because —" she prompted him, and closed her eyes to hear the words, because I love you too.

"Because I want to paint you."

6

When David Meade turned the corner of the Rue St Jean on Monday morning he saw Babette at the fountain. She was bare-headed, with her hair loose and the sleeves of her black alpaca dress rolled up; round her waist she had tied a long apron of coarse blue and black striped material. She was chatting with the other women for whom the fountain was a regular meeting place, but she had turned to go back to the Old Farm, lifting her pitcher to her shoulder with the immemorial gesture of the water carrier, when she caught sight of Meade.

"Bonjour, monsieur!"

The women giggled. David Meade was formally dressed for his working day in dark clothes, with a frock coat and a tall silk hat, such attire as was seldom seen on the Butte Montmartre. They thought Babette's greeting was a *grenouille*'s piece of impudence and were amazed when the stranger came forward raising his hat, and took the pitcher from Babette.

"Let me carry this for you. You're going home?"

"Certainly." She took his offered arm. "Where have you

come from? I thought you'd be out at Versailles."

"Monsieur Thiers isn't expected for a day or two. I've come straight from the Rue des Rosiers. Babette, I've seen Marc Vallon."

She halted for a moment (and in those sabots it was a wonder she could walk at all) and said, "He came to see me yesterday. What did you think of him?"

"He's pretty well, I think, all things considered. Carey told me he was back, when I saw him on Sunday evening at a reception at the Baron de Grimont's. Babette, we've got to talk."

She looked at him coolly, and her black brows met in a straight line over her dark eyes. "Yes, I'd like to talk to you too. But not in the street, and not at the Old Farm. Where shall we go?"

"To one of the cafés in the Place du Tertre, perhaps? If La Mère Catherine's open, shall we go there?"

"It is open. But I can't go in my kitchen dress. Will you wait for me there while I change?"

"Don't be long."

He gave her back the jug of fresh drinking water at the postern door of the Old Farm, bowed, and walked the short distance to the Place du Tertre. There were several cafés open in that attractive square in the very heart of Montmartre, and they were all doing good business, while groups of men were talking earnestly under the budding trees. Meade found an inconspicuous place at the back of the Mère Catherine's *salle*, reflecting that it had listened to confidences and conspiracies since 1793, and took a small sketch book from the tail pocket of his coat. When the waiter brought him a bottle of wine and two glasses he was drawing in charcoal, rapidly and from memory.

When he looked up his subject stood before him in her grey dress and light shoes, the bonnet with the artificial flowers and a pelisse of mauve shot silk. She carried a macramé bag of the same colour, and was rouged to an extent which drew knowing glances from the men at the adjacent tables. Meade pulled out a chair for her, filled her glass and thanked her for coming. "I hope you won't catch cold," he said. "That jacket, or whatever you call it, is too thin for a day like this."

"I've been criticised for wearing Berthe Morisot's cast-offs," she said. "I wanted to wear something of my own today, though it isn't summer yet." She raised her glass. "*A votre santé, monsieur*! I didn't expect you in Montmartre so soon."

"You said I might come to you, and I came as soon as I heard Vallon was back. I wanted to know if you were the happiest girl in the world."

She lifted one little hand and let it fall on the table in a denying gesture.

"Something went wrong?"

"Meade, I'm worried about him. He spoke as if he loved me, next moment he taunted me with Bazille. Then he talked about our friends and where they were, then about my painting; then he asked me to go back to the studio with him – and stay."

"And you refused?"

"Yes. Then Tante Lise came in, and that was that."

"I wondered if I'd find you at the studio today," said Meade lightly.

"Was that why you went to the Rue des Rosiers first?"

"Hardly. Carey gave me rather an alarming account of Vallon's health, so I wondered if he needed a doctor, or invalid food, or anything I could get him."

"And did he? I thought he had fever yesterday."

"He was well enough to be packing up two small canvases to take to the Drouot sale rooms today. He told me he expected you on Tuesday morning – for a sitting."

"He told you that?" said Babette. Her face was crimson.

78

"Yes he did. So I thought – if you were only going to be artist and model to each other, I should come at once to ask if after all there might be hope for me."

"Hope that I might put myself – what did you call it? under your protection?"

"Yes."

Babette shook her head. "I don't know what makes you think you love me. I think you must be very lonely here in Paris, to invent a fancy for a girl like me. There must be someone, somewhere, far more fit to be your true love – a girl of your own sort, whom you wouldn't think you had to buy."

"I never dreamed of buying you."

"Didn't you?" Babette took an envelope from her little macramé bag.

"I want to return this to you," she said, with a sudden assumption of formality very unlike her last impulsive words. "You pretended it was fiacre fare. I suppose you meant it as a down payment."

Too taken aback to reply, David Meade sat staring at the white square with one corner torn off and the words Legation of the United States of America engraved on the other. He saw the slight bulge made by the five gold napoleons which the little *grenouille* had scorned to accept, and heard her say relentlessly:

"What do you take me for – a light woman?"

At that he regained the aplomb he practised daily in his profession, and said "No, no! You mustn't think that. You mustn't feel insulted! I only meant it as a little gift between friends. I knew how hard things looked like being for you when the new rent regulations came into force, and this was just my clumsy way of trying to help you. I'm sorry, dear. I'm really sorry."

She said nothing, but her mouth softened into a smile.

"Don't be upset by my stupidity," said Meade, pressing

home his advantage. He took up the envelope and weighed it in his hand. "Five gold napoleons, one hundred francs. It isn't really very much. And you could earn it, if you wanted to."

"*Earn* it? In what way?"

"By telling me anything you can about the Russians in the Vine House. The Egorovs or Igorovs."

"The Egorovs, Nicolas and Irene. Tante Lise told me that; every concierge has to keep a list of the *locataires*."

"Anything else?"

"Monsieur Egorov is the correspondent for a Russian newspaper."

"Is he though. Then he's on record at the Préfecture de Police, and I've an appointment with Edmond Adam, the Prefect, this afternoon. I'll check up on Egorov. What's the manservant's name?"

"I forgot to ask. But Tante Lise must have it too."

"Sometimes in those émigré Russian households the manservant is more important than the master."

"I don't understand why you're so interested in the Russians!"

Meade sighed. "I know you hate political talk, and you think I'm an alarmist about the National Guard –"

"Don't worry about that. I began to come round to your way of thinking about the Guard on Saturday afternoon. And on Sunday *our* Russians had a visitor I didn't like the smell of – in more ways than one."

She briefly described the speeches in the park and the visit of Louise Michel and her friend to the Egorovs. Meade's inconsequent reply was, "How did you find your sister?"

"Not very well. She thanks you kindly for what you sent." Babette had no intention of involving the Impasse du Drapeau in the Russian story.

"Tell me about the young girl with Michel. How old

might she be?"

"Oh, about my own age – say twenty. Very pretty, very blond, and her first name's almost the same as mine. Elisaveta."

"Elisaveta Dmitrieva, by all that's holy!" Meade said in a low voice. "We knew she'd landed, but she went to ground at once ... So now she's hunting with the Michel woman: that's a clue ... Thank you, Babette." He closed her hands over the Legation envelope. "You've earned that and more too."

"But who *is* she, Meade?"

"Karl Marx sent her over from London to be his *rapporteuse* in France." He looked at his watch. "Excuse me, dear. I'll explain it all to you another time, and soon. Right now I've got to get back to the Legation: I hope I can tell the Minister before he goes home to lunch. Anything more you find out about the goings-on at the Vine House, send me a message at 95, Rue de Chaillot. What are you looking so dubious about?"

"I don't like it, Meade. It feels like being a police informer."

"*Mouchard*'s an ugly word. But this has nothing to do with the police – yet. Oh, I nearly forgot. Before I take you back to the Old Farm, I've got something else to give you." He took the little sketch book from his pocket, where he had replaced it when Babette came in, and held it, closed, while he chose his next words.

"Be patient with Marc, dear. He's had a terrible war, from the wound at Wörth to that awful retreat across the Jura, and the long tramp home. Go along with his moods and pose for him, if that's all he wants for now. But – with my compliments – give him this."

He took two sheets from the sketch book and passed them across the table. The sketches were identical, done in bold, economical charcoal strokes, and showed a spout of water flowing into an iron basin, before which a girl was lifting a pitcher in a lovely fluid movement of one slender arm. Both were captioned 'Babette at the Fountain'.

She wanted to be cheeky Babette, and say "Another of your famous Paris street scenes, I suppose?" but it wasn't possible. She said, "Thank you, dear. Your drawing's wonderful. Are they both for me?"

"No, just one, to give to Marc. The other I'm going to try to get published."

"In a Paris paper? Oh!"

"If that'll make you happy."

<hr />

Babette had been around the studios long enough to know that you didn't show an artist successful work done by another man, even by a talented amateur, when he was on the point of starting a new project in a different medium. She kept David Meade's sketch, enclosed between two pieces of cardboard, in her big wool bag when she reached the studio on the Rue des Rosiers next morning, and produced only the *demi-baguette* and the half litre of milk she had bought along the way. Marc greeted her lovingly. He was wearing the trousers of his brown corduroy velvet suit, a well washed old shirt checked yellow and white and open at the neck, and over everything his painting smock, from which no amount of laundering would remove the stains. He was looking very much better.

"You're none the worse for your trip into Paris?" she said, when he released her from that long embrace. "Did you sell your pictures? Which were they?"

"Sold them both. Two from the Forest of Fontaine-bleau days, and I got five francs for one and seven for the other." He shrugged. "It all helps to keep the pot boiling, though I'm not flat broke like most of the boys used to be. Carey paid rent to Madame Camille on the first of every month without fail, and when I offered to repay him for the second two weeks of March, he refused to accept it."

"So I should hope," said Babette. "He must be very rich." She looked round the studio, restored to the old tranquillity of its bare grey-green walls, and realised what was missing.

"What's happened to Carey's advertisement for Horse-flesh on Sale?"

Marc grinned. "You mean Antony and Cleopatra? A hotel porter came with a wheelbarrow to collect it just before I went out yesterday. I was glad he didn't have his trudge up the Butte in vain. No doubt the thing will grace an English drawing room some day. Now, darling! old Moïse at Drouot told me where to find a little shop where they were selling coffee beans — at a price — and I spent some of my earnings on a kilo. Get out the old grinder and grind us enough for two bowls, and I'll prepare the paints."

"Aren't you going to use the Winsor and Newton stuff?" she asked, with a longing look at the box which Carey had turned over to his friend.

"No, they're for you. But I shan't give you a lesson in oils until I've got your portrait started. Moïse says there's more of a market in portraits than anything else. The Independents are out of favour, he told me, what the public wants are great brawling battle pieces, or troops on parade in the Meissonier style, all cocked hats and sabretaches, so as to make our bellicose public think we won the war."

It was like old times, or better than old times, since she had Marc all to herself, to be sitting on the kitchen stool drawn up to the stove, in which there was now a very small wood fire, and turning the handle of the grinder while the delicious smell of coffee rose up from the iron box. At the table Marc was busy with the work his father taught him in the little artist-colourman's shop he had owned on the Rue Vavin, mixing the paint contained in powder form in the flacons of an old portable paintbox, of which his small rectangular palette was inside the lid. Marc liked the old-fashioned methods, and Babette was surprised when he showed her a commercially prepared canvas, Number 25. She had often prepared canvases for him with a base of silver white, but he explained that he hadn't time to wait for the preparation, he wanted to get on with the composition. This was not the usual practice in his group, for the Independents believed in long reflection on their subject before beginning the *mise en page*. After that, of course, they believed in spontaneity, and Renoir, in particular, was noted for the anxious rapidity of his brush strokes.

When they were sitting on opposite sides of the big table (and Marc placed Babette with her back to the window) drinking *café au lait* from big white bowls with a blue flower design, he told her that he had had bad luck yesterday: he had missed meeting Renoir at the Drouot sale rooms by little more than an hour. However, their friend was still at Louveciennes, and intended to remain there. Suppose Marc and Babette went out to see him there one of these days, if there was any sort of conveyance from their old base at Chatou? Remember how Renoir often slipped away to see his parents when they were all together at La Grenouillère?

"That would be lovely," said Babette, anxious to follow his restless mood. "When shall we go? When it's a little warmer?"

"When the picture's finished."

"Oh, Marc, I'm so excited about the picture! How will

you paint me?"

"Just as you are."

"And call it Girl in a Garibaldi?"

"*Que diable, non*! You'll take off that red waistcoat – a garibaldi, d'you call it? before I start. I saw enough of the Red Flag in Lyon to sicken me of the colour for the rest of my days."

"You've got it right across the street from you now."

"Yes, well, those fellows seem quite harmless," said Marc. "Drinking and singing are about all they're good for."

The invisible National Guardsmen, who all seemed to be indoors on this cold day, obligingly came in on cue by beginning to sing the Carmagnole. The famous song of the French Revolution was very popular, and Marc heard it a dozen times a day.

Dansons la Carmagnole, vive le son, vive le son,
Dansons la Carmagnole, vive le son du canon!

Babette thought of the captured cannon on the Champ Polonais, and shivered. Marc was already in the kitchen, thinking only of his picture. He came ou⁺ with a plate, a paring knife, and some of the ubiquitous green apples.

"Don't move," he said as she got up. "I'll bring the little kitchen table out tomorrow. Now I just want to get the pose. I want to paint you *à contre jour*, with the light from the window behind you, and in front the shadows full of reflected light. You'll be peeling one apple, with three or four others on the plate, and the whole thing will be a study in greys, greens, and violet cobalt. Girl with Green Apples, I'm going to call it, and it'll knock their eyes out!"

The rest of their time together until twilight, with a pause for bread and cheese and a glass of wine, was spent by Babette in holding the pose, with the paring knife and an apple in her hands, while Marc measured, sketched, and made notes on the colours to be laid up on his palette. He intended to work with only a few, including flake white, and for the greens viridian, emerald and chrome, the latter a mixture of Prussian blue and chrome yellow. Violet cobalt, a colour introduced about ten years earlier, and a great favourite with the Independents, was a true dense violet, which would give deep shadows to the grey. When he stopped to light the lamp and say they would go on from there tomorrow, Babette relaxed and stretched, and smiled when he added, "You get a model's pay for this, you know. Regular rates."

"Fine. But before I go, there's something I have to give you."

She found her bag, and told him she had had a glass of wine with David Meade at the Mère Catherine the day before.

He digested this, and said, "Good, I'm glad you told me. I liked the way you told me about having lunch with him and Carey here on Saturday, and going off with him later. Just tell me one more thing. I was mortally jealous of Bazille that first summer; have I got to be jealous of the American now?"

"Marc, how can you even think it?"

"But he's in love with you, isn't he?"

"What in the world makes you say that?"

"I knew it yesterday by the way he spoke your name."

She knew that any sort of admission would be fatal, for the painter was shaking in the grip of a nervous chill. She said as lightly as she could, "He's only interested in me as a subject. Look at this!" And she gave him the sketch of Babette at the Fountain.

He took it, looked long, and smiled in admiration. "When was this done?"

"Yesterday morning, before we went to La Mère Catherine. You can see by my clothes we had no rendezvous. He only came to tell me how you were, because he thought I would be worrying."

Marc Vallon looked again at the sketch, and said, "He really is a draughtsman, isn't he ... I can see I'll have to make Girl with Green Apples a smashing success."

"I know you will, darling."

She was so pretty, with her hair loose and her dark eyes full of light, that the man muttered as he took her in his arms, "I can't bear to take you back to the Old Farm."

"Ah, but you must, or I'll have to go alone. It's getting dark."

"Babette, why won't you stay with me? Tonight, and always?"

"I don't know – I want to – but I can't. Don't force me, Marc. Not yet."

Neither of the men who loved her, not even Babette herself, held the key to her resolute refusal to take a step which would have meant nothing to her in the old careless studio days before the war. The key, of course, was the miserable condition of her sister, the weakness which led to the forced marriage and so to grinding poverty and illness. When she thought of the chances she had taken when she first joined forces with the men of Montmartre – of the risks she had run in the degraded company of thieves and rascals like 'Jo-Jo' Malaval's gang, the little *grenouille* could only give thanks for her good luck. As she tried her hand, under Marc's direction, at a still life in oils, consisting of two apples, an onion, and one of the blue and white bowls, or when she saw her image – subtly altered by another human's visual perception and the calligraphy of an adroit paintbrush – reflected in Girl with Green Apples, she saw new horizons opening before her, not to be closed for the mere satisfaction of an appetite, and disturbed only by fleeting thoughts of Fanny. I've got money to give her now, was the dominant thought. I'll go to see her on Saturday afternoon, and then I'll take her myself to that doctor.

Louise Michel, whom she loathed, and Elvire de Grimont, of whom she had never heard, might have understood Babette's refusal of the love she craved. Both, in their very different ways, were vowed to vengeance on the male sex, Louise because of her mother's seduction, Elvire because of her father's venality. Babette, subconsciously, was avenging her sister's folly, and scourging herself in penance for it. Elvire de Grimont, on the Friday of that beautiful week in March, came closest to understanding when at five in the afternoon, as she was dressing for a rendezvous with her lover, her husband came in a hurry to her boudoir.

He arrived at the moment when she was in the *cabinet de toilette* exchanging the elaborate substructure of chemise, corset, cambric drawers, camisole and lace-trimmed petticoats for a chemisette with suspenders for her silk stockings. It would be the work of a moment to remove when, in half an hour's time, Ned Carey took off her dress in the Hôtel de Bruxelles. When she heard her husband's voice in the outer room she wrapped her feathered négligé close around her and went out to greet him.

"What brings you home so early, Hubert? Is anything the matter?"

"Only this," said the Baron de Grimont, and his sarcastic mouth was twisted, "Monsieur Thiers has taken the advice I gave him at Versailles yesterday and come into Paris. The whole cabinet is summoned to a meeting at the Quai d'Orsay within the hour, so I came home to change and tell them to bring round the carriage."

"How clever you are, *mon ami*! How often have I heard you say Thiers can never govern France except from Paris!"

"Everyone has heard me say it. I hope the old fool hasn't left it too late, that's all ... Now I must hurry."

He went through their bedroom to his own dressing room on the other side and she heard him shouting for his valet. A cabinet council at the Foreign Office – that would take all evening, and she could risk another hour with the young man who for the time being obsessed her senses. Even without help – for her maid, Désirée, was never allowed to be present at these transformations – she had the négligé off and a closefitting dress of crimson cloth on, the matching jacket with its wasp waist and flared basque adjusted, and was smoothing her bonnet strings when her husband came back suitably dressed for a meeting with the Chief Executive.

"Are you going out?" he said, surprised.

"Sylvie de Lhomond has a musicale this afternoon, I thought I might look in." It was the first time since the affair with Carey began that she had ever had to lie about her absence, but there would be so many people at the musicale that she was hardly likely to be caught out.

"I'll send the carriage back for you immediately."

"No need for that, it's only round the corner in the Rue Royale."

"All right, but don't make any plans for going out tomorrow. I wish now I had packed you *and* your mother off in an ambulance to our place in the Sologne."

"Why, are you really expecting trouble?"

"Work it out for yourself, Elvire. Monsieur Thiers is wildly unpopular with the working class, and they have four hundred thousand National Guards, all armed, on their side. He has only twelve thousand troops of the Line, by the grace of God and Bismarck, to uphold his authority. Our meeting will consider what further steps to take for safety; more than that I'm not permitted to say. We have no guests tonight, I think?"

"None. Shall I have the pleasure of your company at dinner?"

He gave a short laugh. "I shall be fortunate to be home for breakfast."

He kissed her hand and hurried out.

Elvire drifted to the window of her boudoir, which overlooked the courtyard of the *hôtel* de Grimont. She saw the carriage at the front door, and her husband descending the steps (he must have run downstairs), the footman holding the door open, and the two matched greys stepping out. What a pompous little man he was! A carriage and pair to cross the Seine from the Rue de Rivoli to the Quai d'Orsay! She watched as the great gates were shut on the Rue St Florentin by two men in the de Grimont livery. Silence fell on the courtyard, where the gardeners had already filled stone boxes with spring flowers. Safety, prosperity, protection – what disturbance could break in here? One more time with Edouard – one more time before Thiers and his cabinet took the 'further steps' Monsieur Pomposity was 'not permitted' to describe.

But I can guess what they'll do if they've any sense, thought Elvire de Grimont. They will spike the cannon of Montmartre.

responsible for building the fortifications – the Sixteen Forts – which were to defend Paris in 1870; so much was to his credit. But to the Baron de Grimont – precisely as to the Central Committee of the National Guard, which posed as an alternative government – he was hopelessly identified with the limited aims and restrictions of the Orleans Monarchy, and nearly a quarter of a century behind the times.

The only comfort de Grimont had from the meeting came early in the evening, when he was congratulated on the part the men from his ministry had played in tracking down an elderly Socialist named Adolphe Blanqui, who had already spent twenty-eight years in prison on political charges, and having him arrested again on a technicality. Before they turned to the business of the guns a light meal was served in another room, one of the vast suite whose windows gave upon the river, and there was sufficient informality in the service to allow de Grimont to take his glass into one of the window bays and look out at the Seine. There was enough gas lighting to let him see across the Concorde bridge and the Concorde square to the Rue Royale, and he wondered idly if his wife had enjoyed the Comtesse de Lhomond's musicale.

Then the soldiers came in and presented their plans for the recapture of the cannon at Montmartre and Belleville. General le Flô, the War Minister, had little to say, but General Vinoy, who was in command, was tough and experienced. With his XIII Corps he had arrived too late on the field of Sedan, but he had led sorties from Paris during the Siege which had given him the utmost contempt for the fighting qualities of the National Guard. He had quelled the Guards' attack on the Hôtel de Ville in January. He was now convinced that twelve thousand troops of the Line, plus three thousand gendarmes, could easily defeat an armed rabble if he mounted a surprise attack. He proposed to divide his forces into four, to attack at Belleville, the Bastille, and the Hôtel de Ville — the last as a covering operation — and commit two brigades to the major objective on the Butte Montmartre. The attack would begin at 3 a.m.

"I think we can leave matters to the military now, gentlemen," said Adolphe Thiers. "We shall meet tomorrow morning and congratulate General Vinoy." Hubert de Grimont, as he bade the Chief Executive goodnight, knew that the goblin-like, little old man would stay awake himself until the gallopers came in with the first account of the 3 a.m. attack, perhaps without retiring to the state bedroom of the Foreign Office. De Grimont walked home. Even with his love of pomp he would not keep his horses out of their stable on a cold March night. His butler, two footmen and his valet were all waiting for his arrival.

Madame la baronne had dined in her boudoir, had complained to her maid of headache, and had retired early, he was told. Their bedroom was in darkness. De Grimont lit a wax candle in a silver sconce, and moved softly through a maze of sofas upholstered in pink satin, cheval glasses, dressing tables, until he stood beside the lace-draped bed. Elvire was smiling in what seemed to be a profound slumber. Her golden hair (she had begun to touch it up a little) was spilled across a pillow also trimmed with lace, and there was a froth of the finest Mechlin on the high neck of her nightgown. Her husband felt no stirring of desire — and she would feel none, he knew too well, when he slipped into the great bed beside her — but he was very tired. He was about to blow out the candle and undress in the dark when something caught his eye in the faint light. Elvire had left undone the three pearl buttons at the neck of her gown, as she often did, but tonight there was a tiny blue mark on the white flesh, such a mark as the light women of Paris called a love bite. He bent closer to make sure, and then with his hand he struck out the candle flame, and made his way in darkness to the bed in his dressing room.

The future Minister of Justice heard the hours strike on the antique clock in the corridor outside his room, while he lay awake in a rage of suspicion, surmise and plans to bring his cheating wife to justice. Subconsciously, perhaps, he was waiting for three to strike, when the dawn attack to recapture the guns was timed to begin, and when the three strokes came he did indeed fall into a fitful sleep. He was awakened by a totally unexpected sound: the ringing of the tocsin from the nearest church, calling the city to arms.

The division sent to recapture the guns of Montmartre was under the command of General Susbielle, with Generals Paturel and Lecomte as his brigade commanders. By the time Hubert de Grimont reached the Quai d'Orsay on horseback, just before seven o'clock, it was the name of Lecomte which was on the lips of the shocked men in the council chamber, and through all the confused accounts which reached them during the next terrible hours, it was Lecomte who bore the burden of the defeat at Montmartre.

Vinoy, who should have known, failed to realise that the 88th Regiment under Lecomte's command was composed of youths who had never seen active service. The flower of the French Army – those who still survived – were either prisoners of war in Germany, mutilated patients in the wards of medieval hospitals or internees in Switzerland. In spite of their inexperience, however, the boys marched up the one road to Montmartre in great

94

style, reached the Champ Polonais where the great guns were parked, and were almost punctual to the hour of three. They opened fire on the National Guards on night patrol, who fled in the disarray Vinoy had anticipated, only one of their number being slightly wounded. A detachment was sent to arrest the men at the command post in the Rue des Rosiers, and it was all over. The cannon of Montmartre were once again in the hands of the government.

It was then that General Lecomte made a devastating discovery.

They had forgotten to bring horses to drag the guns away.

For one wild moment it occurred to the general to transport the guns downhill the same way as they had come up – harnessed to the bodies of his men. He quickly dismissed the idea. They had no ropes, and what was more the guns were now so deeply embedded in mud that only teams of horses would move them rapidly. With men in harness, they could be intercepted before the cortège got as far downhill as the Place de la Trinité. It was a miracle that the National Guard had not turned out already. There was another command post not far away at the Château Rouge, an aptly named building which had been a dance hall. He fell out his gallopers, ordered one to ride to the Quai d'Orsay and the others to make all speed to the two nearest cavalry barracks, requisitioning horses to be sent to the Butte Montmartre at once. After they had gone he remembered that draught horses, not cavalry chargers, would be the right animals for the job.

It was too late. The exchange of fire between his men and the night patrol had been brief but audible in the lanes of the village. It had been caught by the quick ears of Comrade Louise Michel. She put on her uniform, seized her rifle and bayonet, and ran out. She saw the men of the

88th Regiment standing round the gun park, waiting for orders, and understood it all. With wild shrieks of "Treason! Treachery! *Aux armes*!" she roused her fellow members of the Vigilance Committee, and with them the whole able-bodied population of Montmartre.

"*Aux armes, citoyens!*" Never since the *Marseillaise* was written had the heroic invocation been sung with more passion. As dawn came up, while Lecomte and his men surrounded the guns, they were surrounded in turn by a tide of humanity, shouting, swearing, ready for violence, through which the horses, when they came, could well have difficulty in making their way. Louise Michel, now brandishing her rifle, was orchestrating the movement of the crowd, urging them to march to Versailles and assassinate Thiers. And the horses never came.

At dawn, with National Guards arriving from the Château Rouge, from the Place Clichy, eventually from all directions, she persuaded the men to have the tocsin rung.

It awoke Marc Vallon. He had been sleeping very soundly, for in less than a week since his dramatic return he had regained much of his usual health and vigour. The fever had gone from his powerful body, and the therapy of painting had cured his nervous restlessness. On Friday night, after he came back from the Old Farm, he had made up his mind that there was to be no more shilly-shallying with Babette. He was not a rapist, but he meant to have her, and on Saturday night he would make her stay with him.

Now it was Saturday morning, and the tocsin was ringing from the belfry of St Pierre. When it penetrated his sleep he shouted "No!" When last he heard the tocsin he had perforce to cross Paris to the *mairie* of Montparnasse, where for the first time since his conscript service days he was issued with an army uniform, a soldier's kit and a rifle, and sent out on the long road that led from Wörth through Dijon to the Swiss frontier. He was determined never to take such a road again. But the tocsin! Had the Prussians gone back on their armistice agreement? Unbelievably, he had slept through the racket when the troops of the Line occupied the command post on the other side of the street.

He pulled on his shirt and trousers, thrust his feet into his boots, and went to look out. There was no sign of life on the Rue des Rosiers, except for a few birds chirping in the gardens and a prowling cat. The tocsin was silent, and that it had rung at all seemed to be part of a dream. Marc shrugged, and went to brew some coffee. The daylight was growing brighter every minute, and sleep was over for the night.

With the coffee bowl in his hand he sat down in front of the English easel, on which the new canvas stood – half the size of that monstrosity of Carey's. He was pleased with what he had made of Girl with Green Apples. It was not a photographic likeness of the model, rather an impression of Babette, but it was very much what most of the Independents strove for in their painting of ordinary people – ironing, or taking a bath, or sitting over a drink in a wineshop. Darling Babette – she had cleaned his palette beautifully before he took her home the night before, and there it was ready to his hand with linseed oil and turpentine to pour into the little cups. In an hour or so, before she came to pose again, the daylight would be right for some brush strokes on the light *à contre jour*.

Only just out of earshot, there was now a tremendous noise on the Butte Montmartre. General Lecomte's mount, as he waited in vain for the gun horses, was plunging and kicking, and he had an infantryman hanging on to its bridle. His NCOs were being baited by the rabble, who had mistaken Lecomte for General Vinoy, and were urging them to let the old bastard go, and come over to the People's side. His young soldiers had already made up their minds. Convinced by the National Guards who surrounded them, supported by a throng of whores, drunks, thieves, vagrants and respectable citizens, they began to reverse their rifles, turning them butts upper-most as an indication that nothing was to be feared from them. Louise Michel led the shouts of "Long live the Line!" which followed, and in the pandemonium General Lecomte lost his head. He shouted an order to fire on the mob, not likely to be obeyed by mutinous troops, and then shouted another foolish order, "Fix bayonets! Defend yourselves!" It was the ultimate provocation. To cat-calls of "Down with Thiers!" the general was pulled from his rearing charger and hustled through the streets to the command post at the Château Rouge.

The noise of this triumphal progress reached the Rue des Rosiers, to which as a consequence a body of Guardsmen set forth to liberate their comrades held at Number Six. There was no difficulty about their deliver-ance. The troops of the Line were as willing to fraternise as their comrades at the Champ Polonais, and Marc Vallon watching in disbelief saw them leaving the villa with their arms round the necks of their newfound friends, and their free hands brandishing litre bottles of wine. They all went whooping down the narrow street in pursuit of the main body of celebrants, and Marc, hastily putting on a cravat and his corduroy jacket, ran downstairs to confer with the concierge.

Madame Camille, as usual, was well informed. Some of the urchins for whom this was a day of superlative excitement had followed the liberators to the Rue des Rosiers and told her of the frustrated attempt to recapture the guns. "To arrive without horses, monsieur, can you imagine such a folly!" was her comment, and personally she thought the day's disturbance had only begun. The tenants of the ground floor apartment, *des gens bien*, but as you know, monsieur, of a certain age, had already closed their iron shutters and barricaded their door, and she intended to do the same. The tenants of the middle apartment had left Paris at the beginning of the Siege, and Monsieur Marc, of course, had been a soldier, and could look out for himself.

"Yes, but what about Ma'mselle Babette?" said Marc. "I'm going to the Rue St Jean now, madame. I don't suppose she'll have left the Old Farm, but if by some chance she has and I miss her on the way, will you open the door when she rings the bell and let her into the studio?"

"I'll take care of her, Monsieur Marc," said the concierge. She liked Babette, and she had a soft spot for a love affair, although this one, to her way of thinking, was not proceeding along the usual lines.

The Rue des Rosiers, now empty, looked in the full light of day exactly as it always looked. But to Marc it had already taken on the aspect of the ghost towns they had marched through on the retreat from Dijon, the road into the Jura, where the Prussians of Manteuffel's command had passed. Ruin was already in the air. His instinct was to run, but he controlled it. A solitary running man, on the morning of the attack on the guns, would be an object of suspicion to any Reds who happened to be about. So he walked on with long controlled strides towards the Rue St Jean, and then all of a sudden, at a corner, he saw someone who was running as a girl runs, with awkward knees and a big cloak flapping, and it was Babette.

"Thank God you're safe, my darling!" He had her in his arms, and was covering her pale face with kisses.

Not long after Marc led Babette into the haven of the studio (after a shout of reassurance to Madame Camille in her *loge*) Baron Hubert de Grimont rode into the courtyard of his mansion on the Rue St Florentin, threw the reins to a groom and dismounted. Madame la baronne was at breakfast, they told him, and after he had washed his hands he went to join her in the little room kept for the rare occasions when they took this meal together. Normally Elvire had her chocolate in bed, but today she was businesslike and alert in a dark brown velvet dress with a high neck, fastened with a diamond clasp which he had given her.

"You were at work early, mon ami," she said in her languid way, giving him her hand to kiss. "At the Quai d'Orsay again? Coffee or chocolate?"

"Will you give me some coffee, madame?" he said, sitting down. "And a brioche – thank you ... Yes, I've come from the Quai d'Orsay, where I left some very anxious gentlemen."

"Is there bad news?"

He described the events of the night.

"Dear me, what a tale of woe!" said his wife. "Give those animals enough money, and they'll let Lecomte go."

"Elvire, I admired your courage in the Siege days; don't degrade it now by mockery."

She shrugged her shoulders. She was so sure of herself, here in the beautiful little room which his money had furnished, but where the portraits on the Cordovan leather-hung walls were those of her own ancestors: minor Princes de la Treille, suited to a breakfast room but not to the state apartments.

"I'm sorry now," said the Baron de Grimont, "that I didn't escort you myself to the Sologne last week.

However, I did take one precaution. I engaged a suite of rooms at the Hôtel des Réservoirs in Versailles. The carriage will be ready to take you and your mother there within the hour."

"Are you out of your mind, Hubert?" She was not languid now. "It would kill my mother; she hasn't been out of bed for over two years."

"The duchess is not a tall woman," he continued, impervious to her words, "and well wrapped up, with her nurse in attendance, she can be laid flat on one seat of the carriage. Then, whatever happens here, I shall know that you are both in safety."

"And suppose I refuse to go? Suppose I tell you I don't care to lodge at an establishment so recently requisitioned by Prussian officers of the highest rank?"

"Then I shall doubt your patriotism, my dear, and wonder if there is some attraction which incites you to remain in Paris."

"I won't go."

"What it is to have had three great-uncles executed by the guillotine," he jeered. "Are you anxious to make as good a showing as they did in the Place de la Concorde? Because if you are, and if there is a sentimental reason to keep you here, remember this — I won't lift a finger to save you."

"You were very brave to come, darling. Weren't you scared?" It was the first thing Marc said to Babette when he got her indoors.

"Not really, because I came the long way round by the Rue St Vincent, where there weren't many people about," she answered stoutly. But she was scared, her teeth were chattering, and she twined her arms round Marc's neck with all her strength. "Oh Marc, we've been parted so much since the war began! I couldn't be with you on the battlefield, at least I can be with you today!"

"Today is just another flare-up," he said, kissing her. "It'll pass over in a few hours, you'll see. What did Madame Verlet say when you insisted on leaving the Old Farm and coming to me? Is she all right?"

"Tante Lise? She said I was a fool but she understood. She barred the big gate and the postern behind me, and said she was quite prepared to stand another siege."

"She's a game old girl, and with any luck the rabble won't go into the Rue St Jean. She's in a quiet patch, just as we are here." But he looked over Babette's dark head, burrowing into his shoulder as he tried to reassure her, at the red flag drooping on the gatepost of Number Six.

He made more coffee, which steadied them both, but Marc decided to set Girl with Green Apples aside for that day: he saw that she was too nervous to hold the pose which, although seated, demanded professional control of the hands holding the apple and the paring knife. He gave her a lesson in the use of oils instead, and also in the use of paintbrushes, explaining why the Independents preferred those with short, cropped hairs, cut square, for the use of dense colour and also for the 'sign of the brush' which was an artist's individual trademark. She was attentive, and asked intelligent questions, but they were both listening, and they knew it, for ominous sounds from the quiet street.

The quiet was shattered in the early afternoon.

The unfortunate General Lecomte, badly beaten by his captors on his way to the Château Rouge, had become a pawn in the power struggle going on at the *mairie* of Montmartre. The mayor, Dr Clemenceau, was up against a Marxist called Théophile Ferré, a twenty-five-year-old clerk who had served several prison terms. When

Clemenceau told the National Guard commander at the Château Rouge that he would be held responsible for the general's safety, Ferré alerted the Vigilance Committee of Montmartre, of which Louise Michel was the chief ornament, and the Committee, overruling Clemenceau, ordered the transfer of Lecomte to Number Six, Rue des Rosiers.

Under the horrified eyes of Marc and Babette he was carried across the garden in a state of collapse, bleeding and roughly bandaged, and taken into the house, while the whole street was invaded by a mob of the same sort as had answered the tocsin, the rogues and vagabonds, prostitutes and inebriates of the Butte. Yelling, frenzied, they forced an entrance to the garden and courtyard of the command post, and to all the other enclosed premises of the Rue des Rosiers. There was no house-breaking, although Marc, mindful of the concierge, the elderly couple and the empty apartment on the floor below his studio, believed that would be the next step. With his arm round Babette, they knelt on the sofa and watched the throng, which like a tide of hatred seethed round the villa which held the captive of the People.

"What are they *doing* in there?" whispered Babette. They both spoke in whispers, as if they could be heard by the fanatics outside.

"God knows, perhaps holding some sort of court martial. Keep back from the window, Babette. We don't want an invitation to join the party."

But the party givers had a new guest, a tall old man with a white beard who was being hustled along, with his arms pinioned, by a new detachment of the revolutionaries.

"Who's that?" asked Babette fearfully.

"No idea, but he's a damned fool to be out and about dressed up for a garden party." The old man's silk hat was snatched off his head as Marc spoke, and used as a football, and spittle ran down what had been an immaculate frock coat when the foolish old gentleman came out to see what was going on. It was no wonder Marc Vallon did not recognise him, for he was a figure from another age, General Clément Thomas. He was one of the men who had crushed the Revolution of 1848, and while Marc was at the front he had been a detested commander of the National Guard. He was kicked into the villa where Lecomte was held, and when the two appeared again it was to face death at the hands of a maddened and untrained firing squad.

Kill, burn, destroy! General Lecomte was quickly disposed of by a shot in the back. But before it was fired General Thomas stood up to die, shouting at his executioners that they were cowards, assassins, the scum of France, while the random bullets kicked up dust from the wall behind the victim, and the gathering crowd of women howled their contempt for the marksmen. At last General Thomas fell, shot through the eye, and in the momentary silence Babette lifted her head from Marc's shoulder to whisper, "Is it over?"

"I hope so." For here, pushing his way through the mob, came a man Marc did recognise, with whom he had chatted many times at the Café Guerbois; Claude Monet's friend with the strange, almost Asiatic features and black, gleaming eyes, the mayor of Montmartre, Georges Clemenceau. Behind him came a man for whom the mob made way; coming like Nemesis the limping avenger, for Théophile Ferré was a hunchback with deformed legs, and when Clemenceau shouted "No bloodshed, friends, no bloodshed!" Ferré screamed back at him, "Kill, burn, destroy!"

As the mayor of Montmartre was howled down, as men with rifles fired again and again into the two corpses, and those with bayonets hacked at them in a frenzy of bloodlust, Marc Vallon said – and he thought he spoke to himself – "So this is why I was wounded at Wörth and crossed the Jura, this is why Bazille fell at Beaune-la-Rolande – to keep France safe for this *canaille*!" He only knew he had spoken aloud when Babette whispered again, "Is it finished now?" and he was forced to say, "No, not yet. Don't look."

For now it was the turn of the women, and the maenads of 1871 were more vicious and more shameless than the *tricoteuses* of the French Revolution. Babette, clinging to the back of the old sofa, knew every one of the three who had appeared on the steps of the villa, and were urging the harpies in the crowd to still more frenzied demonstrations of the People's power. Louise Michel was there, with blood instead of rust on her bayonet. Pretty Elisaveta Dmitrieva was by her side, with blood upon her dress. And Irene Egorova from the Vine House was there, with blood upon her hands.

They were laughing at the women who were squatting to urinate on the two corpses, at the others who were copulating freely with the men who backed them up against the wall used for the dreadful execution, or flung them down on the soft earth of the trampled flowerbeds. It was an unparalleled scene of butchery and depravity, and Marc exclaimed, as he slammed the wooden shutters shut on the inside of the window, "Come away from there! This is the worst – the worst I've ever seen – even in battle..." But he hardly recognised his own voice, and Babette's, when she replied, was trailing and faraway.

"No, we mustn't – we mustn't watch any more..." He took her up in his arms and carried her into the little room where the curtains were still drawn and the bed unmade, as he had left it in the dawn when the tocsin began to ring. He laid her down on the rumpled sheets and lay beside her, feeling her arms go round his neck and clasp him to the little body that was limp and burning with her own response to all the excesses they had seen. Roused past endurance himself, like the men who had shouted for liberty and turned from liberty to lust, Marc Vallon forgot love and tenderness in the plunging satisfaction of desire. His last sane thought as the dark tide overwhelmed them was, No better than those animals outside. No better than any of them.

8

It was after eight next morning when Marc Vallon quietly opened the inner shutters of the studio window, then the window itself, and leaned out. The Rue des Rosiers was as peaceful as it had been twenty-four hours earlier, except that all the garden fences and gates were broken down, and the pretty gardens themselves were wrecked. The corpses had disappeared from the courtyard opposite, and some cooler heads among the revolutionaries – if there were any such – had seen to the swabbing down of the cobbles. Only threads of pinkish water showed where the blood had run.

Any identification of himself with the human brutes at large the night before had been forgotten in the hours with Babette in his bed. He had proved to himself and her that he had not lost his manhood in the snows of the Jura: he was complete again, and so was she. When he went noiselessly back to his little bedroom Marc opened the shutters and the window there too, and smiled when Babette, with an inarticulate murmur, pulled the blankets round her naked shoulders as a fresh breeze blew in. He took off his shirt and got into bed beside her. There were better ways than blankets of keeping her warm.

It was nearly ten o'clock when she stood beside him at the studio window, in her long white petticoat, her little bare feet chilly on the studio floor, and looked at a courtyard as bare as it was earlier. Even the red flag had disappeared from the gatepost, torn down by merry-makers in search of souvenirs, and Babette acknowledged that it seemed innocent enough. In the stillness they could hear the bell of St Pierre de Montmartre, ringing for the ten o'clock mass.

"I don't suppose Tante Lise went to church this morning," Babette said, when she was dressed in her crumpled merino, and they were drinking coffee by the stove. "I must go along and see her, darling."

"I fancy she knows where you are," said Marc.

"Yes, but I want to get fresh clothes, and we must buy some food."

"If any shops are open."

"Some of the shopkeepers stayed open under the bombardment even, they'll be open today. As for those hooligans, they're all sleeping it off somewhere. It's safe enough to go out, don't you think?"

"It looks like it," said the man who had survived all the dangers on the way home from Pontarlier.

"I meant to go and see Fanny yesterday," said Babette pensively.

"Well, don't go and get any ideas about seeing her today. There were cannon at the Buttes Chaumont, you told me so yourself, and if there was a row there too –"

"Then Belleville went as crazy as Montmartre," she finished for him. "And Didier Leblanc was the craziest of the lot. Marc, I'm *afraid* for Fanny."

"Don't worry, darling, she'll be all right. I'll go and make sure of that myself. Why not?" he said, as Babette

108

seemed to be about to interrupt him, "Fanny knows me, and she'll be glad to have news of you —"

"Didier —"

"To hell with Didier," said Marc Vallon. "I'll take care of him. But you're not running any risks down there in Belleville, darling: we've got enough on our plate here in Montmartre."

There was no sign of any risks to be run as they made their way along the Butte, where the muddy lanes had been churned up by a thousand feet, and the disputed cannon were only lightly guarded. An intrepid baker had opened his doors, and there were women customers in other shops. The male population, as Babette had predicted, was sleeping it off.

Madame Verlet was as firmly barricaded into the Old Farm as when Babette left her on the previous morning, and for the first time in her life she failed to pull the *cordon* when the bell was rung. It was only when Babette put her mouth within an inch of the hinge of the shutter over the postern and called "It's us — Marc and Babette," adding, "Don't be afraid, it's perfectly safe," that she unbarred the door and let them in. She saw at a glance that they were 'us' now, and no longer two. Babette's heavy eyes and softened mouth and Marc's proud satisfaction told their own story. She kissed them both in silence.

"What a night!" she said. "Those devils kept their howling and screaming up till midnight. Some of them came yelling down the street on their way to the Auberge des Assassins — and the right place for them — shouting that two generals had been executed as enemies of the people. Is that true?"

"They were murdered," said Marc in his blunt way. "We saw it happening across the street."

"*You* saw it, Babette? Oh my child! Why didn't you stay

109

at home with me?"

"She came where she belonged," said Marc.

"And I'm going back," said Babette. "I only came to see if you were all right, Tante Lise, and if I could do anything for you – and to get my clothes."

Madame Verlet sat down in her easy chair and put her head in her hands. There was something artificial in the gesture, as Babette well knew.

"I'll take good care of her, madame," said Marc. "Don't you worry. Now if you're sure you can manage without me, I'd like to walk round to the Rue de Norvins and get the newspapers. We know what's happened in the Rue des Rosiers, I think we'd better find out what's happening in Paris. Half an hour, Babette: is that all right with you?"

"I could pack my entire wardrobe in ten minutes," said Babette. "Take your time."

"Some of the shops were open as we came by. Shall I get a bottle of champagne to cheer us all up?"

A muffled groan from the concierge indicated that champagne would be acceptable, and Marc, with a long kiss for Babette, let himself out at the postern gate. As soon as it clicked shut behind him Madame Verlet dropped her mourning pose and rounded on Babette.

"So!" she said. "You silly girl! Going to go Fanny's way, are you?"

"Not Fanny's way," said Babette, shivering. "My own."

"Well, don't come whining to me when the mischief's done."

"I won't," said Babette, and banging the kitchen door she ran upstairs.

Her garret was icy cold, and she hurriedly dragged an old carpet bag from underneath the bed and began to pack. The black alpaca for rough wear, a Paisley shawl worn by her mother, a skirt, a summer dress of pink muslin (if summer ever came again) and that was all. Her

110

small stock of underwear and stockings, her toilet articles and cosmetics took up little room. But now there was a clear space on the mahogany table, and writing materials as well as painting materials, the latter giving her a thrill of excitement as she looked at her old watercolours and remembered what she was learning to do with oils. Then she began a letter to David Meade.

Gazing out of her window at the Vine House, where the shutters were still closed and smoke coming out of one chimney, with her lips no longer soft but set in a hard line, she began,

"Monsieur. Mesdames Michel, Egorova and Elisaveta were at the riot in the Rue des Rosiers on Saturday and cheering on the rioters. With distinguished sentiments, E.M."

She ran downstairs with the carpet bag in one hand and the sealed letter in the other, addressed to Monsieur David Meade, 95, Rue de Chaillot, and saw with amusement that Madame Verlet had washed and arranged on a little tray three crystal champagne glasses, relics of her glamorous past. So she was willing to drink their health! Her face was a study when Babette said quickly, "Tante Lise, I want to send a letter to Monsieur Meade."

"To the American!"

"Yes, and it can't go by post, the mails are so uncertain. I want you to help me find a messenger to deliver it by hand."

"Second thoughts already, eh?" said Madame Verlet. "What's the matter? Didn't the painter come up to the mark?"

"Never mind about that, Tante Lise. This is a message about something Monsieur Meade wanted to know — something to do with his work that you wouldn't understand."

"Too stupid, am I? And where am I to find a messenger,

pray?"

"I thought – Madame Jaloux's schoolboy son. She's sure to send him round this afternoon to find out how you are. Here's one franc to give him for taking the message, and another franc for omnibus fare from Trinité to the Etoile and back again. Look! I'm putting the money and the letter in the table drawer."

"Two francs for running an errand! Have you come into a fortune since last night?"

"In one way, yes," said Babette.

"Of course," said Madame Verlet, "Marc Vallon has money of his own, as all the *quartier* knows. His father had a good business and a good apartment in the Rue Vavin, and even when the mother and the married sister in Biarritz were provided for the son was left well off, as painters go. But I doubt if he gave you money to send a letter to Monsieur Meade." She caught at Babette's hand. "You don't fool me, child, I know you too well. You're not in love with Marc Vallon. 'Take your time', you told him; snapped at him. That wasn't the way a girl in love would speak. You've changed your mind about the American, I only hope he hasn't changed his. I was sorry for you yesterday when you ran off to Vallon. Now, upon my word, I'm beginning to be sorry for ʌim!"

In her impulsive way, Babette dropped to her knees beside her old friend's chair.

"Tante Lise, why are you saying such hateful things to me?" she pleaded. "You know you don't really mean them. You know quite well that I love Marc. I longed for him to come back to me safe and well, and now he *is* getting well I'm so happy! We're both so happy! Why do you sneer at us? Is it because you're frightened? Is that it, my poor dear? Frightened that I won't come back?"

Madame Verlet's face crumpled into tears as she looked over Babette's head at the carpet bag. "You've taken all your things," she faltered. "I didn't blame you for staying with him last night, the Butte was dangerous for anyone, even for two people, out alone. But to *live* with him, Babette – to leave me all by myself –"

"But I'll only be ten minutes' walk away!" cried Babette. "I'll be with you every morning early, to help you with the housework and go to the shops for you, just like always. I'll be here tomorrow morning, all ready for a *petit noir*! Did you really think I could desert you after all you've done for me – for Fanny and me?" She pressed the woman's tear-stained cheek against her own. "And when I'm a famous painter, you'll be proud of me."

Marc came back soon after that, but though they drank the champagne, no one was in a mood for celebration.

"There wasn't a paper to be had," said Marc, "but everyone was bursting with news, and most of it appears to be true. Thiers and all his cabinet have cut and run to Versailles. When they saw the National Guard raging along the Quai d'Orsay they skedaddled one at a time down some sort of hidden staircase in the Foreign Office, and made off. Not very heroic, eh?"

"Did you hear anything about the guns at the Buttes Chaumont?" asked Babette fearfully.

"No, but they say the Red Flag's flying over the Hôtel de Ville, where the troops got out by another secret passage, a tunnel to the Napoleon Barracks. Napoleon must be turning in his grave."

The members of the Central Committee of the National Guard, now startlingly in command of Paris, were incapable of acting as a united whole. Was the 'execution' of the two generals legal or illegal, was the first question to agitate the revolutionaries at the Hôtel de Ville. Was

Comrade Michel right or wrong in insisting that the first objective should be the assassination of Thiers? Ought the National Guard, which was now debating the assumption of a new name, 'the Federals', to be ordered to march at once upon Versailles, and bring Thiers and his ministers back to Paris as political prisoners? Ought the Committee, instead, to begin bargaining for the release of Blanqui? All these views, and many more, were advanced with a remorseless flow of eloquence inside City Hall, while outside, in cold but brilliant sunshine, the Paris of the *petit bourgeois* and the unemployed worker took its normal Sunday pleasure in promenading through the gardens and boulevards where the heroes of the hour, the National Guard, or Federals, were promenading too.

Among the latter there were some who remembered the coup d'état of twenty years back, when Napoleon III, then the elected Prince-President, had come to the throne over the bodies of five hundred men. They had learned then, like their predecessors of 1848, that there was no better revolutionary weapon than a barricade, and the first place they should throw up barricades was the Rue de Rivoli, leading straight to their fortress at the Hôtel de Ville. They recruited enough promenaders to throw up several barricades in the course of the day, the most westerly being erected across the foot of the Rue St Florentin, where that street joined the Rue de Rivoli.

Edward Carey gave it a cursory glance as he strolled out on that Sunday afternoon, easy to take for an English tourist – there were some of the breed intrepid enough to have come back to Paris already. He had remained in the Hôtel St Honoré all morning, discussing with the other Englishmen who had been permanent guests there for months the new situation created by the flight of the ministers. The names of all the fugitives had been given in the morning papers, even in the *Figaro*, and he had not been surprised to read the name of the new Minister of Justice among them. His mistress had told him at their rendezvous on Friday of her husband's proposal to take her and her paralysed mother to the Hôtel des Réservoirs at Versailles. What he didn't know, of course, was whether she had given in at the last moment and gone with him. He wished Mr Wallace were in Paris to tell him what to do.

He made up his mind in the afternoon, when he saw the barricade at the corner of the Rue St Florentin. It was just the kind of gimcrack thing you could expect from Frenchmen. If you wanted to keep troops from bursting out of the Rue St Florentin into the Rue de Rivoli (not that there were any troops left to burst) well and good, but if you wanted to enter the Rue St Florentin itself there was nothing to prevent you. You merely walked round the corner and entered the narrow, aristocratic street from the other end. And this, after dining at his hotel, was what Ned Carey did: dressed for the evening, and carefully groomed, he approached the *hôtel* de Grimont from the Rue St Honoré and was admitted by the only gatekeeper on duty.

The liveried footman summoned the butler to deal with the unexpected guest, and the butler, recognising a young man who had been an occasional visitor under the wing of the illustrious Monsieur Richard Wallace, was very polite when he regretted that Monsieur and Madame de Grimont were not receiving on that Sunday evening.

"I understand," said Carey. "I called to enquire for the health of Madame la Duchesse de la Treille, and to ask if I might be of any service to Madame de Grimont." He produced his card, on which he had already scribbled a message.

"I will enquire," said the butler, from whose sleeve a silver salver seemed to materialise. "Will monsieur be

115

good enough to wait?"

It was an impersonal anteroom into which Ned was shown, with the arms of de Grimont and de la Treille carved in stone above the empty hearth, and it was not long before the butler came back.

"Madame la baronne will receive monsieur," the man said. "Please to follow me."

They went up the grand staircase and into the principal salon, precisely as on all the other Sunday nights, but this time he and Elvire were alone in the suite of rooms which were usually thronged. She was as formally dressed as Ned was, and he had an impression of blond lace and a pointed satin bodice over trailing skirts. The potted palms and hothouse flowers, the marquetry, gold inlay and marble made the salon a very different place from their secret room, but Elvire hardly waited for the door to close behind the butler before she was in his arms with the same ardour, whispering "You came to me! Edouard, my darling, you came to me!" and he was pulling her unresisting towards one of the sofas by the fire. It was a great moment for Elvire de Grimont – to run the supreme risk of being possessed by her lover in her husband's house.

Young Adrien Jaloux earned his two francs and delivered Babette's letter at the American Legation on Monday afternoon. It was not read by David Meade until Friday evening, for he had been in attendance on his Minister all week at Versailles, where Mr Washburne had been in attendance on Thiers. The staff had been kept busy encoding the day-to-day reports sent by telegraph to Secretary Hamilton Fish in Washington. They stressed Thiers's optimism, which nobody shared, and his belief that he could soon get together an army to quell the 400,000 armed Federals who had driven him out of Paris. There had only been one scuffle in the Paris streets since the fatal Saturday — a skirmish in the Place Vendôme between the Federals and a group of moderate citizens calling themselves the Friends of Law and Order. As for the Central Committee of the revolutionaries, ensconced in the Hôtel de Ville, they had found a temporary solution to the problems and dissensions following their unexpected access to power. They were obeying the classic French maxim, 'When in doubt, vote', and on Sunday 26 March Parisians would go to the polls to elect a new municipal council.

David Meade gave Babette's brief message lengthy consideration. What it told him about the Russian women was exactly what he had expected; he was more interested in what it told him about Babette. She had put no address on her letter, but he was willing to bet that she was no longer at the Old Farm. To have seen the Russians at the scene of the generals' murder she must have been in the Rue des Rosiers, in Vallon's studio, and the riot would have been the perfect excuse for him to keep her there. He had to see her as Vallon's mistress, to lay the haunting dream of a little *grenouille* whose love was all for him. He had to accept her as — what were her own words? — 'a light woman', before he could set himself to forgetting her.

Besides, he owed her an explanation.

He went to Vallon's studio on Saturday afternoon, just two weeks after Carey's luncheon party which seemed, in the rush and violence of events, more like two years, and there she was. She opened the door to him, wearing one of Vallon's smocks over her skirt, with the sleeves rolled up and a deep hem making it a better fit; Vallon, who came behind her with a hearty welcome, said he was giving her a lesson in Cézanne's favourite technique, painting with a knife, using a solution of paraffin dissolved in essence of turpentine. Meade was shown Girl with Green Apples and admired it whole-heartedly.

"I had some pretty stiff competition to meet," said Vallon with a laugh, nodding towards Meade's sketch of Babette at the Fountain, which he had glued to a piece of cardboard and nailed to the wall. "You put me on my mettle, mon ami."

"Oh!" said Meade, looking from the sketch to the picture and back again, "did I though? I don't think you've anything to fear from *my* competition. It's a clear case of 'the best man won'."

They were all conscious of the double meaning, and Babette went into the kitchen to fetch wine and glasses. It was not done in a possessive way, like other girls in an equivocal situation, playing housewife (the French called it *un faux ménage*) of whom he had seen so many in the studios: those two intrigued him by their attitude to each other. Babette was looking adorable, with her hair piled on top of her head and held in place with two huge pins, like a Japanese, and Vallon's eyes on her were tender, but there was no touching, no endearments, and they even said *vous* to one another. There was an intimacy between them that went deeper than caresses, and when they talked about the riot he had a feeling that they had been protected from the visual horrors by the strength they took from one another.

"How's your sister?" Meade enquired, when they had all lit cigarettes.

"Not well at all," said Babette. "Marc went to Belleville on Tuesday and found her terribly upset about the little boy. But at least she's been to see a doctor for herself."

"Poor girl," said Meade. "And Madame Verlet?"

"She was fine when I left her this morning," said

Babette. (Now what did she mean by that? Was she living with Vallon or wasn't she?) "But she's worried about the Russians in the Vine House." Her eyes met the American's candidly. She knew he wouldn't say "I got your letter", in the presence of the man who had called him competition.

"What about the Russians? Are they being objectionable?" asked Meade.

"I didn't know you knew them," said Marc.

"We have them on file at the Legation," said Meade. "Nikolai Egorov's the Paris correspondent of *Bread and Liberty*, an anarchist paper published in Geneva, and his wife Irene is his assistant. They're working with Bakunin, who's been stirring up the Reds in Lyon, and their friend Elisaveta Dmitrieva reports on their activities to Karl Marx, the power behind the Second International."

"Is Karl Marx a Russian too?" asked Babette.

"A German living in London."

"It sounds like an international conspiracy," said Marc idly, throwing his cigarette end into the open door of the stove. "I don't see why you should keep foreign anarchists on file, we've got plenty of the home-grown variety in Paris. And do they care a damn about Karl Marx in the United States?"

"Not yet," said Meade, "but at the Legation we think it worth while keeping an eye on the people he's infiltrating here. Dmitrieva's a dangerous woman. She just got out to Switzerland in time after the last plot to assassinate the Czar, and there's another female called Anna Jaclard, whom we've completely lost track of. We think that what's happening in France now is the beginning of something new, what Marx calls the rise of the proletariat, and after this revolution in Paris nothing will ever be the same again."

"I don't agree with you," said Marc, and his pleasant, careless voice was unusually grave. "You're saying class

119

9

"Meade's a nice fellow, but he's a terrible bore about the Russians," said Marc after the visitor had gone. "And as for Karl Marx, who cares a damn for him?"

"I know someone who does," said Babette. "Raoul Rigault, the Red I heard orating in the park a couple of weeks ago. His audience didn't seem to be very impressed."

"Do you blame them?" asked Marc with a yawn. "We need a break after Meade's philosophising. Change your dress and I'll take you out to dinner."

"Out to *dinner*? Wherever could we go?"

"Anywhere in the Place du Tertre. I've kept you shut up in the studio for a whole week now, it's time you had a holiday."

"Oh Marc, don't be silly. I've been out every day."

"Yes, to the shops, and to see Tante Lise. Hurry up, sweetheart, and I'll put all this stuff away."

Babette exchanged her smock for the hard-worked grey merino, worn with the Paisley shawl in graceful folds, and her hair in a chignon confined by a crimson snood. Marc's

121

face lit up when she came out of the bedroom.

"Very, very paintable! But is that shawl warm enough?"

"Oh yes, I think so."

"Next week I'm going to take you to the Printemps and buy you a new cloak. Some day you're going to trip on that old thing of Morisot's."

"Thank you, darling, but you promised to take me to see Fanny next week. She didn't tell you much when you went to see her last Tuesday."

"She was too modest, or too prudish, to tell me what the doctor had to say about a female complaint. Frankly I thought the kid was in worse shape than she was."

He locked the studio door behind them. It was early to go out to dinner, but he didn't want to be too late getting back, in case the Reds began celebrating election eve. They had already made a convincing show of strength by arresting Clemenceau in his own *mairie*, marching him through the streets to the police station wearing his scarf of office, and turning him loose after a few token hours of arrest.

There were several restaurants and wineshops open in the Place du Tertre, all filled with good-tempered customers. Marc and Babette found a table in Le Pichet, a comfortable place with check tablecloths and curtains, where the *plat du jour* was a shoulder of lamb with turnips, and the *pichets* held an honest beaujolais. It was much better than the Siege days, and they ate with appetite. Marc told his girl that she looked lovely, and it was true. The crimson and yellow pattern of the Paisley shawl flung back on her shoulders gave her more brilliance than any rouge, and he saw that men were looking at her admiringly.

One shouted his admiration in the slang of the Butte as he pushed his way between the tables to the door. "Babette, you're looking great!" was a polite translation of what he said as he laid a familiar hand on her shoulder. She shook it off with a cool "*Bonsoir, monsieur*," and a glance at Marc. The newcomer looked too, smiled, said "*Pardon, madame*, I mistook you for someone I used to know," and was gone.

"Who was that?" asked Marc.

"His name's Georges Malaval, 'Jo-Jo' to his friends."

"You seem to be one of them. Where did you meet a *voyou* like that?"

"Dancing at the Moulin de la Galette. He's living with a girl I know – Diane Delorme she *calls* herself – she used to hang about the studios looking for modelling jobs. I sometimes went to the balls with them."

"Living off her's more like it, I should say."

"You'll have to learn to dance, Marc."

Cheeky Babette! In spite of himself Marc grinned, and Babette seized a chance to change the subject.

"Oh look, here comes *monsieur le maire*."

Georges Clemenceau was walking through the crowded square and looking as grim as when he forced his way into a courtyard where murder had been done. Behind him, as then, limped Théophile Ferré with his thick black beard and his pince-nez; and Ferré was the one the crowd applauded.

"Clemenceau did for himself last Saturday night," said Marc. "Ferré looks pretty sure of tomorrow's result."

"Are you going to vote tomorrow, Marc?" asked Babette.

"Not I, my love. I'm going to stay at home and start a new picture of you."

He smiled his good-tempered smile, and Babette thought he had got over his spurt of irritation at the interruption by 'Jo-Jo' Malaval. But she was not at peace with herself, and when a compote of pears had been put before them she said,

"Darling, I want to tell you why Meade came to the studio today."

"Was there any special reason? I thought it was just a friendly call."

"He came because I wrote him a letter."

"Asking him to come? I thought I didn't have to be jealous of Meade."

"Telling him about the Russian women with Louise Michel last Saturday night."

"What the devil for?" asked Marc.

"He's interested in them, and he knows I am too."

"Interested in the people at the Vine House? So he came to pass on his own bits of information, as discreetly as possible?"

"Yes."

Marc pushed away his plate. "These pears aren't nearly sweet enough," he said. "Hard, too."

"Don't eat them, then."

After a silence: "Babette," he said. "I don't want you to get involved in all this political nonsense. You've got a talent of your own, and that's all that matters. Will you promise me to give up dabbling in what's no concern of ours?"

"It *is* our concern. And telling me I've got talent is only a bribe. Bazille told me that two years ago."

"Don't rub it in," the man said. "I know I'm still playing second fiddle to Bazille."

"Oh darling, that's just not true." She coaxed him back into better humour, but they were both quiet as they walked back to the studio, aware of a breach of confidence between them. Babette knew that she had told Marc a little, but not all: she had concealed the story of the five gold napoleons, and when they reached home she went at once to bed. Marc sat smoking in the studio, reflecting that she had been living with him for just one

124

week and was already setting her will against his own. He did not follow Babette to bed until her even breathing told him she was sound asleep.

Next day he was as good as his word. He did stay at home on the Sunday of the municipal elections, he did start a new picture of Babette, and when she asked if Girl with Green Apples was really complete, he reminded her that the Independents believed in finishing a study, not a picture. Even Meade, when he took a last look at the canvas on the easel, had remarked on the artist's impressionistic approach to his subject. Yes, it was complete, his first 'impression' of Babette: the next one would be different. He intended to call it Girl Painting, and the challenge to himself would be the picture within a picture. Babette was to paint the blue and white bowl with a bottle of red wine next to it on a white tablecloth – a nice problem for her; and she was to wear her white painting smock. The three whites would be a nice problem for him.

Towards evening he grew restless, and at Babette's own suggestion he went along to the Café Guerbois, as much to look for old friends as to pick up any reliable news of the election. He came back early, saying there was not a single painter in that great painters' rendezvous except Gustave Courbet, gross, drunk, and raving about Karl Marx and revolution. All he had heard of the election was that the poll had not been heavy. Next day's declaration confirmed this. In a poll of only fifty per cent the Central Committee and the Federals had come to power by an overall vote of four to one, and were now unquestionably in control of Paris. The first act of the new municipal council was to announce that it would be known by a new name:

THE PARIS COMMUNE.

In vain did the calm or the pedantic point out that

'commune' was an ordinary legal term. Montmartre and Belleville had been called communes before they became *arrondissements* of Napoleon III's extended Paris. But 'Paris Commune' meant the French Revolution, meant tumbrils bearing aristocrats to the scaffold, the crash of the guillotine, the excesses of Marat and Robespierre. For some it was an alarming prospect. For the Reds, whose colours, scarves, streamers and banners were everywhere, on statues, arches, monuments and public buildings, it was a victory to be celebrated in the grand style. Tuesday, 28 March 1871 was the appointed day.

One who would not attend the celebrations was Georges Clemenceau. He received only seven hundred votes, and had to give up his post to Théophile Ferré. Too proud after such a defeat to continue as a Deputy for the Seine, he resigned his seat in the National Assembly and went back to his old home in the Vendée.

His defeat shook Marc Vallon's assumed indifference to the insurrection in Paris. For Clemenceau, the friend of Monet, known to the charmed circle of painters for his brilliant talk and personality to be ousted by a little upstart like Ferré, who thought of himself as the new Danton, was an insult to the whole group of Independents, scattered though they were. He complained at such length to Babette that she told him his involvement with politics was far more serious than her own. He kissed her and said she might be right. He went on (it was Monday morning, with a day's breathing space before the Tuesday celebrations), "If you want to see Fanny soon I think this might be the time to go to Belleville, before the Reds start another tremendous drunk. When it's over we'll go and buy you a new cloak."

The former Central Committee, in the intervals of publishing manifestos on human rights, had suspended the mail service and reduced the omnibus timetable both in routes and vehicles. Marc and Babette were lucky to get a fiacre to take them to within a short distance of the Impasse du Drapeau.

"I shan't come in with you, darling," said Marc. "Fanny'll talk to you far more freely if I'm not there."

"But what will you do, Marc?"

"Have a look at the park and think about the night I met you first. I'll be waiting for you at the west gate."

"Be careful then, it's a gun park now."

"You be careful too, if Didier's there."

He little knew how apt that warning was, thought Babette, as she wrestled with the awkward door. But her brother-in-law was not there to harass her, supposing they had been alone. There was another woman in the wretched room, bending over Fanny and the infant in her arms. Babette knew her as Madame Jeanne, the wife of an unemployed labourer and one of the most respectable inhabitants of the Impasse. There was also an older man, in the uniform of a prison warder and with the prison taint upon him, who kissed his hand with greasy gallantry to 'Mademoiselle Mercier'. It was Didier's father, the jailer of La Roquette.

Fanny looked up with an apathetic, "Oh, it's you. Did Marc Vallon tell you about Loulou?"

"He said the poor little thing wasn't very well. But it's you I'm worried about, Fanny. What exactly did the doctor say?"

"I can't tell you with all these people listening," said Fanny pettishly, and Madame Jeanne took the hint. "Come along, Monsieur Leblanc," she said, "my husband will enjoy a chat with you; and Fanny, I'll soon be back." As she urged the jailer towards the door she whispered to Babette, "He had a bad convulsion about an hour ago."

"Wait a minute," said Babette, "where's Didier?"

"Didier's at the Belleville barracks," said his father.

127

"Drilling with the 66th Battalion, getting ready for tomorrow's march past at the Hôtel de Ville. I just happened to look in, to ask for poor Françoise and the baby."

"Didier should be here himself," said Babette.

"Ah, you charming ladies," said Leblanc waggishly, "you never seem to understand that a man's duty must come first! Besides, Didier has his principles, mademoiselle. He says under the Commune all medical care will be free, from a doctor's fees to hospital charges—"

"In the meantime Fanny needs help," said Babette. "Don't listen to that old fool," she told her sister when Madame Jeanne had almost pushed the man out. "Tell me quickly what Dr Bosquet said."

"He said I ought to have an operation."

"Oh Fanny, *no*!"

The very word 'operation' struck terror to the hearts of the rich as well as the poor. Gangrene and pyemia too often followed surgery, and since the war the public hospitals were open corridors to death. "What kind of operation?" asked Babette fearfully.

"An ovary-something, a long word. But Dr Bosquet says there's no hurry, because only one professor at the Maternité can do it, and part of the Maternité's a field hospital now. The doctor gave me some pills to take for the bleeding. He says that must be stopped and my strength built up before I see this professor—I've forgotten his name already. *My* strength!" said Fanny with a sob, "as if that mattered! It's Loulou! He won't eat or drink, Babette, and he's started having convulsions now. Oh, what shall I do? What shall I do?"

If that damned Didier were here I would *make* him fetch a doctor, thought Babette fiercely, although she knew well enough that nobody in the Impasse ever sent for a doctor, and if they did the doctor would only come under police protection, if he came at all. On an inspiration she asked Fanny if 'the Red Cross lady' who had talked to her at the Belleville Ambulance would be allowed, or would be willing, to visit a sick child.

"I don't know."

"It's worth a try," said Babette. "I'll be as quick as I can, and Madame Jeanne will stay with you."

It was no distance to the Rue Montfaucon, but not knowing what delays she might encounter at the field hospital Babette hurried towards the park to tell Marc Vallon of this new development. She was thankful to see his tall figure already standing near the gate of their first parting.

Marc had not lingered long inside the Parc des Buttes Chaumont. The place was so changed that he actually had difficulty in remembering where the *guinguette* had stood when Babette had entered Bazille's life and his own. He leaned for a time on the bridge where she had watched the swans — they called it the Suicides' Bridge now — vaguely aware of accordion music and singing in the distance. He soon identified the tune. It was *Ach, du lieber Augustin* — last heard after the armistice, sung by a platoon of Hessians who had let him warm himself at their camp fire and given him food when he was on the long trek north. He remembered that the soldiers of the Occupying Power were camped, in some localities, close to the walls of Paris. The enemy was still at the gates, while the Federals were preparing to celebrate the proclamation of the Commune! Babette had told him about their speechifying, and there across the lake — where a dead dog, horribly swollen, now floated instead of the swans — was the ramshackle platform of the orators, standing where the *guinguette*'s little orchestra had played in an arbour of flowers. He remembered Babette's innocent face, alive with pleasure at the sight.

Then she had been a new toy. Now he felt responsible for her. He had never cared much for Fanny Mercier — *Françoise l'éternelle victime*, as he privately thought of her — but Didier Leblanc had wronged her, in the idiom of the day, and no doubt believed he made amends when he married her before the child was born. Marc never thought of himself as 'wronging' Babette. They were lovers by their own choice, and he was taking good care that there would be no child, but was that enough? He was keeping her and paying her a model's wages, but was that a generous return for love? If they parted some day, in the casual way such liaisons as theirs ended in Montmartre, what would she become? A light woman, the prey of other men? He didn't take David Meade seriously as a rival, and all that stuff about Russian anarchists was nonsense, but he couldn't forget their encounter with a pimp like Malaval, with whom she went dancing at the Moulin de la Galette. He couldn't forget her casual acceptance of Malaval's 'living with a girl I used to know', and the girl herself 'hanging about the studios looking for a job'. It could be said of any *grenouille* who lost her way in the alleys of the Butte.

His girl — he had known it from the beginning, and so had Frédéric Bazille — was something better than a studio hanger-on. He was surer of her talent every day he watched her handle paintbrush and oils. When the war — when the Commune was over, there must be a place and a time when they could share love and work together. Today, when they were alone at home, he meant to ask her to marry him.

The girl who came running up to him at the west gate didn't seem to be in the mood for a proposal of marriage. Fanny's troubles and Didier's neglect, combined with the urgent need to find a foreign nurse at the Belleville Ambulance had turned his mistress into a small fury, hurrying him along to the Rue Montfaucon. There he was at least useful in impressing an obstructive registrar with the need to see 'Soeur Emilie', for whom 'Miss Emily March' was produced, a young woman who asked in correct if heavily accented French what she could do to help. It was up to Babette then to tell her sister's story.

"I remember Madame Leblanc, of course," said 'the Red Cross lady'. "You say her little boy is the patient now? Well, by good luck I was just going off duty, and there's no objection at all to my visiting him. Miss Clara Barton, who recruited me from Kaiserswerth, always insisted that our first duty was to help civilians."

"Kaiserswerth?" said Babette. "You're not German, are you?"

Miss March smiled. "It's a famous school of nursing, and I'm an American citizen. Wait a minute and I'll get my cloak."

The halls and corridors of the Belleville Ambulance were clear of stretchers and pallet beds, and Miss March, when she returned, explained that there had been a number of discharges in the past week. It was Marc's cue to express his gratitude for the care he received in the original American Ambulance, the genuine field hospital which succoured the wounded on the battlefield of Wörth, and the Red Cross lady said how much she envied the field surgeons their great opportunity. "Surgeon-Major Pasquier has asked for me to be assigned to the ambulance he's organising at Versailles," she said. "There's a good deal of sickness among the Line troops in Satory camp."

"So you're leaving Belleville?" said Marc.

"On Thursday."

Babette listened and wondered if Marc thought Miss March was paintable. She was attractive, certainly: tall and slim, with strong features and grey eyes under heavy dark brows. She wore a dark blue cloak with straps across her breast which revealed her white hospital dress with the red cross on the bodice, and her blue bonnet had a white quilling which concealed her hair as effectively as a nun's wimple. She was probably in her late twenties, and she was like no other woman Babette had ever seen in Paris. Marc was interested in her, that was clear. He liked this girl who talked like a man and worked like a man at her profession. Babette mentally compared her with Louise Michel, the self-appointed champion of women's rights, and began to understand the difference between feminist protest and feminine achievement.

When the American girl turned to her with some questions about little Louis's illness, Babette did her best to answer and then put a question of her own.

"Mademoiselle, you will be going to the American Consulate at Versailles?"

"To see Minister Washburne – certainly."

"Do you know one of his attachés, Monsieur David Meade?"

"Only by name."

"He's a friend of ours – my sister's and mine. Would you be good enough to give him our kind regards?"

The Impasse du Drapeau was a revelation to Emily March. The poverty of Fanny's home was indescribable and she, Clara Barton's protégée, could do nothing to alleviate it. She asked that the window be opened, and the room cleared of interested neighbours, but there was not much she could do to cure a case of febrile convulsions.

"The patient should be plunged in warm water baths," she said. "Have you a bath tub? No? Then how do you keep the child clean?"

"He's sponged every day with warm water from this pan," said Fanny defensively, producing a vegetable pan to which a few potato peelings were sticking.

"I'll borrow one of the big zinc pans from the wash house, that the clothes are soaked in," said Babette resourcefully. She followed the Red Cross lady into the Impasse when the bathing regimen was begun and some medicine administered, and a clean blanket even found to wrap the child in.

"There isn't much hope, is there?" she whispered.

"One must never give up hope, mademoiselle," said Pastor Fliedner's pupil. "But if you know where the father is, I think he should be sent for."

Didier Leblanc was at the barracks of the 66th Belleville. He saw no need to go home to a whimpering woman and a whining child who had friendly neighbours to look after them when he could be with men rejoicing in the triumph of the Commune. He drank less wine than usual when the evening meal was served, because he sincerely felt that tomorrow would be a great day in the history of France and he was proud to play a part in it. Next morning, from clean-shaven face (his imperial and moustache had disappeared with the fall of the Emperor) to well blacked boots his personal grooming gleamed like the barrel of his rifle and his bayonet.

Two hundred battalions of the National Guard, the Federals, marched through the streets of Paris that day. Outside the Hôtel de Ville the newly elected members of the Commune, decked in red scarves, were present on a raised platform to take the salute. Some of the marching men were not sure if they were saluting the living Commune or a bust of the Republic on which had been placed a cap of liberty, and saluted twice to make sure. But the majority snapped off their salutes with the precision of the Garde Impériale, raising their képis on the points of their bayonets as the regimental bands took the *Marseillaise* at a fast pace. Didier Leblanc would have preferred a slower beat as he passed the saluting base. He needed more time to look at his elected leaders. He recognised Delescluze, the veteran Socialist who had spent the best years of his life as a political prisoner on Devil's Island, and Cluseret, an adventurer who had become an American citizen and joined with that hybrid race, the Irish-Americans, in demanding independence for Ireland. He missed Felix Pyat, Grousset, Eugène Varlin, and while shouting *Vive la Commune* failed to see two young men who had been appointed to key posts which would make them the Commune's super-policemen and executioners: Raoul Rigault as Prefect of Police and Théophile Ferré as mayor of Montmartre. Both were dedicated followers of Karl Marx.

It was late in the evening, and he had been the round of the Red cabarets, when Didier Leblanc, his uniform no longer immaculate, returned to the Impasse du Drapeau. Every hovel had its candle lit, every resident was staggering drunk in the gutter. There were drunken women in his own home too. But they were mourning, not celebrating, for in a grocery box on the table, padded with a towel, lay the tiny body of his dead son.

He stood dumbstruck in the accusing group of women. Two were the worse for drink: the creature who served the Impasse as midwife, abortionist and layer-out of the dead, and one of her cronies. Madame Jeanne was crouching on a stool by the fire, and Babette was sitting by Fanny lying on the pallet bed, stroking her sister's hair.

"It's Didier, Fanny," she said softly. His wife, with her back towards him, remained motionless. He knelt down and took her into his arms.

"*Ma pauvre chérie*," he whispered, "when did it happen?"

"While you were gone."

"About eight o'clock tonight," said Babette.

"Did nobody think of sending for me?"

"Oh, I did," said Babette curtly. "I was at your barracks at six. Nobody had any idea where you were."

"Don't you want to see him, M'sieur Didi?" stammered one of the tipsy females. "He's such a beautiful little corpse!"

Didier had been afraid to look at what was on the table where they took their meals. He forced himself to do so now, even to kiss the face twisted in the throes of Loulou's last convulsion. Then he knelt again by the wife who refused his caresses and shut her ears to the words which begged her to forgive him, to be comforted, to believe their poor little boy was better off in heaven. "You hypocrite!" was all she said.

Didier stood up. "What's to be done?" he said. "It – he can't stay here."

Madame Jeanne spoke for the first time, as curtly as Babette. "Monsieur Vallon has gone to the undertaker's," she said. "You'll have to register the death at the *mairie* tomorrow."

He wanted to swear and shout that Marc Vallon took too much upon himself, but the bluster died upon his lips. Didier knew too well that his son would be buried like the girl child born prematurely two months before, in the common grave, with a year to rest there before his remains were shovelled out to make room for others. He sat down heavily on a chair one of the women pushed towards him and covered his eyes with his hand.

"Give him a dram of brandy," said Babette contemptuously. "That's all the comfort Didier needs."

Before he could curse her his wife raised herself from her pallet, and he saw her swollen face before she laid it on her sister's breast.

"Oh, take me away from here when they take Loulou!" she sobbed. "Take me back to the Old Farm, Babette! Take me home to dear Tante Lise!"

Egorova disagreed with her, but failed to understand her resentment of the two young men, Rigault and Ferré, who were twenty-five to her forty, and inclined to laugh at her demands for the murder of Thiers. They had studied more subtle ways of inflicting pain.

She made the best of it. With her Russian colleagues Louise began to develop a revolutionary women's movement, organising Red Clubs for females in every available place from cabarets to churches, where the Red Flag was flown from the steeples. A restaurant called the Boule Noire became (in her frenetic moods, literally) the stamping ground of Louise Michel, and the Elysée-Montmartre, where Babette had stitched the Siege balloons, was open to both sexes as the Club de la Révolution.

Whenever she could she attempted to introduce feminist legislation into the meetings of the Commune. She demanded women's rights to a free union instead of the bonds of matrimony. She demanded that the Federals' marriage allotments be paid to concubines as well as to legal wives, and the new child allowances to bastards as well as to legitimate offspring. When she spoke about women and children she became as emotional about mother love as she was about murder, and the Russian girls, much cooler as well as much younger than herself, warned her that she was boring her hearers with her declarations of love for her own mother, with whom she lived, and repetitions of the mother's story. Seduced and abandoned, the victim of man's lust – it was tedious, they said, and it wasn't even true. The country squire had done well enough by his servant and their bastard daughter. He gave them a home, he gave the girl an education which enabled her to earn her living as a school teacher and even aspire to become a poet. Rejection by magazine editors had given her one more grudge against men. "If I had signed myself Louis instead of Louise Michel," she said bitterly, "my poems would have been published. Look at George Eliot! Look at George Sand!"

"Well, try again, and do sign yourself Louis," said Irene Egorova with a yawn. "Or write something for *Bread and Liberty* and submit it to Nikolai. *My* stuff gets published in Geneva under my own name."

"Alas, my name is too famous for dissembling now," said Louise, to whom the very word 'submit' was an offence. The Russian girls looked at each other expressionlessly. Really there were times when she was a terrible bore. But Mitya said she was too useful to liquidate yet, and Mitya, masquerading as the Egorovs' manservant was, as David Meade had shrewdly suspected, the control from whom their cell, and the Jaclard cell, had to take orders until their plans were complete.

Mitya, otherwise Mikhail Alekseievich Saranov, was accustomed to the anarchists' endless debates on ideology, whether in the Nihilist underground at home or in their Swiss exile. He found it quite natural that the Commune should immediately split into two factions, the Internationalists and the Jacobins, and set up ten Commissions issuing contradictory decrees on subjects ranging from the disestablishment of the Church to the abolition of conscription instead of marching on Versailles. Louise Michel raged that they thought of the twelve miles between Paris and Versailles as some tremendous barricade only influential neutrals like Richard Wallace dared to cross.

The relationship between Wallace and the Marquess of Hertford had intrigued Paris society for years. When it ended, due to the Marquess's death from cancer, there was almost no gossip, for Lord Hertford died in the week before Sedan, when the collapse of the army and the Empire obscured all interest in his funeral or his Will. It became known that the Marquess, who could not leave his title to the bastard Wallace, had left him everything else: the villa amid its rose gardens in the Bois de Boulogne, Hertford House in London, the Irish estates at Lisburne, and the priceless art collection which Richard Wallace had helped him to amass. The beneficiary, a few months later, married Madame Julie Castelnau, his mistress of thirty years' standing, and the mother of his only son. It was hardly a romantic story, and yet when Ned Carey met Mr Wallace immediately after his return from London, where he had gone on business connected with his inheritance, he was struck as always with the youthful, cheerful character of the great benefactor, always the sporting Englishman with his black and tan retriever at his heels.

Mr Wallace himself called the meeting at the Hôtel St Honoré. It was intended to be the wind-up of the British War Charities committee, and the remaining members still in Paris were Edward Carey, two British doctors and Mr Blount, who was once again the British Chargé d'Affaires, Lord Lyons being at Versailles with Thiers. Every man present agreed that the committee must continue active while the threat of civil war in France remained. Many plans were discussed and Mr Wallace had to answer many questions about opinion in London, but as chairman he kept the meeting short, only asking 'Mr Carey' to remain behind when the others left.

"I want to tell you something, Ned," he said, dropping the formality at once, "your father came to see me in London."

"My father did!"

"Yes. There was something in the papers about my visit to town, and he came up from Manchester especially to see me and ask about you and your safety in Paris. I told him you were well and had done first-rate work in organising our charities. His amiable reply was, 'So the lad's not such a fool after all!'"

Ned chuckled. "I can just hear him!"

"But he's very anxious about money matters. He's got it into his head, and he may very well be right, that the Commune will seize the Banque de France and confiscate all private accounts, including yours. He asked me to be your banker if the need arises, to advance you cash for all reasonable expenses, and present my account for such expenses, with interest at three per cent, for his repayment in six months' time. I agreed, of course."

They both smiled at the stilted quotes, and Ned said, "I think that was damned decent of him, sir, and very good of you to take me on. I'm not strapped for money, and I hope there'll be no trouble at the bank."

"*You're* not in any trouble, are you, Ned?"

"Should I be?" – defensively.

"You know best," said Wallace drily. "Heaven knows I've no right to moralise, and Madame de Grimont is very lovely. But I wonder if it's wise – for the lady's own sake – to *afficher* yourself with her so publicly. Madame Julie – I mean my wife – and I saw you both in her carriage yesterday afternoon, driving round the lake in the Bois and with eyes for no one but each other."

"The honour was mine," said Ned, flushing. "I hope you and Mrs Wallace found nothing to criticise in Madame de Grimont."

"I didn't mean it as a criticism," said Wallace, getting up and laying his hand affectionately on the young man's shoulder. "I meant it as a warning. Hubert de Grimont can be a vicious enemy."

Ned lit a cigarette and sat on in the empty room he knew so well, which still smelt, as it had done all through the Siege, of tobacco, snuff, spirits and assorted medicines. Wallace had put his finger on a sensitive spot. He was not afraid of de Grimont's enmity, but his passion for de

Grimont's wife had cooled since she insisted on the carriage drives and the meetings, known to all her servants, in de Grimont's house. In a boyish way he felt it wasn't quite fair play. A secret rendezvous – fair enough; there had been plenty of them in his life, even in puritan Manchester, but he felt like a paid boy when he sat in Elvire's boudoir and accepted a glass of champagne from her butler. Damn it, the man was bound to know what was between them! He meant to insist that their next meeting should be in his studio at the Hôtel de Bruxelles. But that evening Madame Delphine's hat shop, Elvire's way to their secret room, had its windows broken, and Delphine herself was arrested by the police of the Commune on a morals charge.

That was comparatively easy for de Grimont to arrange. His next step required more finesse, and the persuading of Surgeon-Major Pasquier, the head of the new Sanitary Commission at Versailles, to provide him with a *laissez-passer* for Paris, an ambulance and two stretcher-bearers, and – as an afterthought – a Red Cross worker for window-dressing.

"So no sooner have we got you here than we send you back to Paris, mademoiselle," said Dr Pasquier cheerfully to his new assistant. "The Minister of Justice needs your help in conveying his ailing mother-in-law to the Hôtel des Réservoirs. You'll only be away for a few hours, and tomorrow your duties here will begin in earnest."

"Very good, sir," said Emily March. She hoped, as she went to her quarters, that her new civilian assignment would be more successful than her last. She was trying to be professionally cheerful when she took her seat beside the two stretcher-bearers in the ambulance with the Red Cross on its white canvas hood.

"Sit here beside me, mademoiselle," said the gentleman who introduced himself as Monsieur de Grimont when the ambulance picked him up outside the Préfecture. She had been expecting someone more official, but the Minister of Justice was unobtrusively dressed in a grey sack suit, with a thick scarf twisted round his neck and chin. He put her through a pleasant but complete interrogation as they drove out of Versailles. What had induced her to take up military nursing? The example of Florence Nightingale, she supposed; at least, she had followed Miss Nightingale to Pastor Fliedner's school at Kaiserswerth. In the United States she had been impressed by all Miss Dorothea Lynde Dix had done for the Federal troops in the Civil War. But she owed most to Miss Clara Barton, a neighbour at home in Massachusetts, who had persuaded her parents to let her go so far away to study. Miss Barton had also worked on the American battlefield, and now she was in France trying to organise help for civilian victims of the war with Prussia, in close collaboration with Henry Dunant, the founder of the Red Cross. Monsieur de Grimont had met Monsieur Dunant many times. He had also met Miss Barton at the home of Monsieur Richard Wallace, and admired her. This harmonious conversation brought the ambulance to the Pont de Neuilly.

There were many more Federal troops guarding the bridge than when Emily left Paris with three Sisters of Charity on Thursday afternoon. In forty-eight hours sentry boxes had been set up, two at each end, which meant that the Surgeon-Major's *laissez-passer* was inspected by four armed men when the ambulance arrived from Versailles. Emily March, who had keen eyesight, saw that it was made out to 'Dr Hubert and his team (*équipe*)' and not to Monsieur de Grimont, but it was accepted at its face value, and the ambulance rolled on across a bridge lined with troops. At the Paris side 'Dr Hubert' got out, and had a brief conversation with a Federal lieutenant, whom he seemed to know quite well.

"We have one stop to make before we reach the patient," said de Grimont, as the ambulance proceeded towards the Arc de Triomphe. "It shouldn't detain us longer than half an hour."

"Is the patient quite helpless, monsieur?"

"Not entirely, but she lost the power of speech after a massive stroke two years ago." De Grimont smiled. "Don't worry, she won't be your responsibility. Her personal attendant will be with her, and perhaps another lady too."

Then what am I doing here, Emily March wondered during the time, much longer than half an hour, which she spent alone in the small salon of a shabby old house on the Rue de Lille. The woman who brought her a cup of coffee told her that the house belonged to Prince Pierre de la Treille, a name which meant nothing to the American girl. She began to feel that she was being used as a pawn in some devious game, a political masquerade which had nothing to do with nursing, and was glad when de Grimont himself came to tell her that they were going to his own home now, and might bring the duchess back to this quiet courtyard on the Rue de Lille. It was the first time she had heard of the patient's rank. "The duchess of what, please?" she asked.

"De la Treille."

An elderly gentleman, presumably the prince of the same name, was being helped into a pony carriage in the courtyard, and the stretcher-bearers, who had been drinking wine in the kitchen of his house, were running towards the ambulance with the driver. The pony carriage followed as they took a roundabout way to the Rue St Florentin, avoiding the barricade at the foot of the street and another barricade in the Rue Royale. These were the only signs of strife in the heart of fashionable Paris on that brilliant Saturday, the first day of April, when the confectionery shops remaining open had their windows full of chocolate fish.

The butler, welcoming his master, regretted to inform him that madame la baronne was not at home.

"That makes it easier," said de Grimont to Prince Pierre, who had joined him in the hall. "Miss March, wait in the ambulance. You men, get upstairs as fast as you can."

There was no delay here. In less than ten minutes Emily was arranging pillows and blankets under the direction of the 'personal attendant', a middle-aged woman who seemed to resent her presence, and the orderlies were transferring a tiny bundle wrapped in ermine from their stretcher to a couch inside the ambulance. The driver had his orders, and they started back at once to the Rue de Lille. Emily wondered dazedly if she had assisted at a kidnapping.

Prince Pierre de la Treille, miserably waiting for de Grimont in the library, had the same illogical feeling that there had been a kidnapping. He knew that de Grimont was less concerned with the old lady's welfare than with using her as a weapon against his wife, and he dreaded the scene he must witness when Elvire de Grimont came home. Luckily he had not long to wait. She sauntered into the library half an hour after the ambulance left, not seeing him at first, but saying to her husband:

"They told me you were here, Hubert. Pray has Monsieur Thiers dispensed with your services?"

He ignored the sarcasm. "And they told me you had gone out, Elvire," he said. "Were you at another of the Comtesse de Lhomond's musical afternoons? Or choosing a new bonnet at Delphine's?"

It was a declaration of war. "Delphine's is out of business," she said. "You managed that, of course."

"It wasn't difficult. Don't you intend to greet your

145

cousin Pierre?"

"Pierre! Why are you lurking in the shadows?"

"Bonjour, Elvire," her kinsman murmured. "Hubert invited me to be present as – as –"

"As a witness," said the Minister of Justice. "Pierre is your nearest male relative in Paris. I wanted him to be here when your mother was removed from my house for her own good –"

"*Mother*!" It was a shriek, whether of despair or fury Pierre de la Treille could not have said. "What have you done with her?"

"She's in a safe place, with her own woman and another nurse to look after her, and she'll soon be on her way to the Hôtel des Réservoirs at Versailles. This is your last chance, Elvire. Will you come with me to join her, and – in the eyes of the world at least – preserve the fiction of our happy married life?"

"Never!"

"Then, since divorce is out of the question, you must prepare yourself for a judicial separation, which I shall seek when the rule of law is re-established."

"Elvire," said old de la Treille in his quavering voice, "think what you're saying. Don't throw your life away. You can't live separated – disgraced – *déclassée* –"

"How much did Hubert pay you to come here and say all that?" the woman cried, and her husband sneered that it was only one more payment he had made over the years to the de la Treilles.

"My brother never was your debtor," said Elvire. "I'll go to Hyères, where the duke will give me a home, I know."

"You forget," said de Grimont, "–not that you ever bother to remember – Alain is at Hyères. And I shall make sure, by due process of law, that you never see your son again."

"Elvire," the old man intervened again, "this is not a question of exchanging insults, it's a matter of life and death. Take a night to sleep on it and think it over well. Let me come back tomorrow morning and take you to the Rue de Lille. Marguerite and I would be glad to have you, to give you a place for rest and tranquillity, and who knows? You may decide after all to join your mother at Versailles."

"You've said one sensible thing, cousin Pierre." She never lost her nerve, the Minister of Justice thought; the bravado was always there. "You recommend a good night's sleep. It isn't bedtime yet, but I find you boring, messieurs; I shall excuse myself and retire to my rooms."

"Sleep well," said de Grimont, "but don't expect to find the same comforts surrounding you tomorrow morning. I intend to dismiss all the staff, with compensation, before I leave the house tonight. It will no longer be run for the pleasure of yourself and your English lover. And mark me, madame" – he seized her wrist in his first violent gesture – "I can break him as easily as I broke Delphine the procuress. We shall see how his ardour survives a stay in a Commune prison."

On that same Saturday Marc and Babette decided to be selfish. The whole week had been given up to the concerns of Fanny, and Babette was very tired. Marc persuaded her to stay in bed all morning, while he went into Paris on some vague 'business', and not to go near the Old Farm. Fanny was in their old room at the top of the house, with Tante Lise in devoted attendance, and her friend Madame Jaloux, the midwife of the Place du Tertre, plying the sick girl with remedies which she vowed would do more good than an ovariotomy performed by Professor Stéphane Tarnier of the Maternité.

"I am tired," Babette confessed. "I haven't caught up on those two nights without sleep when the poor child died. But you've been an angel, Marc. I don't know how we could have got through it without you."

"All I did was kick those two Leblancs into finding a horse and cart to get Fanny back to Montmartre; Tante Lise did the rest. Oh, and the pathetic funeral; yes, I saw to that."

"And the priest, Marc; that too." She knew that her lover had paid the fee for the burial service when Loulou's body was committed to the common grave.

"I'd have been glad to break Didier's jaw for him if he had kicked up a fuss about Fanny's going away. Actually the swine is looking forward to life in barracks. So their problems are settled, and now you and I are going to enjoy ourselves."

She had had her sleep out and was painting when Marc came toiling up the long hill to Montmartre, carrying a heavy parcel, which he presented to her with a flourish as her *poisson d'avril*.

"That's far too big for a chocolate fish!"

It was the new coat he had promised her, and he had chosen it all by himself at the Printemps, with some advice from the saleslady, who said the shoulder capelet was the latest fashion. The colour was the violet cobalt beloved of the Independents, which suited Babette's vivid looks, and the fit was perfect.

"You see I know your measurements by heart," said Marc slyly, and after the squeals of pleasure, the hugging and kissing were over, Babette's old dress came off with the new coat, and Marc explored the little body which clung to his in love. They slept, and woke drowsily, they drank wine and slept again through the warm spring afternoon. Much later he took her to dine in the grand manner at the Reine Margot, where they were hardly likely to be interrupted by an apache like 'Jo-Jo' Malaval and where the cloakroom attendant hung up the new coat as respectfully as if it had been the ermine wrap of the Duchesse de la Treille. While they ate and drank Marc made love to his girl with voice and touch until he was sure, as sure as he had been in bed, that she was utterly his, and that this was the night he would ask her to marry him.

The evening was so warm and their happiness so complete that Babette's lover wanted to prolong it, savouring the moments ahead, and they walked back to the Rue des Rosiers by the long route down the Rue St Vincent. There were lights burning in the windows of the Vine House which fronted on that street, but no other sign of life, and the Russians were not mentioned. They were in the mood for entertainment and stopped for a final glass of wine at a little place more like a country cottage than a wineshop at the corner of the Rue St Vincent and the Rue des Saules. It had been a *chansonnier* before the war, and once again the sound of singing was coming from the Auberge des Assassins, so called from a series of murals depicting the murderous career of one Troppmann, who had died by the guillotine in 1869.

Some day it would be known by the more cheerful name of the Lapin Agile, but the sinister background did not depress the customers, who joined in the singing when they could and applauded all the satirical songs, usually celebrating Thiers's flight to Versailles and the ex-Emperor's simultaneous flight to England. Babette was in great spirits. She had one glass of wine too many, and kept saying it was like old times, fun times come again. They walked home with their arms round each other, stopping in the shadows of the Montmartre buttresses to kiss and

149

caress with such fervour that Marc was on fire for her, and thought a pit had opened at his feet when an armed man in uniform ordered them to halt.

"Who the devil are you?" he began, and then as he came out of his trance of happiness and faced reality he saw that he was very near his own building, where a light still burned in Madame Camille's window, and that the Federal who had accosted him was the sentry at the gate where the Red Flag flew.

"Corporal Lemoine, citizen," said the sentry. "I've seen you before. I need your name, rank and age."

"Vallon, Marc, former sergeant, age twenty-six."

"Eligible for conscription in the National Guard."

"I thought the Commune had abolished conscription."

"For the royalist army, not for the Guard. Every able-bodied man must serve the People's cause. Nature of *your* service, sergeant?"

"I was with MacMahon's division at Wörth, and wounded in action."

"Discharged?"

"Passed *bon pour le service* after six weeks, and later served with Bourbaki when we took Dijon. Where did *you* stand fire, corporal?"

"I was wounded in the Great Sortie last winter," said the Federal. "You needn't think you're the only one who's been to war."

"I don't, but at least you and I were fighting Prussians."

"What does that mean? You object to fighting the Versaillais?"

"I object to fighting Frenchmen, whoever they are."

"Better not let our new mayor, Comrade Ferré, hear you say that. He'd have you in the *taule* as fast as he could get the bracelets on. Look here," said the man, "take my advice and get your discharge papers ready. The Conscription Law will soon be passed, and then we may be

150

obliged to come and get you." He had ignored Babette, who was clinging to Marc's arm, during the whole exchange. Now he sketched a salute and said, "I hope I haven't alarmed the little lady."

"Not in the slightest," said Babette coldly, and the man smiled.

"*Alors amusez-vous bien tous les deux*," he said.

Nothing was further from Marc Vallon's thought than the sort of amusement his interrogator had in mind. When they reached the studio he relieved his mind by swearing and kicking the furniture before slumping down on the old window seat to watch Corporal Lemoine on sentry duty.. He was pacing up and down in a regular cadence quite unlike the slouching of the usual drunken louts on duty. Marc could see him by the light of a waxing moon, and decided that for all his gibberish about a 'royalist' army, the man had been a regular himself. By the very tone of his interrogation he might have been an officer of the Line.

"Marc, where did you *put* your discharge papers?" fretted Babette. "I've never seen them anywhere."

"Look in the table drawer."

The drawer was crammed with odds and ends, but there was a big envelope which looked promising, for Marc's mother had marked it 'Personal Papers' when the home in the Rue Vavin was broken up. It contained nothing but his birth and baptismal certificates and a copy of his father's Will.

"They must have given you *some* sort of paper when you were discharged at Montparnasse."

"Darling, I was so dead to the world that day I can't remember what they did ... Let's try the kitchen drawers."

Babette laid aside her new coat carefully, and they tackled the kitchen table and cupboards and a bureau in

151

the bedroom, all without success. Then Marc said quietly, "Light a candle, sweetheart. We'll try the *cagibi*."

"There's nothing up there but cobwebs."

The *cagibi* was a glorified closet beneath the eaves of the building, in which a tall man could hardly stand upright. Reached by a short staircase from the landing it held, as well as cobwebs, an old easel, a few warped canvases, Babette's carpet bag and a leather trunk with a broken strap. On top of the trunk's contents, when the lid was lifted, were the blue tunic and red breeches of Marc's army uniform, and in the breast pocket of the tunic was the missing discharge certificate.

"*Voilà*!" said Marc. "Now I'm all ready to face Comrade Ferré."

Babette did not echo his laugh of triumph. In the wan light of the *cagibi*, criss-crossed by the wavering candle flame and the stars shining through the grimy skylight, he saw a peculiar excitement on her face.

"I thought you were through with war," she said.

"So I am."

"Then why did you keep your uniform?"

". . . I don't know."

When he awoke next morning Babette was beside the bed with an expression on her face which spoke of danger.

"Marc, please wake up! Can you hear the guns? Has the war begun again?"

He had to strain to listen, for the noise came from the western perimeter of Paris, but both he and she were perfectly familiar with the sound.

"Don't be afraid, darling," he said. "Yes, it's started."

152

11

The Baron de Grimont's official report of his visit to Paris lay on the desk of the Chief Executive within an hour of his return to Versailles in the Red Cross ambulance. Monsieur Thiers turned the sealed envelope over more than once before he opened it, and he asked the secretary who laid it on his desk if Madame de Grimont had arrived with her husband. The man said no; only the Duchesse de la Treille was reported to be at the Hôtel des Réservoirs. Thiers sighed and shrugged. He was not a sensitive man, and assumed that his Justice Minister was able to handle his own matrimonial affairs. But he had a moment of pity for poor Marie de la Treille. He remembered dancing with her in her bridal gown at a Tuileries ball in the days of King Louis Philippe.

The report was concise, and contained the information de Grimont had received from the young officer at the Paris end of the Neuilly bridge, a clerk from his own ministry whom he had infiltrated into the National Guard.

"I am reliably informed," it ran, "that the leaders of the so-called Commune intend to attack Versailles five days from now. Their fighting force is only half of what it was, and is now less than two hundred thousand men."

Thiers had done wonders during the two weeks that the Commune's concern with ideology had put into his hands. He had halted the desertions among the regulars, welcomed deserters from the moderate National Guard, and brought in militia from the provinces, where the local Communes were petering out. Gendarmes, *gardes-forestiers, gardes-champêtres* had rallied to the Tricolore which waved defiance to the Red Flag. But the Government force still numbered only 60,000, which on paper was not equal to the Federals' strength. And then there was the question of leadership. Monsieur Thiers was installed in the Préfecture of the Seine et Oise, recently occupied by the newly proclaimed German Emperor, but if he were at home in the Place St Georges in Paris, he could put his finger on the quotation he wanted in an instant. He was a distinguished scholar, who had written history while he was making it, and in his *Histoire de la Révolution Française* he knew exactly where to find his own evocation of the glorious days when 'France was mistress of all the lands between the Rhine and the Pyrenees, the sea and the Alps ... and twenty heroes led French soldiers to victory...' Bonaparte, Hoche, Kléber, Masséna – the roll of honour seemed to stretch out indefinitely. All he had were Vinoy, Cissey, Clinchant, Gallifet and of course MacMahon. Patrice MacMahon, a man over sixty, whose victories in the Crimea and Italy were well in the past, and whose defeat at Wörth and Sedan too brutally in the present. Nevertheless Vinoy, a failure in command, would have to be replaced by MacMahon, the Marshal-Duke of Magenta, if the Commune meant to attack in five days. He called a council of war, and informed his generals that they must attack tomorrow.

This was the sound of firing which Marc and Babette heard, like everyone else in Paris, on that Palm Sunday morning. The attack took place at Courbevoie, some miles north-east of Versailles and not far from the Fort du Mont Valérien, one of the strongest of the Sixteen Forts which the prescience of Thiers had caused to be built in a bygone age. The Federals were in strength at Courbevoie, and fought back with all the artillery and small-arms fire at their command. They were doing well when a battalion of Zouaves charged them with shouts of *Vive le Roi*! It was not clear which king the Zouaves meant, Bourbon, Orleans or even Bonaparte, but to the Federals, some drunk and all indisciplined, it was a terrifying voice from the past of France. They broke ranks and fled, dropping their old-fashioned 'snuffbox' rifles as they abandoned the vital bridge across the Seine to the regulars and ran back into Paris. It was a rout as complete as any the National Guard had known in the sorties of the Siege, and the usual excuses for cowardice, that they had been 'sold' or 'betrayed', did not impress their horrified supporters in the capital. The leaders of the Commune promised tremendous reprisals on the next day, when the largest army they could muster set out for Versailles. Unfortunately, with a forgetfulness equal to the late General Lecomte's, they forgot to take with them the cannon of Montmartre.

The government troops met them with a fury like their own. Among the fallen at Courbevoie was Surgeon-Major Pasquier who, not content to wait in his 'ambulance' at Satory for casualties to arrive, accompanied the attacking troops and was killed on Neuilly bridge. That he had been shot down while carrying a flag of truce became one of the legends of a civil war destined to be rich in legends, and 'Vengeance for Pasquier!' was the slogan behind the reprisals which began as soon as the Federals were routed. One shell from one of the cannon of Mont Valérien made their defeat certain, and while the rearguard fled back to Paris the vanguard was cut to pieces on the plain of Versailles. Next day two of the Federal 'generals' were found hiding in the neighbourhood and executed on the spot. Other prisoners were shot as soon as captured, and the Commune was informed that war would be waged 'without truce or mercy'.

"That does it," said the American Minister, alone with David Meade in his office in Versailles. "When you start shooting prisoners of war there's no going back, and Thiers means to be as bloody-minded as the Reds. I've no hope of being a successful mediator, but I've got to let Secretary Fish know I tried. You're due to go into Paris this morning, aren't you?"

"I am, sir. Have you any instructions about the passes?"

"Yes, hang out a notice saying no more will be issued at present. All the American citizens left in Paris have their letters of protection as well as their passports, and I'm sick of bogus Alsatians trying to pass themselves off as Germans. Secretary Hoffmann's been having the devil of a time with them."

"Am I to come back to Versailles with Mr Hoffmann, sir?"

"No, stick around for a day or two. I want to get a first-hand impression of the real feeling in the city. Keep moving, and keep your eyes and ears open for any Russian interference. Oh, and Mr Meade —"

"Sir?"

"Two young Americans, Dr Quimby and Dr March, have joined poor Pasquier's ambulance out at Satory. Stop by on your way into the city, and see if they need any help from us."

As a neutral diplomat David Meade had of course his own *laissez-passer* between Paris and Versailles, and the attachés now shared the use of a driver and a closed cab with the arms of the United States on the door. He was glad of the privacy as the cab jogged towards Satory, for the three days' fighting had taken an unexpected toll of his nerves. The Siege had not affected him to the same extent, because this conflict was a civil war, arousing old memories which he had tried to bury. He was even agitated at meeting two strange American doctors, probably of an age to have served in the War Between the States and on the Union side.

A tent city was rising on the plain of Satory, and when Meade asked for the *médecin américain* the doctor who came from one of the tents to greet him was a cheerful youngster who could only have been a schoolboy when Lieutenant Meade was inside besieged Richmond. He had 'done a turn', he said, with Dr Swinburne in the great American Ambulance, and he pointed with pride to the ventilation in the French tents, which were heated only by a stove inside a hole in the ground which kept the earth dry. The French wounded complained bitterly, he grinned, but the method was tried and true, and prevented septicaemia, as Mr Meade was no doubt aware. Mr Meade was aware: he had been nursed back to life in just such another tent after Richmond fell.

"Is there anything the Legation can get you, Dr Quimby?" he asked. "We have a substantial war comforts fund for our own nationals."

"Poor Dr Pasquier had everything organised," said the young man. "But if we have another couple of days like the last we're going to need more *charpie*, I mean shredded lint."

"I'll make a note of it," said Meade. "And how about your colleague, Dr March?"

Dr Quimby smiled again. "It's *Miss* March," he said. "I've a Red Cross lady for one of my colleagues. She's a

157

first-rate surgical nurse."

He crooked a finger at a hovering orderly. "Go to Tent B and tell Nurse March I'd like to see her if she's free," he said, and to Meade, "She should be free. Dr Lautrec finished his last amputation half an hour ago; they'll have washed up by now."

"Tough job for a woman."

"She's got a steady nerve."

The girl who appeared between the flaps of a nearby tent had a steady walk, the quick, almost military step of one accustomed to a sudden summons. She had a clean hospital smock over her Red Cross uniform, and her sleeves were turned down and fastened at the wrists, but she either had no mirror or had not looked in a mirror, for in the washing up she had missed a tiny smear of blood at the edge of her cap, as if she had at some time wiped the sweat off her forehead with the back of a blood-stained hand. The drawstring of the cap was pulled so tight that it was impossible to tell the colour of her hair. Her eyes, red-rimmed with fatigue, were the shade of grey sometimes confused with green.

"Yes, Dr Quimby?" she said.

"Miss March, let me introduce Mr Meade, from the American Legation, come to find out what they can do to help. I told him we need *charpie* more than anything."

"It's very kind of you, sir," she said, and he had a feeling that out of uniform and in his mother's new parlour on Staten Island she would have dropped a lady's formal curtsy. "*Charpie is* badly needed, and would it be possible to get a quantity of lemons to make cooling drinks for the patients? They're suffering terribly from thirst."

"I don't think I can promise a quantity, whatever quantity you have in mind," said Meade, "but I know where I can lay my hands on *some*, and I know there's *charpie* at the Legation. I'm on my way to Paris now, and I'll do the best I can."

"That's very good of you." She hesitated. "Are you Mr David Meade?"

"That's my name."

"Then I have a message for you – kind regards from Madame Didier Leblanc and her sister – I think her name's Babette."

"From Babette Mercier! How in the world did you come to know her?"

Emily March described Madame Leblanc's original visit to the Belleville hospital and its sad sequel, her little boy's death from febrile convulsions. "I could do nothing for him," she admitted, "and when I went back to ask for him just before I left Paris, he was dead, and a woman told me his mother and her sister had gone to live at an old farm in Montmartre."

"I know the place, Miss March. What about the husband? Did he go too?"

"I never saw the husband."

"Was there no man to look after them in their trouble?"

"Oh yes, a Monsieur Vallon, who was very anxious to help."

The candid grey-green eyes betrayed no intimate knowledge of Monsieur Vallon's reason to help.

"Well, well," said Meade, "life takes strange turns, doesn't it? To think of your meeting Babette and her poor sister . . ."

Emily could not have told what spark of jealousy made her say,

"She's very pretty, isn't she, mademoiselle Babette?"

"She's lovely."

The man, and he was not a very young man, for Emily had noticed his greying hair, blushed like a schoolboy as he spoke, and the spark of jealousy kindled to a tiny flame.

She was ashamed of herself, and when the 'goodbyes' and 'good lucks' were said, and she was hurrying back to a draughty tent full of wounded men she wondered what her heroines, Miss Nightingale and Miss Barton, those spinsters supreme, would have thought of a military nurse who allowed herself to be charmed by the first attractive American she had seen for months. She couldn't help wondering what he had thought of her.

David Meade's thoughts were not of women as he was driven across Neuilly bridge, which had changed hands more than once during the action of the previous days and was now in the hands of the government troops. The great avenues were empty, as if the life-blood of Paris was slowly draining away, and the brilliant boutiques of the Champs Elysées shuttered and bolted as when Paris was besieged by the Prussians. There were a few loafers outside the American Legation, but not the lines of passport applicants Meade had expected, for Mr Washburne's instructions had been anticipated, and a hand-printed notice nailed to the door stated that the issue of passes had ceased. The Assistant Secretary, Wickham Hoffmann, told Meade he had acted on his own initiative after the bad news came that morning.

"What bad news, for heaven's sake?"

"The Reds arrested the Archbishop of Paris and chucked him into the Mazas prison."

"I don't believe you!"

It was incredible but perfectly true. Raoul Rigault had arrested the saintly Monsignor Darboy on the vague grounds of 'hostility to the Commune' and 'Bonapartist sympathies', for the archbishop had been Grand Almoner at the court of Napoleon III. With him Rigault arrested the aged *curé* of the famous Madeleine church, who had been the Empress Eugénie's confessor, and a number of minor clergy. The real reason, revealed by Rigault a few days later, was revenge for the summary execution of the Commune's 'generals' after the failed attack of April 3.

This was not the only piece of bad news Hoffmann had to impart. At the Hôtel de Ville the Commune was debating a Hostages Law, calling for the imprisonment of anyone guilty of 'complicity with Versailles' as a hostage of the people of Paris, liable to execution when any Commune prisoner of war was executed. Complicity with Versailles was capable of wide interpretation, and so that the zealous Prefect, Rigault, and his policemen could keep their eye on all suspects, the Gates of Paris were to be shut and all rail traffic halted.

"Looks like we're in for another siege," said Meade with a sigh.

"You and I are old siege hands," said the Assistant Secretary with a mocking smile.

On the surface his words were innocent enough, for both Americans had been inside the Legation when the Prussians were bombarding the Sixteen Forts, and had worked together in harmony. But there had been a time, not so long before, when their siege experience had been conducted on different sides: Colonel Hoffmann as one of General Grant's officers at the siege of Vicksburg, Lieutenant Meade with the Confederate forces besieged in Richmond. Old siege hands! At that moment old passions flared again, and Meade had to choke back furious words. If I feel like this, he thought as his fury ebbed in silence, about Hoffmann, who's a decent fellow, what can we expect of the French, who hate each other's guts anyway?

"The Minister must be told as soon as possible," said Hoffmann, who felt the tension in the air. "He didn't say anything about getting Mrs Washburne and the family out of Paris?"

"He seems to think they're safe enough at the Porte Dauphine. This may change his mind, of course."

"And the duty clerks are to stay on here with you?"

"Unless we have to shut up shop. Hoffmann, will you do me a favour? The Minister wants us to look out for two Americans working for the Satory Ambulance, Dr Quimby and a Miss March, a Red Cross nurse. I saw them both this morning. Do you know anything about them?"

"I issued their letters of protection ten days ago. Young Quimby's a Bostonian, and Miss March comes from a little town in Massachusetts, where her father's a Methodist minister."

Northerners both, just as he expected. "They're doing a fine job," said Meade, "and all they've asked from us is *charpie* and lemons for the wounded. Could you take some stuff down to them?"

"In the *cab*?"

"How else?"

"Can't it wait till tomorrow, and go down in the waggon?"

"The waggon may be needed for the Washburne party, bag and baggage."

"Oh damnation," said Hoffmann, "I suppose you're right. Which reminds me, I'd feel happier if I sent a note by hand to Mrs Washburne, telling her how we're fixed. While I write it, rustle around for what you want."

Of shredded lint there was an ample supply in the storeroom where some of the destitute Germans had been housed by the Protecting Power, and Meade reflected, as he filled bags with a servant's help, that much of the stuff had been prepared by German hands. He found fifteen lemons, put three of them aside with a few tins of meat extract, saved the others for Miss March, and then went to the desk in his own office. There was something he needed in a locked drawer.

It was not until the afternoon that David Meade turned into the Rue St Jean. He had carried out Mr Washburne's order to keep moving. He had walked miles through the streets of Paris, listened to conversations, lunched at the Hôtel St Honoré, where the regulars were always well informed, and had heard the pros and cons of the archbishop's arrest and the threat implied in the Hostages Law. He never thought he could pass for a Frenchman, nor ever tried, but he knew better now than to appear in Montmartre wearing a frock coat and a silk hat, and in a well-worn ulster he was unobtrusive enough to get up to the Butte without being asked to show his identity papers more than twice.

When he rang the concierge's bell at the Old Farm it was Babette's voice which asked who was there, and when he answered "David Meade" she was ready with a kiss for him as soon as the door was opened. "I've found you!" he said. "I went to the Rue des Rosiers and found nobody home. How are you, dear?" She looked pale and anxious, dressed in her black alpaca and working apron just as he had drawn her in his sketch of Babette at the Fountain.

"Marc went to the Banque de France to cash a cheque," she said. "Now the fighting's started he wants to have some cash in hand. He'll be sorry to have missed you — but do come in."

The kitchen was warm and empty. "Tante Lise has gone to church to pray for the archbishop," Babette explained. "Isn't his arrest a dreadful thing?"

"Terrible. But how about your sister? I was sorry to hear about the child's death."

"She's still in bed, and a friend of ours, Madame Jaloux, is sitting with her. They say she's getting better, but I don't know ... she doesn't speak much, or seem to care for anything. Didier came here last night to tell her he hadn't been in the fighting, and she only said 'Better luck next time!' and then lay looking at the wall."

"Poor creature. I brought a few little things for her—"
He was emptying the pockets of his ulster, crammed with
tins of Liebig, that standby of the Siege, and the three
lemons kept back from the fruit for Satory.

"You *are* kind, Meade!" She stood on tiptoe to kiss his
cheek. "But who told you about our trouble?"

"A young lady I met for the first time this morning. You
knew her, Babette; you sent me your kind regards by Miss
Emily March."

"The Red Cross lady!" She was smiling now, the cheeky
smile of the little *grenouille* he had fancied himself in
love with, and she said "I thought you'd like her."

Now what was she up to? Was Marc Vallon's lover
trying to be a matchmaker? He thought it was time to ask
for Marc. Gone to cash a cheque—no wonder; the man
might have three women on his hands if the fighting went
on, and there was no one left in Paris to buy paintings.
Babette said Marc was well, but had been tackled by a
Red from the command post, and told he would be
conscripted into the National Guard.

"That's rubbish," said the American, "the Commune
hasn't passed the Conscription Law yet."

"But they will do?"

"Unless Thiers recaptures Paris first—I'm afraid so."
Before she had time to sigh he asked if Marc Vallon
carried a gun.

"*Marc*? You know how he feels about firearms since the
war."

"Yes, but firearms can be a useful means of defence."

"I don't think it would have been very useful if Marc
had shot that Red soldier who stopped him in the street."

"Just give him this and see what he says." He put his
hand in his jacket pocket. At least he knew better than to
offer her money and have her ask if he took her for a light
woman—he hadn't forgotten that searing phrase; what he

164

laid on Madame Verlet's kitchen table was a short-barrelled derringer, from which Babette instinctively recoiled.

"Don't worry, it isn't loaded."

"It won't be much use if it isn't loaded."

He laid a small box of ammunition beside the gun.

"Show me how to load it, Meade . . . please."

"Oh no. A derringer isn't a toy for pretty girls to monkey with."

"Not even when they're living next door to Russian anarchists?"

The words brought him back to that phase of his duty which he had forgotten in the spell of her nearness, and he said almost guiltily:

"Have you found out any more about that manservant?"

"His name's Ivan Ivanovich, his master told Madame Verlet, but I hear Louise Michel calling him Mitya. You can find out quite a bit by sitting at the window in Fanny's bedroom – our bedroom, it used to be, and I hear him talking French with Louise Michel. Do Russian servants speak foreign languages?"

"Not as a rule. What does he do with Michel – walk up and down the garden?"

"He's doing some work in the gardener's shed at the side of the house next the vineyard, where the tools are kept, I mean. I see the Red Virgin brandishing a saw and probably wishing it was a bayonet. They're as thick as thieves, the lot of them, but they won't fool me. Now do I get shown how to load a what d'you call it – a derringer?"

Against his better judgment Meade showed her how. It was amazing how quickly her neat little fingers caught the knack.

12

Lunching with good friends at the Hôtel St Honoré on any other occasion, David Meade would have been more aware of the silence of Edward Carey than on the day when the arrest of the archbishop and the debate on the Hostages Law were the prime topics of conversation. The young Englishman hardly joined in the talk, ate little, and excused himself before the meal was over on the grounds of an engagement with Mr Wallace. Meade thought he was probably regretting not having left Paris before the Gates were shut and the train services cancelled. There was no disgrace in that, he would not be the only neutral to be appalled at the idea of living through what was obviously going to be a second siege.

Ned certainly had an appointment with Richard Wallace at the Grand Hotel, still in use as a war hospital, but not until four o'clock. He left the dining room at half past two, weary of the talk and arguments he had listened to so often before, and thinking of nothing but the letter received that morning, which he already knew by heart. He took it from his wallet as soon as he was in his own room overlooking the courtyard of the hotel, piled with the heavy leather portmanteaux and valises of his fellow Britons who, at half past midnight rather than at the eleventh hour, still hoped for an exit permit and transportation to the coast.

The letter paper was thick, pale grey in colour and embossed with a coronet in gilt, and it ran:

Dear Monsieur Edouard Carey,

With what regret must I bid you adieu! The Minister of Justice requires my presence at Versailles, where my invalid mother is already under his care, and I must go where both duty and affection call me. Our Paris home, where we have often welcomed you with pleasure, will be closed until the defeat of the vile Commune, which I know you desire as ardently as we do. Your tranquil England awaits you, where I hope that in the bosom of your family you will often spare a thought for your sincere friends,

E. and H. de Grimont.

Only the first sentence of the letter made any sense. The rest was a fake, written for all Ned knew at her husband's dictation as a means of saving his own face, or proclaiming the victory of money and prestige. But *with what regret must I bid you adieu* – that rang true, that echoed exactly what he felt himself, in spite of his furtive, unworthy feeling that he was glad the affair had come to an end. I'd better get my Louvre copies out of that room I took in the Hôtel de Bruxelles, he thought, or my father will think I never completed a single painting while I was in Paris. And then give up the room and the key to the corridor door, useless since Delphine's establishment was closed. He felt the stirrings of desire as he remembered all the passions they had satisfied in that secret room, but at the same time he wished Elvire had made up her mind sooner. He might have been at Dover by this time. Now, he supposed, he would have to ask Richard Wallace for a job in the Hertford Ambulance.

He had no idea, as he replaced the letter in his wallet, of the time and thought Elvire de Grimont had given to its composition, any more than she realised, as she searched for a formula of friendship to save him from her husband's enmity, that she was writing what might some day be Edward Carey's death warrant.

Elvire's gesture in sweeping from the library and ignoring the arguments of her husband and Prince Pierre de la Treille had been not without its dignity, but unfortunately it was a tactical error. It gave her husband ample time to dismiss the servants after the state rooms had been put in dust sheets, and arrange for the transfer of the horses to a livery stable. One of the footmen, still in silk stockings and powdered hair, was told to take a supper tray to the boudoir of madame la baronne, and this appeared so normal that Elvire decided her husband was only bluffing when he threatened to deprive her of her comforts. She made a pretence of reading for a time, decided to avoid her maid's inquisitive eyes, and took two grains of chloral to make her sleep instead of ringing for Désirée to undress her. By that time Désirée, with de Grimont's gold in her pocket and two of Elvire's silk dresses in her bags, had been out of the house for over an hour.

Elvire woke to the sound of horses on the cobbles of the courtyard. Unrefreshed from her drugged sleep she went heavily to the window to see them go: the carriage horses, her husband's mount, and the petted mare she had ridden so often, and with so many admiring cavaliers, along the bridle paths of the Bois de Boulogne. He meant it then! He was stripping his house of everything, to punish her, and if he went so far, what might he do to Edouard? Furious tugging at the brocade bell pull brought no maid, no preparation of a scented bath or fresh lingerie, no dainty chocolate equipage. Elvire dressed quickly in a plain dress, knotted up her curls as best she could, and started with relief when a knock fell on the outer door of her boudoir suite.

It was the butler, no longer in his stately black and white, but in a respectable brown suit with a silver salver in both hands, a salver which held the silver chocolate pot and Sèvres china of every morning, with a rose in a crystal vase and a letter propped against it.

"Forgive me, madame," the butler said with a low bow, "I couldn't leave the house without making sure that madame la baronne was served as usual –"

"Have the others left?"

"Most of the indoor staff left last night, madame, and the stablemen are leaving now. Of course, as monsieur le baron explained, it's only a temporary arrangement until the end of hostilities –"

She nearly laughed in his serious face. Which hostilities had Hubert meant? The Commune and the Government? Or the de Grimonts, man and wife? She said, "Am I alone in the house, except for you?"

He had been a good servant, and he was perspiring with embarrassment. "Oh no, madame, there are two people in the kitchen and a watchman on duty, and of course monsieur le baron's message" (he indicated the letter, still on the salver he had set on a table) "will describe the travelling arrangements he has made for madame. May I wish madame *bon voyage*, and a speedy return to her home in Paris?"

She thanked him and let him go; he had done his best.

She drank some chocolate and crumbled a brioche before she opened Hubert's letter, which was headed Midnight, and went on: 'Elvire. I placed a sum of money in the safe in your boudoir which will be enough for your immediate needs. The Commune intends to prepare the city for a siege, so I strongly advise you to accept Pierre's invitation to the Rue de Lille. Unless, that is, you prefer the safety of a convent. G.'

The safety of a convent? The jibe was characteristic, but when she remembered that she had been taken from her convent school to marry de Grimont at fifteen, with the blessing and entire approbation of the Mother Superior, she thought she had found no protection there. That he had 'placed money in her safe' was more surprising, and proved that he had been prowling round the house before their encounter in the library, for she had never left her rooms until the butler brought her chocolate. The key to the wall safe was in a casket, also locked, and that key was attached to the gold chain bracelet she always wore. There were no important jewels in it, for after the fall of the Empire these had been transferred to Hubert's strong box in the cellars of the Ministry of Justice – "and much good may they do him there if the Reds take over the place," she thought, as she began the complicated process with the keys.

There was an envelope on the velvet shelves, when the safe was opened, and that was all. Her husband had filled his pockets with the pearl necklace and tiara, the diamond clasp she was fond of wearing, and the ornaments of amethyst, tourmaline, lapis lazuli and other semi-precious stones suited to the Sunday evening soirées when the enemy was at the gates. "The brute!" she said aloud, "he has left me nothing! Nothing but money, and not much of that!" Her immediate needs would have to be modest indeed to be satisfied with the sum in the envelope. What could she do? Where could she go? Anywhere but to that old leech, my cousin Pierre, she thought, and started downstairs to find someone who would tell Prince Pierre de la Treille, when he called, that madame la baronne was not at home.

It was a shock to see the state apartments, where all the furniture was sheeted, the flowers wilting in their vases, and the marble statues already seeming to be covered with a fine film of dust. There was little left to remind her of her famous receptions, or of the hours she had spent alone with 'Edouard', the splendid folly which had ruined her, and yet it was of Ned Carey she thought. She found pen and ink under the dust sheet on her own escritoire, and sat down to write the letter intended to warn him and advise him, while there was time, to flee.

With the letter in her hand she began to explore the house. There was no change in her husband's apartments, except that the huge wardrobe had been emptied, and in her mother's room the bed had been stripped down to the mattress, as if a death had taken place. The difficult tears came to Elvire's eyes at the sight. Her mother was no more dead to her now than when she lay there yesterday, a helpless, speechless paralytic, but there had sometimes been a spark of recognition in her eyes, a faint warmth in the hand her daughter kissed. There were daguerrotypes of her father and her brother, the present Duc de la Treille, on the dressing table, and a modern photograph of her son, sent last Christmas from Hyères. "That's where I'll go!" she vowed. "Hubert shall not keep me from my son!" Then she remembered that she could go nowhere. The Reds held the city and had closed the Gates and she was as much a prisoner in her own house as the Archbishop of Paris in his Mazas cell.

The butler had told her there were two people in the kitchen, and she found them when for the first time in

171

years Elvire de Grimont descended the service stairs. Unexpectedly she recognised them both. The scullery maid was called Anne and the lame boy in charge of the lamps was Bernard (she had forgotten their surname), a brother and sister from the Sologne, whose father had been a gamekeeper at the château in the days of old Henri Grimont, and who for some sentimental reason Hubert had brought two years ago to Paris. They were bowing and curtsying now, and Bernard explained to the lady they had only admired from afar that monsieur le baron had told them they might stay on when the others left, because they had no way of getting home, and because Bernard had learned how to keep the house heated — there was a good supply of mazout for the *chaudières*. If the heating failed the ormolu furniture might begin to crack.

The furniture, of course; trust Hubert to remember that! Elvire said briskly, "Well, make yourself tidy, Bernard, and take this letter at once to the Hôtel St Honoré. When you come back, tell the watchman to bar the gates behind you and admit no one else until I give permission. Anne, there's plenty of food in the house, I suppose?"

"Enough for a few days, my lady. Oh, will it be for longer?"

"The Government troops will soon be here, and then you'll both be sent safely home. Be quick, Bernard!"

The last prisoner of the Second Empire hardly realised, as she watched Bernard in his Sunday jacket limping across the courtyard with her letter to Edward Carey, that whatever the outcome of the letter might be, in writing it she had performed one of the few unselfish acts of her life. Her principal concern was the arrival of the Government troops. After two victories over the Federals in two days' fighting, Monsieur Thiers should have no difficulty in entering Paris before the end of the week.

Monsieur Thiers took a more realistic view of the military situation. He knew that his successes on Palm Sunday and the following day were due to incompetent leadership of the Federal troops and their own cowardice in breaking as soon as the battle went against them. But they were still numerically far stronger than the Government forces, and now, with their first two leaders dead, they were commanded by a man who had at least had a professional training.

The soldier of misfortune named Gustave Cluseret, then forty-seven, had had a chequered career. A graduate of St Cyr, he had fought with distinction in the Crimea, was cashiered in Algeria for black-market activities, and served on the Union side in the American Civil War. When it ended he had become an American citizen, and joined forces with the Irish, then called Fenians, whose successors would be known as the Irish Republican Army. With them he planned to invade Canada, and though that came to nothing he did join a Fenian group operating in England in an attack on Chester Gaol. He turned up again in France after the fall of the Empire, and proclaimed the Commune of Marseille.

Setting all the rest aside, the St Cyr training and the combat experience in the Crimea gave General Cluseret (his Irish rank) a considerable advantage over the officers who aspired to lead the National Guard, and Thiers was not misled by the sarcasms of Minister Washburne, who despised what he knew of Cluseret in America, into taking him less than seriously. He made MacMahon and Vinoy keep up the pressure they had gained under the protection of Mont Valérien while General Cissey prepared to invest the next of the Sixteen Forts, called Fort Issy. The army must take care of Cluseret; Monsieur Thiers regarded as his principal adversary a man nearly fifty years his junior, the twenty-five-year-old Prefect of

Police, Raoul Rigault.

It took Rigault nearly a week before he was ready to confront Thiers on the subject of the imprisoned archbishop, now the prime hostage under the newly passed Hostages Act. He had to let his prisoner experience a few days of the treatment reserved for criminals in the Mazas prison before he could persuade him to write a letter to Thiers protesting against the summary execution of the Federal leaders on 4 April. With a similar letter extracted from the *curé* of the Madeleine it was forwarded under safe conduct to Versailles, and as summarily as the executions were carried out, the protests were rejected by the Chief Executive. Nothing more or less than a cry for help, they were accompanied by an offer from Rigault to exchange the priests for Auguste Blanqui, the veteran Socialist imprisoned on the eve of the uprising. Thiers refused the proposal on two counts, first that Blanqui was as good as an army corps to the Reds, who venerated him, and second because it came from Rigault as the leader of a rebel faction calling itself the Paris Commune. "I will have nothing to do with rebels," he said, when the American Minister made one more useless attempt to act as mediator. "All I require from the so-called Commune is unconditional surrender." When Mr Washburne had gone he added to one of his few confidants that a man who accepted the archbishopric of Paris must also accept the risks he ran. Archbishop Affre had been killed while preaching peace on the barricades during the revolution of 1848, and Archbishop Sibour was murdered in church in 1856. The new victim would have to take his chances like the rest.

Thiers was looking beyond the Mazas prison and the sappers inching their way across the glacis of Fort Issy. During the war with Prussia, and later, he had been a tireless traveller round the capitals of Europe in search of help for France, going as far as St Petersburg to implore the Czar to join the French in opposing the German lust for dominance. He was everywhere unsuccessful. All the chanceries of Europe agreed with the British Prime Minister that the quarrel between France and Prussia must not be allowed to escalate into a European war. Now he made one more overture, through an envoy, to the last statesman a Frenchman might have been expected to approach: to Bismarck, the Chancellor of Imperial Germany.

Bismarck would have endorsed David Meade's view of the Commune as the beginning of something new. Although he lacked the American information about the Egorov cell, the Jaclard cell, and other Russian groups who had crept in from England or Switzerland to infiltrate the Commune, the Red leaders in their speeches made no secret of their devotion to Karl Marx. A victory for the Commune would give immense encouragement to German Socialism, a blow for Bismarck in the very hour of his triumph; and diverting though it had been to watch Frenchmen fighting Frenchmen the time had come to bring the farce to a close. He agreed to Thiers's request that the French Army, limited by the armistice terms, be increased to 170,000 men, and that 100,000 of the French prisoners of war be immediately repatriated from Germany.

As the railway lines in north-eastern France, a region controlled by the army of occupation, had been cut or destroyed during the fighting, Bismarck sent the Frenchmen to seaports in Hanover, from which they embarked on all the boats Thiers found available at Brest and Cherbourg. Although many newspapers, headed by the *Figaro*, had been suppressed by the Commune, it was impossible to keep such news out of the remaining papers, and once they landed in France most of the men managed to get messages through to their families. Those, of course, were scattered up and down the land, and the provinces were growing sick of the Commune's assumption that Paris was the centre of the universe, flouting the authority of the elected members of the National Assembly. Even though the repatriates were not allowed to go home, but were drafted into special camps for retraining and rehabilitation, they were back in their own country, which at first induced such euphoria that their new officers failed to see what a stubborn and vengeful temper they had brought from their German prisons, or how they had transferred their anger from the Emperor who led them to disaster to the Red bastards who wanted to turn Paris into a battlefield.

Madame Jaloux, who had nursed Fanny Leblanc back to reasonably good health, was one of the happy parents whose son had been repatriated. She received his letter on an April evening when Thiers's first victories were two weeks old, and came hurrying to the Rue St Jean to tell her crony Madame Verlet the great news, with her schoolboy son for escort. She found all her friends in the kitchen ready to share her joy. All except one, for Marc Vallon, who was sitting at the kitchen table with a sketching block and a stub of chalk, was .ess enthusiastic. He said Roger Jaloux had been released only to go to war again, and what sort of shape was a man likely to be in who had spent six months in a German prison camp after being captured at Gravelotte?

"That's true, Monsieur Marc," said Madame Jaloux, beginning to cry. "Oh, if only his own mother could nurse him back to health!"

"He'll soon be home again, *maman*," said young Adrien Jaloux gruffly, and Babette said of course he would, now the Government had seasoned troops to rely on Monsieur Thiers would surely increase his snail's pace

176

towards Paris. She thought Marc was being unreasonable, but then he often was these days, and now that Fanny was downstairs again it was not easy to persuade him to visit the Rue St Jean. Fanny had always irritated him, and he told Babette roundly that she was 'working' her sister and Madame Verlet for all she was worth, and had done from the moment of her *opéra-bouffe* appeal to be taken back to the beloved Old Farm. Yes, he agreed she had been ill, yes, he was sorry she had lost two children, *but* if she had the good luck to lose Didier too, he bet Madame Leblanc would be a most attractive widow.

"I'm not going to fight with you about my sister, Marc," said Babette after an argument in the studio. "She's changed a great deal since poor little Louis died. She seems so sweet and sad and gentle on the surface, and she never flies out at me the way she used to or says I'm trying to break up her marriage, but underneath I think she's just a little bit, what shall I say, *détraquée*."

"Crazy is the word you're looking for," said Marc grimly, and on the night when Madame Jaloux came to tell them all the good news of her son's release Babette saw that the chalk sketch he was making of Fanny in the big chair by the stove (and she was deliberately posing for it, arching her neck and laying one hand on her heart like the illustrations in the Books of Beauty she used to read) showed *Françoise l'éternelle victime* as a practised voluptuary with greedy eyes. It wasn't like Marc to be so cruel, and Babette was thankful when he crumpled the sheet and put it in his pocket, saying "No, you shan't see it, Fanny. Chalk doesn't do you justice. Babette must paint you in oils someday."

"Babette indeed!"

"I haven't tried my hand at a portrait yet," said Babette to cover the offended tone. Marc jumped up to open a bottle of wine for Madame Verlet, and they all drank long life to Corporal Roger Jaloux, who at present had no other address than somewhere in France.

The wine must have been too much for young Adrien, who when Babette and Marc were about to leave before night fell on the now darkened streets of the Butte Montmartre, asked the painter if he proposed to go into hiding.

"No, why should I?" asked Marc.

"Because of the new Conscription Law, monsieur. 'Jo-Jo' Malaval and his gang have taken to the *maquis* already."

"Best place for them, keep the streets cleaner," said Marc. "I'm not going into hiding to dodge a bunch of Reds. If they want me they'll have to come and get me, Adrien boy."

"But monsieur —"

"Hold your tongue, Adrien," said his mother. "Roger would be ashamed of you if he heard you talking about that apache Malaval. Really, Lise dear, I think it's time for us to be going too."

In the kitchen, where everybody had been talking at once, the sound of the guns was muted. In the street the steady firing in the south-west was clearly audible: the government artillery covering Cissey's sappers was exchanging shots with the Federals defending Fort Issy. It was the sound to which Parisians had become accustomed, as a few months earlier they had been accustomed to the far noisier exchanges between the Prussians and the Sixteen Forts. There was no immediate danger in Montmartre, and no likelihood that Marc and Babette would be stopped on their way back to the studio, for the Red command post on the Rue des Rosiers was empty now. The men who occupied it had been engaged in the first attack on Versailles, where the aggressive corporal was among the fallen, and after that defeat they had been ordered to the Château Rouge. New concentration of his forces was one of the reforms introduced by General Cluseret – reforms resented by men prepared to fight for their own sector of Paris but less willing to serve at a distance from their homes. Marc Vallon had been left in peace for two weeks, but now that the Conscription Law was in force, and a house search instigated to draft all able-bodied men between the ages of nineteen and fifty-five into the Federal ranks, Babette thought it was time to tell him what she had kept secret since David Meade's last visit to the Old Farm.

It was not the best time, for the real reason for Marc's ill-humour was that his painting was not going well. He was entering a white phase, thanks to the varied shades of white in his last canvas, and he was working on a still life of white flowers in a white Belleek vase on a white linen tablecloth, all the whites giving the impression of an inner colour. He went to his easel as soon as they entered the studio, and dismissed his morning's work with one fecal adjective.

"Marc, I've got something to tell you." He was too absorbed to hear her the first time, and repetition brought only a discouraging "H'm?"

"Darling, you remember my telling you about Meade's coming to the Old Farm, after the Red Cross lady told him where to find us? The day you went to the Banque de France?"

"Meade and the Red Cross girl, of course I remember. How's that romance coming along?"

"I don't know if it *is* a romance! I haven't heard about either of them, from that day to this."

"Oh, I thought you were going to say Meade had dropped in on another of his social calls. Don't tell me he's lost interest in the Vine House Russians."

"I only wanted you to know that when he did come he left you this."

She rummaged in her big wool bag with the embroidered lilies and roses, which she had carried to the Old Farm with a shirt she was mending for Marc. In everyday use the bag held bread, milk, wine, apples and cheese, and showed it; now, besides the shirt, it held only half a kilo of potatoes, Babette's purse, a pair of shoes back from the cobbler wrapped in newspaper, and underneath the detritus a deadly weapon.

"What the devil—"

Babette did not meet his eyes. She said apologetically, as she fished out the box of ammunition, "Meade said it wasn't loaded."

"So I should hope." Marc broke the derringer open, satisfied himself that what she said was true, that no cartridges were missing from the box, and tossed the weapon and its ammunition into the litter of miscellaneous objects in the table drawer. The look he turned on Babette was as hard as his voice.

"Meade gave you that thing to give to me?"

"Yes."

"Why didn't you hand it over then, two weeks ago?"

"Because you said when you came back from the war you never wanted to handle a gun again as long as you lived."

"Yes, but a man says things he doesn't mean ... I was dead beat then, not seeing straight ... you should have trusted me, Babette. *Shown* me the thing, at least, given me a chance to send it back to Meade. What the devil did he expect me to do with it, anyway?"

"Use it in self-defence if *they* tried to conscript you."

"Shooting it out with twenty Federals taking me into the post where we saw two murders done? What a fool that Yankee is! Doesn't he realise that if a man like me, known to be opposed to the Commune and taken in for questioning by a man like Ferré, were found to be carrying a gun he'd be next in line for a summary execution?"

"I'm sure Meade carries a gun himself."

"A neutral gun — who cares?"

They had both remained standing since they entered the studio. Now Marc flung himself down on the sofa, sighing and running his fingers through his hair, while Babette took off her Paisley shawl and sat down on the little stool beside the stove, like a nervous pupil waiting for the master's questions. The first was:

"Have you been carrying that thing in your bag for the past two weeks?"

"Only since Fanny came downstairs."

"What's Fanny got to do with it?"

"Marc, please let me tell you how it was. When Meade went away that day I put everything in a kitchen towel, took it up to my old room and hid it there. Madame Jaloux was giving Fanny stuff to make her sleep, and she didn't know what was going on half the time. But after she was better I thought what if *she* started poking about, and found the gun, and took it, then —"

"Then what?"

"You know — she was acting so strangely whenever Didier came . . ."

"You thought she might pull the gun on Didier?"

"Yes."

"My God!"

"So then I thought you were the best judge of what to do."

"How very kind of you."

The icy sarcasm was too much for Babette. She faltered. "Please don't be angry. I thought I was acting for the best," and her lips quivered like a punished child's.

This is hopeless, thought Marc Vallon. Things are going wrong, and we've started to get across each other. He remembered the night when he had set the scene for his proposal, with a grand dinner, a cabaret and all the romance of the old pre-war Montmartre village ending in fiasco. Now they were in a cold shabby studio, with his Study in White on the easel, a failure, and a derringer in the table drawer between them. No romance, only Paris 1871; only love.

He crossed the floor and knelt down beside the little stool, putting his arms round her hips and laying his head on her young breast.

"I'm not angry with you, darling," he said. "I'm angry because we're boxed into such a hopeless situation, and because you and I are living like two fools. It's the Montmartre way, it's not our way. Marry me and let's face the world together." He lifted his head and smiled at her confidently.

"Face the world, with two wedding rings?"

"As many wedding rings as you like, my darling."

Then Babette smiled too, the ghost of her old cheeky smile, and said,

"Ask me again when we're out of danger."

13

To be out of danger was a dream which receded with the closing days of April. The artillery duel continued, shells from both sides doing fearful damage to the pleasant villages of Neuilly, Passy and Auteuil, and politically the Commune went from one excess to another. After three days of fierce debate their assembly voted to set up a Committee of Public Safety as in the days of the Terror, and Raoul Rigault was elected *Procureur* of the Revolutionary Tribunal.

The American Minister was growing impatient. Ever since his Legation on the Rue de Chaillot had been hit by shell splinters on a day when he was in Paris and actually working at his desk he had been anxious for the end of hostilities, and indignant at the need to remain in Versailles. There, having consistently advised Thiers to accept the Commune's proposal to exchange Blanqui for the imprisoned Archbishop Darboy, he knew that he was in disfavour, and that this was giving pleasure to his rival Lord Lyons. Finally he persuaded Mrs Washburne that their residence at 75 Rue Unruh was no longer safe for her and their children, and arranged for them to travel via Versailles to a peaceful retreat in the country.

On the night of their arrival Mr Washburne gave an informal dinner party at the Hôtel des Réservoirs. He wanted his wife to meet Emily March because of her position as a protégée of Miss Clara Barton, whom they both admired, and also Dr Quimby, as an up-and-coming young American whom they had not met in Paris. Mr and Mrs Richard Wallace were invited, although 'Madame Julie', not quite accustomed to her legalised position, begged off on the grounds that someone had to stay at home to guard the beautiful Villa Bagatelle, which the Commune's exponents of 'Property is Theft' had threatened to burn to the ground. Secretary Hoffmann and Mr Meade were invited as makeweights.

Richard Wallace was the first to arrive. The great philanthropist's right to move freely between Paris and Versailles was never challenged by either side, but the endless problems of transportation made him either early or late for his appointments, and he came into the hotel foyer in time to encounter the Baron de Grimont on his way to a cabinet meeting. After the usual courtesies the Englishman enquired for the invalid duchess, and was told there was no change in her pitiable condition.

"And Madame de Grimont?"

"Should have arrived at Hyères by this time. Our son – h'm – has been outgrowing his strength according to his aunt and uncle, and Madame de Grimont, you understand a mother's feelings, thought her place was by his side."

"A courageous journey to undertake these days." Not by the twitch of a muscle did Richard Wallace reveal his disbelief in the baron's invention. He had seen Elvire de Grimont walking briskly up the Rue d'Antin only the day before, and obviously not wishing to be recognised. He explained his dinner engagement, said goodnight to de Grimont, and crossed the foyer to greet David Meade who, out of courtesy to his chief and his wife, was early too.

David Meade was eager to see the Red Cross lady in evening dress. He had sketched her with Dr Quimby at the door of a hospital tent, and again inside the tent between the beds of wounded men who, being from the government and the federal side respectively, had agreed to stop quarrelling for the occasion. He thought the sketches were a failure, because Emily March had not Babette's gift of posing and looked alarmingly stern, but they were going to *Harper's Weekly* in New York with others of the sturdy Yankee Minister and the shell-pocked Legation under the blanket title of 'American Help for France'. If he could ever get them out of the country and into the United States in time to be topical, that was. Mr Washburne had said they could go in the pouch carried by a courier he was sending to an American steamship due to berth within the week at St Nazaire.

Emily March in evening dress was a revelation. The dress itself was simple, with a tight bodice and a flowing skirt in soft grey moiré, but the neck was cut low, the better to display a necklace of green peridots each set in gold, which emphasized the grey-green of Miss March's eyes. But her hair, always invisible under her close-fitting bonnets or nurse's caps, was the marvel. As simple as her dress, brushed smoothly into a chignon, it was the colour of chestnut leaves in autumn, a true bronze which made her pale face glow. She blushed as she made her curtsy to Mrs Washburne, resplendent in crimson velvet and cameo brooch and bracelets.

It was her deference to the older lady which first roused David's admiration. She listened attentively to all Mrs Washburne's complaints about the obvious fact that

185

the government troops were firing on their own supporters in the rich suburbs of Paris, led on to do so by the need to return the Federal fire. The food blockade, in which as the good lady said 'the just and the unjust suffered alike' (for farmers to the west of Paris refused to cross a field of fire to take their produce to the city, and the Prussians had now stopped supplies coming in from the east) was making housekeeping as difficult as during the Siege days, and Emily assented to these lamentations too. Probably Dr Quimby, enjoying an unusually good dinner, and Mrs Washburne, enjoying her audience, were the only two whose minds were on the occasion and not elsewhere. The American Minister, as his Assistant Secretary well knew, was thinking about high finance, specifically the loan made by Rothschilds to the Commune, and the determined refusal made by the Marquis de Ploeuc, one of the aristocrats they despised, to put the Commune in possession of the Banque de France. The marquis was smuggling out money to the government, along with plates for printing banknotes, but this was not a topic for dinner table conversation, especially in a restaurant. Richard Wallace, seated on Mrs Washburne's right, would have been interested in the bank situation, but for the first part of the dinner at least his mind was on Elvire de Grimont. Edward Carey, when he asked to be taken on as a stretcher-bearer or a driver in the Hertford Ambulance, now on active service again, had said in answer to Wallace's blunt question that Madame de Grimont had gone to join her husband at Versailles. The husband said she was on her way to her brother at Hyères. The lady herself was walking purposefully along the Rue d'Antin. Mr Wallace decided not to tell Ned that she was still in Paris. The affair was over; better to let sleeping dogs lie than stir up more trouble by giving young Carey the sort of news which might send him off to learn the truth in the Rue St Florentin. He was doing fine work in the ambulance, and clearly acquiring a new compassion.

Emily March, for her part, was waiting for a break in the general conversation which would give her a chance to put forward her particular interest. She had seen Mr Washburne only twice since coming to Versailles, once in a duty call at his own office, and once when he came to visit the Satory ambulance tents. She wanted to tell him about Miss Clara Barton's great ambition, to start a branch of the Red Cross in America, and to have the United States government sign the Geneva Convention drawn up by Henri Dunant when the International Red Cross was created in 1864. She was in a strong position to argue with the Minister for, as he knew, it was the International Red Cross which had brought her to Paris as a military nurse, but Mr Washburne was too experienced a diplomat to commit himself. He knew that signing any international agreement would be opposed in Congress by those who dreaded any 'foreign entanglement', even on a humanitarian level. David Meade admired the way the girl kept her head when the old man administered the mildest of snubs, saying this was a matter for the President and his cabinet, certainly not to be decided in an overseas legation nor by the most charming of young ladies. She talked well, David thought, and didn't run a controversial subject into the ground, but threw the conversational ball in Hoffmann's direction with a question about the famous Dr Swinburne, whom she had never met.

The dinner party was broken up early by the sound of firing from the direction of Fort Issy, which was rumoured to be on the point of surrender. Mrs Washburne was anxious to get back to her family in preparation for an early start to the country, and Mr Wallace to the Hertford Ambulance. David asked leave to escort Miss March to her quarters. She was going on duty at ten o'clock and had to change into uniform. For a wrap she only had her uniform cloak, which partly covered the becoming grey dress. David Meade, as he laid the cloak round her shoulders, remembered that Babette wore a grey dress too, but Babette wore a dashing red garibaldi instead of an antique necklace of peridots and gold. He was glad it was dark enough to hide his expression when they arrived at her 'quarters', which were in one of the furnished cottages where he had wanted to establish Babette Mercier as his mistress.

"What do you take me for — a light woman?" That was how she had dismissed him, and yet somehow they had stayed friends. His last words to her at the Old Farm had been that she was to come to him at once if there was any problem about Marc's conscription, and she had thanked him with a kiss. The memory of that kiss obliged him to say "I beg your pardon?" to Emily March's last remark.

"I said we really had a delightful evening, didn't we?"

"I — yes, certainly we did. We must get up another little party soon, wouldn't you like that? With Dr Quimby too, of course?"

"If it doesn't interfere with our duty," she said primly. It might have been her father, the Methodist minister, speaking, thought Meade, who was an Episcopalian.

"I wish you didn't have to go back on duty tonight," he said. His eyes were accustomed to the darkness now, and with her bare head and arms, so white beneath the straps of the cloak, he thought she looked magnificent. Her looks belied the prim voice and the stilted sentences. Over her "I mustn't be late," he said, "When can I see you again?"

"I thought you spent most of the time in Paris."

"Only two or three days a week."

"Well, you know where to find me." She gently drew her hand from the crook of his arm. "Please don't come up to the door with me. The nuns wouldn't like it."

"The nuns?"

"I share the quarters with three Sisters of Charity. So good-night, Mr Meade, and thank you for your pleasant company."

"Good-night, Miss March." The shining bronze head was out of sight at once among the tall shrubs of the cottage garden. Meade had only gone a few yards along the road before he thought, "Pleasant company be damned! I ought to have waited and seen her safely to the ambulance." A few more steps, and he heard her calling. "David! Help! David!"

He shouted, "I'm coming!" and ran back, pulling out his gun as he raced up the garden path. She was struggling in the arms of a man in uniform, whose hands were round her neck as he tried to pinion her to a tree, and her voice when she tried to call for help again was an incoherent gurgle. David Meade pulled her assailant away and hit him with the butt of his pistol. There was no need to fire, for the first blow made him reel and the second knocked him out on the flagged path, insensible, while Meade took Emily into his arms and held her close.

"Are you all right?"

"He – he scared me, David. He jumped out at me, and he hurt my throat – oh, my necklace! Is it broken? It belonged to my grandmother –"

Amazingly, the necklace was intact. The green peridots gleamed on the white neck, and the marvellous hair, released from its chignon, streamed over Emily's shoulders. The man on the ground was beginning to stir and mutter, but there was no sound from inside the house.

"Your nuns are sound sleepers," said David. He was still holding her closely, and she made no move to draw away. "Now don't worry about this rat. He wasn't out to get

189

you, he was just a sneak thief, trying a fast in and out to a civilian house. I'll turn him over to the provost marshal, he and his boys are never around when they're needed, and that'll be the end of it as far as you're concerned. But you've had a shock, you mustn't try to work tonight. I'll tell Quimby what happened, as soon as I've run this fellow in, and you go to bed and rest."

She rubbed her cheek against his, like a child, and whispered, "Thank you, David. Thank you for taking care of me."

In the same low tone he murmured "Emily!" and kissed her. The lips he touched responded very slightly, as if savouring a new sensation. A virgin mouth was something new to Meade. He felt the primness, the stern devotion to duty melting beneath his caress, and as he kissed Emily March again he felt that he might at last have found someone he could protect.

Fort Issy was evacuated on 30 April, and although it was reoccupied almost at once by General Cluseret and a troop of belated reinforcements, the Fenian general was relieved of his command. His attempted reforms of the National Guard had made him too unpopular, and as Cissey and his sappers pushed their way to the very moat of Fort Issy, supported by fifty-three batteries of guns, the cry went up at the Hôtel de Ville that Cluseret the incompetent was 'sold' to the government side. In all French political squabbles the word *vendu* is fatal, and Cluseret was not only dismissed but arrested and thrown into prison.

He was succeeded as Delegate of War and commander by his Chief of Staff, Louis Rossel, a competent engineer officer who had served in the war with Prussia. He found that owing to casualties and desertions he could count on only 30,000 fighting troops, a quarter of the effectives under MacMahon's command, and in handling them he was no more fortunate than Cluseret. The government pressure on Fort Issy was steadily increased. The 55th Battalion of the National Guard was caught sound asleep at the redoubt of Moulin-Saquet, the railway station at Clamart was captured, ten shells a minute were fired into the ramparts of what was now a mass of rubble and corpses, and on 8 May the Tricolore was planted where the Red Flag had flown over the ruins of one of the Sixteen Forts. Remembering the fate of Cluseret, Rossel declined to wait to be arrested, and following the example of so many deserters from the Commune, he too deserted and was seen no more.

One who never dreamed of deserting, and who fought better than most men in the struggle for Clamart station (where the government troops were again accused of shooting prisoners of war) was Louise Michel. She had rallied her comrades, she had shot and bayoneted the enemy, she returned to Montmartre more than ever a heroine of the revolution. It was a great surprise to Babette Mercier to find her banging at the kitchen door of the Old Farm on a May morning when the lilacs were in bloom, having walked up the garden from the Vine House to demand attention.

"What do *you* want here?" was Babette's indignant greeting. "You're supposed to ask admittance at the concierge's *loge*."

"I want to know by what right you've put padlocks on the big gate and the postern. You're denying freedom of passage to Comrade Egorov, his wife and their servant."

"The padlocks were put on by a written order from the landlord, Monsieur Renard. There are so many bad characters about these days that he wants his property to be securely protected."

"Don't bandy words with me, young woman—"

"Or you'll have me sent to the Mazas prison, eh? The Egorovs haven't used the great gate since their luggage arrived from London."

"They want to use it now, so find the key and be quick about it, or you'll be sorry."

"What's the meaning of all the noise in the yard?" said Madame Verlet at the back door.

"This girl is refusing to open the great gate," said Louise Michel, glaring at Babette.

"And quite right too, you're not one of the tenants," said the concierge. "But keep your voice down, madame. There's a sick woman in this house, and she mustn't be disturbed."

"There are women sick of hunger and despair in every dwelling in Montmartre," said the Red Virgin, but she did speak more quietly as she explained that the Egorovs' manservant requested the free passage of a cart carrying wine for domestic use, in containers too unwieldy to be carried up from the other entrance on the Rue St Vincent.

"When's the wine expected?" asked Babette.

"This morning, between ten and eleven."

"If the carter rings the bell in the usual way, I'll take off the padlocks," said Babette. "Till then, no key."

"You little vixen," said Louise, "any more of your impertinence and I'll make sure that lover of yours is up before a conscription tribunal—"

"Meeting where?" asked Babette. "Fort Issy? Or Clamart station?"

At the taunting reference to the Commune's defeats the woman seemed ready to unsling her rifle, but before she could reply by word or bullet a heavy tread was heard on the flagged path, and the Egorovs' manservant appeared. It had rained in the night, and the raindrops from the lilacs sparkled on his bare head. He was a short man with broad shoulders and a tanned, expressionless face, so stolid that he seemed like an image carved out of wood.

"Having trouble, comrade?" he said to Louise.

"Just the usual bourgeois obstructionism. These lackeys of the property owners are making difficulties about removing their padlocks from the gates."

"Shall I try a little gentle persuasion?" The man's wooden face relaxed into the imitation of a smile.

"There's no need for that – yet," said Louise, and Madame Verlet, who had not understood, said, "And there's no need to be abusive, Madame Michel. Bourgeois obstructionism, indeed! Who are you, monsieur? Is your name Ivan Ivanovich, in the service of Monsieur Egorov?"

"Also known as Mitya," said Babette flippantly, and when the man growled "What do you mean?" she answered, "That's what Corporal Michel calls you, when the two of you are strolling in the garden, isn't it? Mitya's a nice name, short for Mikhail I'm told."

"Come back to the Vine House, Ivan," said Louise. "Comrade Egorov ought to complain to the landlord about the way his reasonable requests are treated. You" – she rounded on Babette – "have the big gate open in an hour from now, or else –"

"Or else you'll call the police. I thought the Commune had abolished the police?"

"That's enough, Babette," said Madame Verlet. "Come indoors." And once inside the kitchen, she asked why the girl went out of her way to irritate those people. "We're at their mercy here," she sighed. "It's all very fine to have padlocks and keys to keep out the street rabble. What we need is something to keep out the Russians. This is worse than the Siege days, I declare."

The wine cart arrived with unexpected punctuality, and in answer to the carter's shouted request Babette unfastened the padlock and swung back the heavy bar across the gate. 'Ivan Ivanovich' must have been on the lookout, for he came up to help as the driver eased his two-horse team through the archway and into the cobbled yard. Babette stepped out of their way and watched from the kitchen doorstep.

The wine cart was one of the old sort still to be seen in the alleys of the Butte, plying from wineshop to cabaret with huge containers of the cheap red wine poured into flagons for the over-the-counter trade. Such waggons smelt of wine, but this one, which had no name written up on the tilt, reeked of wine, as if a couple of bottles had been broken in transit. But what came out, when the horses had been given nosebags as if the proceedings would take some time, was not bottles nor even baskets of bottles, but the huge receptacles called *les bonbonnes*, encased in wicker, which the Russian and the carter, both silent, had difficulty in manhandling down the garden path to the tool shed against the wall of the Vine House, where the manservant had been observed at work. When the fourth and last *bonbonne* was taken in the door was shut, and Babette with a shrug went back to the kitchen. Underneath the heavy smell of spilt wine she had detected another smell, not at once identifiable, but which decided her to wait until she heard the horses and cart clear the archway and start up the Rue St Jean. She would be late at the studio, for painting and for food, but it couldn't be helped. She intended to replace the padlock with her own hands and hang the key on the board in the *loge* before she left the Old Farm to the tender mercies of Mitya and the woman she had sneeringly called 'Corporal' Michel.

Fanny was sitting, sleek and comfortable as a cat, in her favourite chair by the stove where no fire burned.

"I wish you'd remember to bring us some candles,

Babette," she said in her complaining way. "Tante Lise and I would have been in total darkness last night if we hadn't had the bedroom candles. And I don't suppose there's a drop of paraffin to be had, unless you bring us some from the Rue des Rosiers."

"We've only a drop left for ourselves," said Babette, and stood stock-still on the flagstone floor. Paraffin! That was it, of course, the smell the spilt wine was intended to disguise. The *bonbonnes* delivered at the Vine House contained paraffin, known in France as *le pétrole*.

14

Babette had no idea of what the delivery of *pétrole* in such a quantity could signify. She thought it possible that the Russians were about to indulge in a bit of profiteering, for during the Siege paraffin had sold at four times its market value. She decided not to mention her suspicions to Madame Verlet, who would certainly think there was a fire risk in the storage of such a combustible on Monsieur Renard's property. At least the *bonbonnes* were in the stone-walled gardener's shed, and not in the cellar of the Vine House, where someone looking for a bottle of wine by the light of a guttering candle might start a blaze leaping from the wooden wine-racks to the wooden stairs. She said nothing about it to Marc, and *le pétrole* was forgotten when early next morning, as Babette came in from shopping, Didier Leblanc arrived at the Old Farm.

It was not his first visit. He had come twice to ask for his wife since their child's death, and his father had come once, all three visits for the laudable purpose of handing over the allowance paid by the Central Committee to the wives of National Guardsmen. Didier was in uniform, complete with rifle, bayonet, bandolier and knapsack; he was also in a highly emotional state.

"I'm ordered to the front," he said to Babette and Madame Verlet in the kitchen. "I want to say goodbye to my wife."

"Which front is that?" Babette enquired. Not one of the five Belleville battalions had been in action yet, their officers claiming that they had to protect their home district from a possible attack by the Prussians occupying the eastern perimeter of Paris and now suspected of 'complicity with Versailles'.

Didier chose to ignore the sarcasm. "We're ordered to the Point du Jour," he said. "The weak point on the road to Versailles, where the monsters Thiers and MacMahon hope to enter Paris. We muster at three o'clock at the Hôtel de Ville, so there's no time to lose. I've come a long way to see my wife, where is she?"

"She's not well this morning, so I made her stay in bed," said the concierge. "Babette, you'd better run up and see if your sister's awake."

"I'll go myself," said Didier.

"Oh no you don't," said Babette with her back to the door. "She hadn't much of a welcome for you last time, remember? The fever came back after that and now she's so much better I'm not going to let you worry her again."

"Why should it worry her to see her husband? A man has the right to embrace his wife, hasn't he? Especially as it may be for the last time ..."

"We'll go upstairs together, then," said Babette. She knew what her brother-in-law meant by 'embrace' – he wanted to make love to Fanny, and in her present unbalanced mood she was just silly enough to let him. Then the whole thing starts over again, thought Babette grimly, as they mounted the wooden stairs in silence. She didn't expect her sister to be asleep, nor was she; Fanny was propped on her pillows, finishing the *café au lait* her sister had carried up to her before she went to the grocery shop.

"Fanny, Didier's here," she said briskly, and took the empty bowl from her sister's limp hand.

"Oh – Didi!"

"My regiment is ordered into action, Fanny," the man said. "I've come to say goodbye before I strike a blow for liberty."

There was something so false about his speech that Babette turned her back on both of them and looked out of the window at the Vine House. She was aware that Didier had fallen on his knees at the bedside.

"Into action?" Fanny said. "You mean – fighting?"

"Fighting the tyrants, darling. Have you forgotten what you said to me after you came back to the Old Farm, when my regiment wasn't engaged at the very start? You said 'Better luck next time!' as if you hoped next time I would be killed."

"No, no, Didi, I couldn't have said that! I was ill then, and so unhappy –"

"I know, I know, dearest, but we're young, we'll try again –"

It was the old cajoling tone Babette remembered from the wonderful summer of 1869, when Didier Leblanc came courting, and Frédéric Bazille and Marc Vallon were rivals for the favours of pretty, pert Babette Mercier. She moved involuntarily, and Leblanc jumped to his feet, saying in his old violent way, "Babette, why the devil don't you clear out? Surely you realise that a man has the right to be alone with his wife?"

"When he's about to strike a blow for liberty? I think we'll let the man's wife be the judge of that. Fanny, shall I stay or go?"

"Please stay." Fanny started to cry, and when Didier

198

took her in his arms she had the strength to push him away. "It's no good, Didi. I wish you well, today and always, but it's too late for us to try again. What we had once, you destroyed, and you almost destroyed me too. Please go away, and don't come back."

Babette stayed with her sister until the man's angry words, and the expostulations of Madame Verlet, had sunk to silence in the rooms below, and then went back to the Rue des Rosiers as quickly as she could. She was glad her lover was not in the studio, because if she had had to give him a true account of the scene in the Old Farm she would have seen the curl of the lip which revealed his belief that Fanny as well as her husband had been acting a scene from a Palais Royal farce. She knew he had gone down to the Drouot auction rooms, not so much in the hope of selling a canvas, an impossibility since the fighting started, as of finding a reply to the letter he had written to Renoir. Someone at the Brasserie des Martyrs, whose doors were still open, told him that the painter had left Louveciennes and come back to Paris, but where he was living or if he was working was not known. Vallon had offered help and hospitality, little knowing how soon he would be taken at his word.

It was that very afternoon, on one of those cloudless May days through which France so often lives her hours of crisis, that the arrest and liberation of Renoir created one of the legends of the Commune.

It was quite true that the man whom some called the greatest of the Independents had come to Paris and was prevented while the battle raged from returning to his parents' home at Louveciennes. At thirty he was still unmarried, with no home of his own, impoverished and completely dedicated to his art. That Paris was a hot-bed of political passion and spy mania had not occurred to him, nor did he realise that a man painting on the banks of the Seine, and constantly looking westwards towards La Muette, where shells were actually falling, could be mistaken for a government spy 'drawing plans' for the invasion.

A few National Guardsmen stopped to watch him from the upper *quai* above the river, where the bookstalls had been shuttered since the days of peace. They saw Renoir's solitary figure on the lower promenade from which the amateur fishermen had disappeared, not far from the Pont Neuf, and jumped to the conclusion that he was a traitor – ignoring the fact that to sketch the war zone at La Muette and the Bois de Boulogne he should have been equipped with a powerful pair of binoculars or a telescope. Renoir was absorbed in painting light on the Seine. The time was towards sunset, and the gold light on the water was changing with every moment that passed. He was painting it with rapid strokes and did not hear the clatter of booted feet down the nearest flight of stairs. When he did hear the shouts of '*Halte-là!*' he looked up in genuine surprise. He was standing still, and had no intention of moving, but the Guardsmen treated him as if he were in flight, seizing him by both arms and shouting a challenge to the 'spy'.

The *quai* above their heads had been almost empty, but as the Guardsmen yelled and Renoir himself shouted expostulations, it quickly filled with a rabble of men and women who ran down to join the growing group. They were all convinced of his guilt, and no one listened long enough to examine the entirely unmilitary painting of the river bank and the ripples of gold on the Seine. It was flung into the water along with the artist's palette and portable easel: when he objected he was struck in the face and stomach, and while several women (always fiercer than the men) urged that he follow his paints and brushes into the Seine he was dragged bruised and stumbling up the stone stairs to the *quai*.

Several newcomers to the scene advocated a summary execution, 'the way the Versaillais shoot their prisoners of war', but one of the Federals, more litigious than his comrades, was all for going through the motions of a trial before the firing squad was called into action. The usual argument developed: should the prisoner be hauled to the nearest commissariat or the nearest *mairie*? Renoir's lucky star was in the ascendant. With a yelling crowd at the heels of the prisoner and his escort, they made for the *mairie* of the Sixth Arrondissement. Renoir was slightly built and weak from lack of food. He lost his footing more than once as he was dragged along, and fell full-length on the uneven pavement, with more bruises and fresh dirt on his clothing when he was dragged up and on. He was so battered that he failed to recognise the speaker when a new voice hailed him from inside the *mairie*:

"What are you doing with my good friend Renoir?"

"Who – who are you?"

The jutting beard on the arrogant chin, the pince-nez on the vulture's eyes, all added up to the image of Raoul Rigault, the terrible Procureur of the Commune, whom a trick of fortune had brought to the *mairie* of the Sixth at that moment, to inspect the men and weapons of the emergency firing squad.

"I'm Rigault, comrade. Don't you remember how you saved my life in the forest, years ago?"

"At Fontainebleau ... I remember now."

"Of course you do." Rigault turned on the prisoner's escort. "Let this man go, you damned fools. He's no spy! He rescued me from the emperor's police, long before the war; rescued me with clothes and money; he deserves the best I can give him now."

"Shall I bring some wine, comrade?" asked one of the Federals obsequiously. He had been the loudest to shout

"Spy!" and spit on the prisoner.

"Wine, and a sponge with warm water, and – do you need any food?"

"I'm not hungry."

"Where are you living in Paris, Renoir?"

"Here and there. I should be with my family in Louveciennes."

"In the war zone. If I give you a safe conduct, will you use it tomorrow?"

"Not today?"

"It'll soon be dark, better wait until the morning. And then *stay* in Louveciennes till the fighting's over! When the Commune's victorious come back to me, and I'll make you Minister of Fine Arts instead of Gustave Courbet."

Ten minutes later, still dazed and aching, but with a *laissez-passer* in his pocket, Renoir was walking back by the way he came, towards the river, and still followed by an eager crowd. But this time the hangers-on were cheering him – '*Vive Renoir! Vive le camarade de Raoul Rigault!*' was the slogan now, instead of 'Drown the traitor! Shoot the spy!' He had no idea how to shake them off, and the draggle-tailed procession was nearly at the empty Chamber of Deputies – empty, that is, except for a contingent of the light women of Paris, who had been conscripted to sew sacks for the barricades – when he had his second stroke of luck that day. A small waggon with the Red Cross on the canvas roof, and the insignia of the Hertford Ambulance on the canvas sides, drew up alongside the kerb, and Edward Carey, pulling the team to a halt, leaned out of the driver's seat to shout, "Renoir, by all that's holy! Want a lift?"

The painter scrambled aboard thankfully, and when Ned whipped up the horses they soon left the crowd behind. Renoir explained what had happened, and Ned shook his head. "You were mad to go painting along the

Seine," he said. "I'm glad I found you. This is only our supply waggon, but if you open that white enamel box you'll find bandages and a bottle of brandy. I think you'd better drink some and then hold a bandage to that cut on your face until we can get it cleaned up properly. Where can I take you? Where are you living now?"

"I got caught when the Gates were closed, and I've been living pretty rough. But I was planning to go to the Drouot rooms today, there's a chance of meeting Marc Vallon there. Now I've got a pass, maybe he can give me a bed for the night—"

"The studio's big enough, I sublet it myself for a while. But—did you know Babette Mercier was living with him now?"

"Little Babette? But I thought Bazille was the favourite ..."

"Bazille's dead, more's the pity."

The cutting tone chilled Renoir. He began to ask Ned about his work as a stretcher-bearer and relief driver for Mr Wallace, and that lasted until they came to the door of the famous auction rooms, where old Moïse came out to greet them with behind him Marc Vallon beaming and holding out his hands to his friends.

Ned Carey drove Renoir and Marc as far as the Rue des Rosiers, sent his love to Babette and declined to come in because the supply horses had had a bad day and needed to be rubbed down, fed and watered in their temporary stable. He advised Renoir, not for the first time as they drove, to cross in the morning at the Porte de Clichy, where there was far less chance of being caught in a skirmish than further south, although it was a longer way to Louveciennes. "Doesn't matter if I have to spend a night on the road," said the artist cheerfully. He had recovered much of his gentle good humour since the reunion with Marc. "The woods near the village are full of gipsies, who all adore my mother because she gives them food and good advice. I'll get shelter in any one of their encampments, it wouldn't be the first time. Or the first time I've painted them. Damn those Communards, they threw my paintbox and palette into the Seine – the kit I've had since the old days at Fontainebleau. Like the one you have belonging to your father, Marc."

"I left a pretty good one upstairs when I cleared out of the studio," said Ned. He seemed in no hurry to drive away, as if there was some comfort in talking to old friends of his student days.

"Babette's using it now, *and* the Winsor and Newton paints," said Marc. "I'll find a spare one for Renoir."

"*Babette*'s painting now – ?" Renoir said. "I must see this, first thing."

But when they said goodbye to Carey and climbed the stairs, he hung back while Marc unlocked the door, as if he were suddenly abashed by his bruised face and dusty clothes, and stood on the landing until the younger man called, "Babette! Darling! Look who's here!" Then such a pretty girl, prettier than ever, rushed out to kiss him and drag him into the studio, pouring a glass of wine, bringing a bowl of warm water and some clean rags to sponge his face, and agreeing with Marc that he must sleep on the old sofa until it was time to start for the Porte de Clichy in the morning.

"But tell me exactly what happened," she said when they had all settled down comfortably. "What was the good turn you did Rigault which saved your life today?"

"D'you know, I'd almost forgotten about it," said Renoir. "It happened years ago, in the old Fontainebleau time. I suppose he was just a kid then, but he was in trouble with the emperor's police, or secret police more likely, and he was on the run. He came panting into a glade in the forest, where I was painting alone, and asked me to help. Well, I didn't know what the row was all about, but I hated to see a fellow-creature hunted, so I lent him an old painting smock and he escaped from the woods disguised as one of us. That's all there was to it."

"It's one thing to his credit," said Marc. "That's why he saved your life today."

"And that's also why Rigault was saved to become the Procureur de la Commune, the most dreaded man in Paris," said Babette.

Renoir's smile faded. "That's another way to look at it," he said. "Believe me, I thought of that when all those roughs were shouting after me, 'Long live the comrade of Raoul Rigault!' "

"All's well that ends well," said Marc. "Look here, don't you want to take off your jacket and have a proper wash?"

The studio was modern enough to have a lavatory with a separate entrance on the landing, and when Marc came back from showing Renoir the way he found Babette spreading two wool blankets and a cushion on the big sofa. The table, as it happened, was already set for their meagre supper, and Babette looked at it anxiously. "Will that do?" she said. "I wish we could give him a decent meal, but there's only soup and bread and salad."

"And a good bottle of wine," said Marc. "Hurry up and lay your own place, darling."

"I'll get something from Tante Lise. I think I'd better sleep at the Old Farm tonight."

"Not stay here when Renoir's our guest?"

"I'll ask him to excuse me, and you must too, of course. You're the one who's been longing for a good talk with him. You don't need a *grenouille* hopping around."

"Stop using that ridiculous word!"

His tone was so rough that Renoir stopped in the doorway. "Am I interrupting something?" he said, and Babette went close to him and stroked his arm. "Dear

Renoir, I wish I hadn't got to go out. My sister's sick at the Old Farm and needs me; will you forgive me for hurrying away?"

"I won't let you go until I've seen your paintings." The artist's gentle vitality seemed to be restored, and his encouraging smile enchanted the girl. "All three of my paintings!" she said. "A gallery!"

Renoir looked long and silently at the three still lifes. "All filled with light and colour," he said. "Well done, Babette! What you need now is hard work and technical skill, and you've got two good teachers – Marc himself and Berthe Morisot. She hasn't come back to Paris yet, has she?"

"Not so far as we know. But do look at Marc's pictures, please!"

Girl with Green Apples and Girl Painting were highly praised; Study in White was called 'difficult and very ambitious', and Marc went into the bedroom to find the old box of paints and small palette which had come from his father's shop on the Rue Vavin. When he came back, Renoir was helping Babette on with her long black cloak, for the skies were heavy with rain.

"I wish you wouldn't go out, you silly girl," said Marc.

"I wish I didn't have to. *Au revoir*, Renoir, until soon."

"*A bientôt, Babette, bonne chance*!"

They heard the light footsteps running downstairs, and Renoir said, "You don't think it's dangerous for her to be out alone?"

"Babette's a law unto herself, and she thrives on danger ... I'm trying hard to persuade her to marry me, but it's uphill work. Talk to me about *your* work, and what you were doing by the Seine this afternoon."

Renoir paid a silent tribute to Babette's tact as they lit cigarettes, filled their glasses, and pulled their chairs up to the wood embers in the stove. The rain drizzled against the windows and the soup was warming, while the two men who had so much in common lived again through the experiences which had shaped their art. They were the only two of the Independents left in Paris, Renoir commented; he had heard that Degas was still at Château-Mesnil Hubert and Manet at Arcachon, while Cézanne, of course, had never left Provence. But Claude Monet's flight to London with Pissarro looked as if it would bear fruit. They had met another French refugee called Ruel, or possibly Durand-Ruel, who was interested in their work and thought he could sell it. If he liked their friends' work too, perhaps the lean years were over for the Independents whose work was so rarely accepted for the Salon.

Marc Vallon wondered at his optimism. Renoir seemed to have forgotten that a short time before he had been within five minutes of a firing squad, or that their friend Monet, for all his genius, had been in dire poverty before his flight to London. He had made himself responsible for a woman and their child while he was painting *Les Bains de la Grenouillère* in 1869, and Renoir, desperately poor himself, helped them out. "I'll never be their equal," thought Vallon the realist, "but if Babette'll marry me I'll work as a labourer if I have to, and let painting take second place. And Monet's no business man, whatever this Monsieur Ruel may be."

"Our time's coming, Vallon *mon vieux*," the optimist was saying. "When this crazy war is over it's *our* work they'll want to see. Not Meissonier's with his *opéra-bouffe* hussars. Not the imitation Watteaux and Fragonards, and thank God no more Winterhalter. But the gold lights on the Seine, and the fisherfolk at the seaside, and racehorses coming up to the start, and women at their washing tubs – all that explosion of light and colour, of flowers and waves, of lovely rosy girls and their plump infants – that's what we'll give them when there's peace in France again."

"Just you keep clear of the explosions you nearly heard this afternoon," said Marc gruffly.

Renoir laughed. "I was thinking about that," he admitted. "That crazy mob yelling *'Vive Renoir! Vive le camarade de Rigault!'* Wouldn't it be the devil if I went down in history as the comrade of Raoul Rigault!"

"No danger," said Vallon. "You'll go down in history as Pierre Auguste Renoir, who painted lovely women — and the gold lights on the Seine."

Babette, hurrying towards the Old Farm with Berthe Morisot's voluminous cloak held high above her ankles, was for once not interested in a painter's view of the reflections on the river which had first beguiled her. There was something in the painter's happy-go-lucky acceptance of the 'good turn' he had once done the man now guilty of murder in fact and in law which jarred upon her, but she thrust it to the back of her mind. She intended to make the most of the rare opportunity to be out alone after dark.

The long way round to the Old Farm by the Rue St Vincent was deserted on such a wet night, and most of the bourgeois houses were standing empty. Across the vineyards she could see the farmhouse buildings, with one of the tallow candles she had bought for Fanny shining like a pinpoint in Fanny's window. To the garden wall of the Vine House next door a more powerful light was fastened, although the open flame was protected by shutters like a policeman's lantern, and Babette slid through the gate of the vineyard and up the narrow path to see better. Yes, it was a stable lantern, hung above the door of the shed where the carboys of petrol had been stored.

Babette stopped at the sound of footsteps, moved in among the vines and dropped to the ground. She seemed to be lying in a marsh although the thick stuff of the old cloak gave her some protection, and the scent of the newly opened vine leaves was as heady as wine. Between the branches she saw four men coming down the path at regularly spaced intervals, each carrying a large tin can with a cork stopper. They disappeared on the roadway, and were replaced by four and again four more, after which Mitya, quite recognisable in the lantern light, blew out the lamp and barred the door. Babette waited ten more minutes, wet through to her chemise, and then wriggled out of the vineyard on her hands and knees. All she had learned was that if the Egorovs were selling black market *pétrole*, it was a well-organized operation.

15

When Richard Wallace saw Madame de Grimont on the Rue d'Antin at the end of April, plainly dressed and unwilling to be recognised, she was on her way to the *étude* of the de la Treille family solicitor, Maître Gaucher, whose law offices were in the Second Arrondissement, the principal banking and business district of Paris. The mayor, Monsieur Tirard, had resigned from the municipality when the Commune was elected, and there were fewer signs of democracy rampant there than elsewhere.

Elvire had not once gone beyond the gates of the hôtel de Grimont since her husband had stripped her of her possessions and her dignity. Her one unselfish fear was that in the neighbourhood where he lived she might encounter Edward Carey before he had time to leave the city. She knew that a chance meeting after her lie about going to Versailles would end in the old way, perforce in a cheap hotel and a kind of degradation she had never known before. And in winning Carey again she would lose him, to prison or worse, for Elvire was as much a victim of spy fever as anyone else in Paris, and had made up her mind that the watchman left by de Grimont at the gates of his house had been put there to spy on her comings and goings. He was in fact a promoted postilion whom she had never noticed on her carriage drives.

Anne, the former scullery maid, bought food for their needs each morning at the Marché St Honoré, and she and her brother rearranged two of the smaller salons for the comfort of their mistress, but no guests were invited and Elvire, once the queen of Paris society, paid no calls. One day she decided to visit her good friend Sylvie de Lhomond, who lived close at hand on the Rue Royale, but was kept back at the last moment by the fear of gossip. Suppose Hubert himself had spread the news of their separation? To be called *déclassée* was the worst thing that could befall her – that, and the little smiles and sneers of the women she considered her inferiors. At the end of April the matter was settled when she received the cards of the Comte and Comtesse de Lhomond '*pour prendre congé*'. So they were leaving the doomed city too! No doubt they had bought an exit permit for London, where Sylvie had relatives. It could be done with money and influence, and she wasn't stripped of either in spite of Hubert's threats.

During the weeks since she defied him, Elvire had expected to hear daily that the government troops had burst into the city. This was the time when General Cissey was bogged down in front of Fort Issy and the Federals were shelling the western suburbs: there was no prospect of a speedy relief. In spite of Anne's economies there was no longer enough food in the house for four people, and such food as there was, the potatoes and the starchy rations of the Commune's siege, had begun to take its toll of Elvire de Grimont's slenderness. The situation was becoming too difficult to face alone, and she decided to seek help from the counsellor who knew more about the private lives of the de la Treilles than they knew themselves.

It was strange to walk out into the Rue St Florentin, where all the government buildings were closed (she supposed the Reds were huddled together in the Hôtel de Ville) and the barricade at the Rue de Rivoli end was now fifteen or sixteen feet high. She saw another great earthwork being thrown up on the Rue Royale. Barricades everywhere, on the Place de la Concorde, on the Place Vendôme, across the broad avenue leading to the new Opéra! But the way was clear across the boulevards to the Rue d'Antin, an ancient street with the heavy new façades of Second Empire Paris. She had heard her brother speak of Maître Gaucher's *étude* as the sheet-anchor of his business life, so it was disconcerting to find that although the law offices were open, the lawyer himself had retired.

She knew that he and his wife had been bereaved, for their mourning cards had been received months ago. Their two elder sons were career officers, and in the war with Prussia one had fallen at Wissembourg in the first week of hostilities and his younger brother with du Preuil's Cuirassiers at Mars-la-Tour. That seemed a long time ago to Elvire as this scruffy new war dragged on, but she produced delicate words of sympathy to the surviving son, a man of forty, who now sat at his father's desk.

Maître Roger Gaucher was a clever lawyer, but the de la Treille affairs were new to him, and he hedged for time in his talk with Elvire. She was offering him what might well be a *cause célèbre*, were it not for the fact that the object of her matrimonial complaint was also the Minister of Justice in the cabinet of Monsieur Thiers who, at his own snail's pace, would presumably come to power some day. Maître Gaucher asked a few obvious questions. Was Madame de Grimont prepared to seek a divorce *a mensa et thoro*? A legal separation? The custody of her son during his minority? An alimony or an out-and-out settlement? "Because with all due respect to the Minister, madame, he cannot be allowed to deprive you of the dowry secured to you by your marriage contract –"

"I have very little money left, monsieur."

"The Etude Gaucher will of course be your banker –"

"And the Duc de la Treille will of course stand security."

"Ah! I was coming to your brother. Permit me to say that before there is any question of legal proceedings, you should be established under the duke's roof with your son."

"But how can that be with no trains running, and all the Gates of Paris barred?"

Maître Gaucher made a steeple of his well-manicured hands and smiled. "There are ways and means," he said. "Expensive, but quite efficient. The best way out is by the Porte St Denis, which is held by the Occupying Power; that eminent French novelist Emile Zola left his country on a Prussian passport. But travelling by St Denis means making a long detour to the north-east, and you are bound for the Mediterranean."

"But by what way am I to go, then?"

"You must leave that to me, madame." He had no intention of telling a scatterbrained society lady that a *passeur* would take her out by the Porte d'Italie, and then by the back roads to Orléans, where the telegraph service had been restored between Paris and the south, and where she could be met by the servants of the Duc de la Treille. "The one thing I insist upon is that you wait for a few days, until everything can be arranged, at the residence of Prince Pierre de la Treille in the Rue de Lille."

"I could have gone there a month ago."

"And so you should. That long stay alone may tell

against you in a court of law, if the Baron de Grimont brings suit and you defend it. Promise me you'll go to the prince's home tomorrow. Can you walk as far as the Left Bank, madame?"

"Of course I can."

"Then leave your house as quietly as possible, saying nothing to your servants—"

"I promised to send them home to the Sologne."

"They're your husband's responsibility. I'll see that they receive board wages as caretakers, and charge the baron accordingly when he returns to Paris. Now here is a sum sufficient for all your current expenses and your journey to the coast—sign this receipt here, please—and wait at Prince Pierre's until your guide comes to fetch you. I'll send you one line with his name and the date of departure, and that's all. Tell nobody about your plans, and don't come here again."

She said with the first touch of her old insolence: "You are taking every possible precaution, maître, no doubt for your own sake as well as mine?"

"Yes, for my own sake too, Madame de Grimont. My brothers gave their lives for the emperor, but I decline to die for any of the émigrés, even when they happen to be the honoured clients of our house. You have lived out of the world for a month, and it may have escaped your notice that those who help the refugees are guilty in the eyes of the Commune of complicity with Versailles. They are liable to imprisonment followed by execution under the Hostages Act now in force. Will you try to remember that I have a right to my point of view?"

She assented sullenly, and they parted after he had rehearsed her in the details of her journey. There were so few people on the boulevards that a solitary woman attracted no attention, and Elvire was free to brood on the humiliation of asking the old de la Treilles for shelter, and the further humiliation of being spoken to so abruptly by 'young' Gaucher, whose father would never have dared to take such a tone with her. "Are you prepared to admit to marital indiscretions on your own part?" he had said, and when she replied that she preferred the word 'imprudence' he snapped that in a court of law the petitioner would use the word 'infidelity'. If it came to court proceedings she would choose another barrister, more susceptible to the charm of Elvire de Grimont.

She walked home, as quickly as the barricades allowed, by the new avenue and the Rue de Rivoli. The big barricade at the foot of her own street was not impassable, she was pleased to find, for a gate of furze and sharpened wire was ajar at one side, and the unarmed Federal standing guard merely nodded as she went through with a friendly inclination of the head. Nothing was as bad as rumour made out! Even the intermittent shelling in the west had stopped. She enjoyed the cup of tea Anne brought her, and spent the evening sewing large patch pockets into the lining of a light summer cloak – it would grow warmer as she went south – to hold her remaining valuables and the larger part of the money borrowed from Maître Gaucher.

It was not until later that she began tryng to remember exactly what she had said in the letter giving Edward Carey his dismissal. If it fell into the wrong hands, was there anything in it which might cause him to be accused of the fashionable crime, complicity with Versailles? She didn't think so. The purpose of the letter was to show him as her husband's friend as well as her own, and to give him an oblique warning to return to England. He was sure to be already there and far beyond the reach of Hubert de Grimont's spite.

Before noon the next day she told Anne that Maître Gaucher had lent her money, the smaller part of which she gave to the girl for her current household needs. She knew that a confidential clerk from the lawyer's office would call in a day or two to explain the board wages plan, of course without revealing the whereabouts of the lady of the house, and she said no more to Anne or Bernard, not even goodbye. The watchman, who had to open the heavy door on the street to let her out, was the only one who saw her go, and then she only said, "Tell Anne I've gone to pay some calls and may not be back until late"—the man bowed. The reticule in her gloved hand was all she carried, and Elvire thought with distaste of the need to borrow one of fat old Cousin Marguerite's voluminous nightgowns until the unknown guide came to take her out of Paris.

She would have preferred to leave the house where she had frittered away nearly twelve years of her life by the left-hand pavement and turn into the Rue Royale to look once more across the Place de la Concorde. She was not sentimental about Paris, but—as Hubert in his sarcastic moods had exploited time and again—she was proud of her family's royalist traditions and the forebears who had died courageously on the scaffold when the guillotine of the French Revolution stood on that vast square. But the sentimental pilgrimage was not to be, because a new barricade had been erected across the top end of the Rue St Florentin, and remembering the other barricades on the Rue Royale, Elvire shrugged and turned towards the foot of the street. It was a grey afternoon, and the two rows of sombre houses seemed to lean towards her like the granite circles of a millstone.

The shortest way to the Rue de Lille was across the public gardens of the Tuileries, under the windows of the empty palace, over the Pont Royal and straight on down the Rue du Bac. Elvire pictured the gardens as still the haunt of nursemaids, children and lovers, and her spirits rose at the idea of losing herself among the afternoon strollers, going to new adventures and a new way of life. She thought of Alain, her boy on his way to manhood who would be her best protector, and of Gilbert, the much older brother who had taken her side since she was a child. She would be with them in the old haunts where some day inevitably there would be a new lover for Elvire.

She heard the shouting long before she reached the immense barricade which stretched across the Rue St Florentin. Where there had been one unarmed guard the day before there were now twenty men with rifles, and ten of them were keeping back a crowd which had gathered on the Rue de Rivoli, some clinging to the high railings of the Tuileries gardens. Other spectators had prudently retreated to the shelter of the Jeu de Paume, a classical building erected during the Second Empire which a hundred years later would hold the priceless paintings of the artists once known as Independents. On this day of 1871 it looked as heavy and dismal as a mausoleum.

The shouting resolved itself into bursts of applause punctuating the sound of a single voice, as if a public meeting were taking place, but Elvire, as she came up to the furze and wire gate, could see no platform and no speaker. The gate was barred, and as she stood beside it in perplexity she saw, through the shifting hedge of National Guards, a hunchback standing in the middle of the Rue de Rivoli. It was from his twisting mouth and frothing lips that the words of denunciation were pouring.

"Can I go through?" she asked the Federal with his hand on the latch of the gate. He was a decent-looking man who might have belonged to the respectable artisan class before the war.

"Not now, citizeness," he answered, civilly enough.

"Can't you see the Prefect of Police is holding a summary trial?"

"Is *that* the Prefect of Police?"

"That's the *new* prefect, Comrade Ferré. Never seen him before? He lays it on good and thick once he gets going. He'll have those three traitors before the firing squad before they know what's hit 'em. Look – that big fellow and the two old folk."

Elvire now saw, in front of the hunchback and loosely tied, a tall young man whose face was covered in blood, standing between an older man and woman who were vaguely familiar, and holding them protectively.

"But what have they *done*?" she asked.

"Sheltered one of Thiers's men, seems like. One of them sent back from Germany, he deserted, and crawled into Paris to see his papa and *maman*. A neighbour denounced them, and there they are."

Elvire recognised the old couple now. She had bought gloves in their tiny shop at the corner of the Rue Cambon. "But can they be arrested for giving shelter to their own son?" she asked, and the man's eyes narrowed.

"Complicity with Versailles," he said. "Citizeness, if you know what's good for you, you'll go back to wherever it was you came from and stay away from the Rue de Rivoli. What're you doing here anyway?"

"Trying to get across to the Left Bank to see an old friend who's ill, and needs help –"

"Forget it." But his hand moved on the latch, and Elvire in her imperious way pushed the gate open. She was promptly stopped by another Federal, but the little scuffle attracted the attention of Ferré and his prisoners. The woman recognised Elvire, and so did others in the crowd of spectators; it was she who cried out, "Princess! Help us, for the love of God!" and received a heavy blow across the face.

"Bring that woman here!" Ferré had no need to shout, for Elvire was through the gate and in the roadway, with her arms round the terrified mother who had dared to give shelter to her son. As she forced her way across the pavement a woman snatched the reticule from her hand, another tore off her bonnet, and the golden hair which Ned Carey had twined round his wrists and kissed spilled over her shoulders. One of the viragos shrilled, "*Regardez la pute!*" and others took up the cry, but Ferré himself said "*Regardez l'aristo!*"

"Are you a princess?" he asked, when she was dragged away from the old woman and stood before him.

"I'm a citizen of Paris, like yourself, *monsieur le préfet.*"

"I ask again, are you a princess?"

"What has that to do with it? I'm a woman and a mother, like this poor creature, who has done no wrong. If her son is your enemy, imprison him, but set his parents free."

"For the last time, are you a princess?"

"I was born the Princesse de la Treille."

What pride of race, what atavistic sense of responsibility for the weak and dependent had forced her into this admission, Elvire could not have told. In frozen horror she heard the deformity condemn her to death for contumacy and 'aristocratic contempt for the Commune', she felt the coat torn from her shoulders and the laces from her breast as she was hustled across the street and back to the barricade. She felt the deserter who had brought them to disaster seize her hand and press a kiss on it – the last touch of a man's lips that she would ever know. She knew it was useless to ask for a priest, although the old man was mumbling a prayer which might be heard on high. All Elvire could find for comfort was the thought of the young princes who had died so near this place, on the guillotine of the Concorde, and try to be worthy of her ancestors.

The firing squad was forming; they were far more efficient now than in the time of the two generals, and mercifully she failed to understand Ferré when he shouted to a sergeant, "Make sure you have enough quicklime!" She had not lost her sexual awareness, and she understood by his slack lips and brilliant eyes that the prospect of a killing was giving him a special form of sexual satisfaction. She closed her own eyes in disgust, but opened them again when she heard the Federal who had held the gate ask if she would like a bandage to hide the sight of the levelled rifles. He was holding out the red neckerchief which was part of his own uniform.

"No thank you," she said clearly, "I don't care for the colour," and with that last show of bravado Elvire de Grimont, born a princess, took a rain of bullets in her naked breast.

16

Marc Vallon accompanied Renoir to the Clichy Gate after his friend spent the night in his studio, saw Rigault's personal exit permit respectfully accepted and the painter waving a cheerful goodbye as he set off for the woods, the gipsies, and the forest trees he loved. He was back in the Rue des Rosiers before Babette, and when she came in he was in the act of putting away Meade's derringer in the table drawer.

"Marc, you carried it!"

"My darling, you came back to me!"

They both spoke together, and although Marc was quick to take her in his arms Babette was quicker in pulling off her cloak before he could feel, on this sunny morning, that it was still wet with the damp of the vineyard. "Did you think I wasn't coming back?" she asked, as he covered her face with kisses.

"I wasn't sure. You ran away so fast. It wasn't all because you thought Renoir and I should have our talk alone—"

"No, it wasn't all unselfishness," she admitted. "It

was – you'll think I'm very silly – but I couldn't imagine being in bed with you while another man was lying awake just two metres away on the other side of the wall. It would, somehow, I don't know, be like being in bed with two men at the same time – don't laugh!"

Marc was too clever to laugh outright, or call her a prude: he said, "You *are* silly, but you're very sweet. If we were married, would you object if a friend of ours needed a bed for the night?"

"That would be quite different –" She saw the trap, and stopped while Marc, free to laugh at last, said, "Isn't that what I've been asking you for weeks? Marry me, and all those imaginary difficulties would be ended. We'd be two against whatever danger lies ahead –"

"It's not so far ahead."

Then she had to share it with him, the story of the wine cart which delivered petrol, and the men who carried the stuff away in single containers after dark. As usual she told it obliquely, knowing that Marc might jeer at her suspicions of the Russians, always associated in his mind with the influence of David Meade. She said nothing about her reconnaissance in the vineyard, but let him think she had seen the furtive comings and goings from Fanny's window. She knew what he would say to her escapade, and in fact she had been badly frightened after it was over. If Mitya, or Ivan Ivanovich, or whatever he called himself, had caught her crouching among the vines, what kind of 'gentle persuasion' would he have used to make her tell why she was spying on his movements? But for once Marc neither sneered nor cross-questioned her, but sat smoking silently, thinking carefully about what she had told him. Finally he said,

"Petrol, eh? Do you know that petrol can be used in warfare?"

"I thought war was all shooting, and cutting off food

222

supplies. What do they do with petrol?"

"Make incendiary bombs, or flame throwers, to set fire to enemy emplacements, as we did at Dijon. Old Garibaldi and his sons taught us a lot of ways to handle petrol. My God! the Commune published an official notice last week, ordering all petroleum products to be registered by their owners —"

"Maybe the Egorovs have registered theirs."

"I doubt it. What you saw makes it look as if they were dividing up their supplies, but what for?"

She saw that her account of the petrol delivery and dispersal had done more to convince her lover of the Russian threat than all the political philosophy of David Meade.

"I wish Clemenceau were still at the *mairie*," he muttered. "He's the sort to take action on this sort of thing. But Ferré —"

"— Would be the first to throw a petrol bomb."

Marc got up and walked restlessly across the room. "What are they *doing*, out there at Versailles?" he grumbled. "Why all the delay, after Fort Issy fell? They're all too old for the job, that's what. Do you remember what MacMahon was supposed to have said in the Crimea, after he took the Malakoff: 'Here I am and here I'll stay!' So he sticks in the mud on the far side of the Bois de Boulogne —"

He calmed down after a while, and they made a *petit noir* from the grounds of the breakfast coffee pot, to be enjoyed while Marc told his girl everything Renoir had said about her paintings, which he looked at several times, and the diffident suggestions he had made for Study in White. Babette listened greedily. She had thought of Renoir as well as of the Russians during some sleepless hours at the Old Farm, and of what he said about her need of hard work and technical skill. She had been around the studios long enough to know how deficient she was in technique, and how badly she needed what was open to no woman – planned study in a teaching atelier. Berthe Morisot had copied the Raphaels in the Louvre, as any young lady was free to do, but it was the teaching of Corot first and then Manet which had made her a painter, and theirs of course was private tuition. It was the men who went daily or nightly to the ateliers: Renoir with Gleyre, Manet with Couture, and Monet at the Académie Suisse. Even David Meade, a gifted amateur, had gone regularly to the Life class at poor old Dupuy's. She had Marc for a teacher, who had recanted from the orthodoxy of the Beaux Arts to join the Independents, but he had held a Beaux Arts scholarship, and it was possible that where he led she could not follow. Or was it? He had taken up his brush and palette to illustrate what Renoir had said about Study in White, and presently Babette put on her painting smock and turned to her own easel. There was a happy silence in the studio as a man and a girl escaped from the danger which threatened on all sides.

After the desertion of Rossel the Commune's Ministry of War had passed into the hands of Delescluze. He was about the same age as Marshal MacMahon, younger than Thiers, but he was dying of tuberculosis contracted during the long prison terms on Devil's Island and elsewhere which had left him devoid of any military knowledge or experience. He had some competent field officers, two of them Poles, but as the month of May advanced the most vigorous fighting done by the Commune was at its own headquarters, where the Committee of Public Safety was now virtually dictator, and Rigault and Ferré were directing a reign of terror far removed from the gentle ideology of Charles Delescluze. The time was ripe for Thiers, on 8 May, to warn the inhabitants of Paris of a general attack on the city, to be followed by what he called 'expiation in the name of the law'.

This declaration was received in Paris with fury. The Commune, aware by this time of imminent defeat, had been trying like many another despotism to keep the people happy with bread and circuses, and although bread was in short supply there were several forms of circus available. The destruction of the Vendôme Column, that monument to Bonaparte imperialism, had been for long the pet project of Gustave Courbet, only delayed in its execution by engineering problems; while waiting, there was a new attraction, the opening of the Tuileries palace to the public. It was announced that a series of concerts would be held there to raise funds for the Federal wounded, and the challenge issued by Thiers followed immediately after the first of these had delighted the Paris proletariat. The songs and recitations by professional entertainers were applauded, but of course the real attraction had been the sauntering through the banqueting halls and ballrooms where Napoleon III and Eugénie had entertained their royal guests. Then there were the bedrooms, both state and private, the private chambers, lined with satin, slobbered over as the scenes of those 'nameless orgies' to which the broadsheets and lampoons of the Reds were only too willing to give explicit names. The throne room, the Galérie de la Paix, the Rose, Blue and Green Salons of the Empress were all explored, and exhausted republican behinds sank gratefully on to the spindling gilt furniture once supporting the crinolines of her ladies-in-waiting. When the great clock in the dome of the palace marked closing time a happy throng streamed out, most of them concealing some small article purloined as a souvenir. It had been a triumph for the People, and then, on top of it all, to have to listen to the threats of that old devil Thiers!

It was not Louise Michel who thought of a good way to get even with Thiers, but she supported it enthusiastically. It was Henri de Rochefort, a journalist and rabble-rouser who had been a thorn in the flesh of the emperor and had transferred his satirical attacks to Thiers, who first proposed the destruction of Thiers's own home in Paris. It was in the Place St Georges, this home of forty years, and contained all the books collected and written by the scholar-statesman, as well as his paintings, drawings, bibelots and family treasures. The Committee of Public Safety published a decree of destruction on 11 May and Comrade Michel, with her female followers, hurried down from Montmartre to see the fun. The house was first looted systematically, under the Committee's order to distribute the valuables to the museums and the linen to the field ambulances, and then tile by tile, stone by stone, a house which was not a palace but had held the record of one man's life was razed to the ground.

"Spite and nothing but spite, damn them!" swore Marc Vallon. He declined to go near the Place St Georges himself, but he got the news of each day's progress from young Adrien Jaloux, who was as regular in attendance as Louise Michel herself. The boy was just at the age to be carried away by mass excitement, and only the fact that his brother was serving on the government side kept him from taking to the adventurous life of the maquis with 'Jo-Jo' Malaval and his gang. Adventure lost its charm when he saw the gang and its leader rounded up by a posse of Federals and removed to the nearest barracks, and Adrien's respect for Marc Vallon rose to its old level. He was always ready, during the few days that the destruction of Thiers's house lasted, to answer Marc's regular question, "Are they using fire?"

No, they were not, the house was taken to pieces by hand, but on the last day Adrien had heard one of the demolition squad say to his mate that a drop of petrol would sort out this lot faster, to which the mate replied that they didn't want to set fire to the whole damned square, did they?

"Very interesting," said Marc, and to Babette, later, "So they're thinking about it. They probably mean to use it later on. 'Kill, burn, destroy' – the Russians are on the arson detail, not the ideas." When he went out later Babette saw he was carrying the pocket pistol he had last taken from the drawer to protect Renoir.

In the excitement of destruction, and planning vandalism, the general public hardly noticed that on 13 May another of the Sixteen Forts had fallen to Marshal MacMahon. This was Fort de Vanves, the next of the forts on the south-east of Fort d'Issy, which meant that the Point du Jour Gate which the Federals were defending in strength was now menaced from the south as well as from the great cannon, La Jeanne Marie, of Mont Valérien on the north. The general public was concerned only with the next circus on the Commune's programme, the demolition of the Vendôme Column.

The Place Vendôme, under the Commune, had been re-named the Place Internationale, and the monument itself had changed in appearance several times since it was first erected by Napoleon I. The current version of the great man showed him in imperial robes on top of a bronze column cast from the enemy cannon of 1805, and this double symbol of Bonapartism and militarism was to be felled like a huge tree on the sixteenth of May. The private citizens still living in the Place Vendôme (or Internationale) were to have their windows protected by paper strips, their pavements by bracken and straw; the individuals who might want to join in the festivities were to do so by invitation only.

"You're looking disgruntled, Mr Meade. Are you thinking Monsieur Courbet was out of line when he sent you two invitations to the smashing of old Boney's statue?" asked Mr Washburne on the day before the much-advertised event.

"Considering I hardly knew the fellow, I think he had his nerve, but in fact I was wondering if *you* thought I ought to show up or stay away."

"Oh, as far as I'm concerned I think you should go by all means. Let the readers of *Harper's Weekly* know we've a man in the Legation who can show them the truth of what's going on in Paris now. I presume you'd like to take Miss March with you?"

"If she's not afraid to go into Paris after Monsieur Thiers's warning."

"I'm sure she'll trust herself anywhere with you."

David Meade flushed with annoyance. Ever since he had saved Emily March from attack by a man who as he had surmised was a returned prisoner of war, trained by six months in a German prison to snatch at whatever seemed like profit for himself (and a prisoner again, since that night, under the provost marshal's tender care), the whole community at Versailles, thirsting for any sensation to relieve the uncertain days, had invented a romance between them. Emily herself had been perfect. She met him as if those cries for help, those grateful embraces had never been. Her only concession was to agree that they should be 'David' and 'Emily' to each other, and to accompany him with a group of other people to the occasional entertainments, mostly private theatricals, got up by the officials who were as much prisoners in Versailles as the Communards were prisoners in Paris.

"I've known Miss March for a very short time," he said.

"War and love go hand in hand," said the Minister briskly. "You've done good work here, Mr Meade, and you deserve promotion. But in the Service promotion comes faster to the man with the right wife, and Miss Emily is the ideal wife for a rising young diplomat. Besides her devoted work for the Red Cross, she's the right age, with the right background —"

"Unfortunately *not* the right background," David interrupted.

"What the devil d'you mean, sir? She's American and Protestant, a minister's daughter —"

"And her only brother fell at Antietam, fighting with the Union Army."

"Did she tell you that?"

"Dr Quimby did. He also said that in his opinion it was the brother's death in action that made Emily take up military nursing, and not the inspiring example of Miss Nightingale and Miss Dix."

"Quimby talks too much," growled Mr Washburne.

"I'm not so sure," said David. "I doubt if the Methodist minister and his lady would welcome a former Confederate officer as a suitor for their only daughter's hand."

"They should if they're true Christians. The French, now, they're going to keep this Commune hatred going for the next two generations, maybe more. Get along and organise your trip to Paris, and Meade my boy —"

"Sir?"

"I don't want to rush you."

Mr Washburne in the unusual role of matchmaker had the effect of making David Meade feel very rushed indeed, and self-conscious in Emily's presence as the Legation cab carried them across the Seine and through the tragic streets of Paris. She was in her Red Cross uniform, worn less uncompromisingly than before, since as it was now too warm for a long cloak she had only an elbow-length

229

shoulder cape of white material over the emblem on her breast. Her bonnet, too, was set further back on her head, allowing strands of the glorious chestnut hair to appear, and the strings were tied at a piquant angle. They were to be the guests of two English doctors, members of the Hertford Ambulance, who shared a flat on the Place Vendôme and were eager to share their windows for a view of the descent of Bonaparte. Giving Emily some account of the people they might meet kept David on safe conversational grounds, and her replies were as polite and conventional as ever. She only made one original remark as they drove, endlessly showing their invitations, adorned with a cap of liberty, to Reds in and out of uniform, but to Meade it was striking.

"Don't you think it's funny, David, that they never call each other Frenchmen?"

"Why ... but of course they're Frenchmen!"

"Not since the civil war began. The government troops are always called *les Versaillais*, as if Versailles were a separate country, and the others are called *les Communards*, or the Federals, or the National Guard; it's very confusing."

"Not to Mr Washburne. He calls them all Commun*ists*."

"He must have made up that name. But you see what I mean: none of them ever says *les Français*."

He made an effort – he had to bring it out in the open – and said, "We were all Americans, ten years ago."

"And we are again. But we had our Federals, in between; only we called them the Union Army, or the Boys in Blue."

Lieutenant Meade had called them the Bluebellies.

"And then your friends in the Confederate States Army," Emily went on coolly, "we called *them* the Johnny Rebs. But the French call us all *les américains*, they've got more sense about us than they have about themselves."

A conceited man might have thought that a pretty broad hint. David Meade put it aside as he concentrated on piloting Miss March across the crowded pavement in front of the doctors' house, and up the equally crowded stairs. One of their hosts, who had a turn for statistics, estimated that there were ten thousand human beings milling around in the Place Vendôme, and as many more in the side streets, held back by the rifles of the National Guard. The proceedings were due to begin at three, but it was now nearly four, and nothing had happened: Napoleon I still stood on his bronze monument, dressed by Napoleon III in imperial robes, with a globe sur-mounted by the figure of Liberty in his victorious hand. Street boys were climbing round the scaffolding at the base of the statue, and three bands were playing patriotic airs, but the capstans with ropes running to the top of the column had not yet been winched.

"Trust the Froggies to make a muck of it," said one of the doctors, but he spoke in a low voice, for there were ladies present, three of them English and one a woman of title, whom Meade knew slightly. They were of the arrogant, overbearing sort, who thought they had acquired merit by remaining in Paris and doing a little voluntary work in the private 'ambulances', and jeered at the act of vandalism they had come to see as if they were at the play. They soon tired of looking out at the heaving mass of humanity and the engineers arguing round the capstans and windlasses, and were ready for the sherry and *petits fours* handed round by their hosts. Their attitude to Emily March, at first supercilious, soon became friendly and even respectful – that white uniform, Meade thought, was a great asset. And then Emily looked so well, talked so well, was so completely a lady – what had old Washburne called her? the ideal wife for a rising diplomat. She had everything, was everything, except – she wasn't an impudent little Paris gamine with brown eyes, and a smile he had never been able to forget.

While workmen were driving in extra wedges on the side of the column which had already been sawn through, and Meade was making charcoal sketches of Gustave Courbet, sober but beside himself with impatience, and other Commune leaders, Ned Carey appeared in the apartment and was introduced to Emily March.

"Ambulance life suits you, Carey," said David Meade, and it was true. The Englishman seemed taller, burlier, with shaggy hair and cheeks browned by the sun of the splendid summer. "I like my job," he said, "it makes more sense than painting Antony and Cleopatra, eh Meade?"

"The Hertford Ambulance is famous," said Emily (and indeed it was to be the nucleus of the Hertford British Hospital in Paris). "What exactly do you do?"

He had begun as a stretcher-bearer, said Ned modestly; well, that was just a matter of brute strength and an acquired knack of lifting and walking, but the doctors had begun to give him lessons in first aid on the battlefield, and he could do simple things like splints and tourniquets.

"But you're a surgical nurse, Miss March," he protested. "I've heard about you from Pat Quimby, and I know I'm not in your class, so don't let me bore you with my tourniquets. Sometimes I drive the supply waggon; that's really more in my line. Oh, by the way, I had Renoir and Marc Vallon in my waggon, only the other day –"

There was a shout that something was really happening out there at last, and in the Place Vendôme the bands struck up the *Marseillaise* for the twentieth time. It was another false alarm, but it ended the adventure of Renoir, and left Edward Carey alone to stare across to the Ministry of Justice, and remember how on winter afternoons he had watched for the light of Hubert de

Grimont's lamps. He hoped Elvire was happy at Versailles. Remembering Renoir and his admiring followers on the *quai*, he remembered too that just before he saw the painter he had the annoying sense of being followed by two men in civilian clothes with red scarves, one of whom reminded him of a footman in the de Grimont house. They had disappeared when the crowd came up, but Ned thought he had seen them again when he was alone in the one-horse supply waggon and even (but he was probably imagining things) in the crowd outside, now howling 'Sold!' and 'Treachery!' because it was nearer six o'clock than three, and Bonaparte still stood on his column with the globe of the world in his hand.

The monument was brought down by manpower at six o'clock, fifty extra men on the ropes having proved more useful than machinery, and fell without damage to life and limb in a mass of broken bronze and stone on the tons of bracken and straw put down to receive it. The cheers and shouts of *Vive la Commune* were deafening, the struggle for souvenirs began, and the English doctors, producing hoarded refreshments, begged their guests not to think of leaving for another hour.

"It'll take that long to clear the square," they said, but Edward Carey said he would have to take a chance and go. "I'm on duty at half past six," he explained. "Surely it won't take me long to fight my way round the corner to the Hôtel St Honoré, where we use the stables." He was so determined that they had to let him go in a flurry of pleasant goodbyes and thanks, and watching from the windows they lost sight of his tall figure immediately in the clouds of dust which had arisen from the fallen monument and the scuffling of so many feet round the tribunes on which leading Communards were making speeches which none of the souvenir hunters wanted to hear.

"Carey, Edouard, *anglais*?" said the official, writing.

"Precisely!" said Ned. "*Je suis anglais*! And I demand to be put in touch at once with the British Embassy!"

"There is no such place in Paris, your ambassador has thrown in his lot with the Versaillais."

"But what the devil am I supposed to have done?" said Ned. "I work for Richard Wallace's ambulance, and he cares for the wounded of both sides."

"Read the charge against this man," said the lieutenant governor to a little clerk by his side.

"Complicity with the Versaillais."

"What damned nonsense!" shouted Ned.

"Denounced by whom?"

"Citizeness Elvire de Grimont."

He went mad at that and started to struggle with his guards. Ned was big and strong and they were taken by surprise, he got in a few heavy blows before they wrestled him to the ground and hauled him up again bleeding from a long shallow cut above one eye, made by a metal bar, and a punch to the jaw which loosened several teeth. He was still conscious when they dragged him down a stone corridor and threw him into a cell with bunks for four men, now occupied by twelve standing crushed together to suffocation point. Someone considerately made a little room for him on a bottom bunk, and there he sat with the blood dripping from his forehead and his handkerchief pressed to his aching mouth. Ned Carey's senses came and went during that long night without food or the water for which they were all begging, while the bucket which was the only sanitary provision filled to overflowing; and he found, when one or two of his fellow captives asked his name and why he was there, that he had forgotten all the French he ever knew.

It had been after six o'clock when he was taken in the Place Vendôme, and the clock of the Mazas prison at least

236

told the hours of darkness and announced the haggard dawn. By feeling in his pockets he knew his watch was gone, with his wallet, his ambulance identity card and his British paper of protection, so that Edward Carey, born in Manchester, residing in Paris at the Hôtel St Honoré, had now no means of proving his identity. He was an accomplice of the Versaillais, denounced by Citizeness Elvire de Grimont – that was the point at which reason stopped, and once in the dead of night tears came.

But he was young and strong, and possessed of the arrogant British belief that one Englishman was equal to ten Froggies, at least (the blood was dry now) in a fair fight, and when he had eaten one of the pieces of stale bread thrust between the bars of the cell about seven o'clock Ned felt better able to face what the day might bring. It brought, at nine, the governor of Mazas himself, who read a statement about the Jury of Accusation which was about to sit in the prison, presided over by Comrade Rigault, the Procureur of the Commune. "Be sure to look your best, *monsieur l'anglais*," he said sarcastically to Ned. The Englishman looked no better for the heavy fetters fastened on the wrists of himself and his cellmates as one by one they were led through the barred gate.

The Mazas was a prison, not a hall of justice, and therefore contained no room of a size suitable for trials by jury. 'Jury of Accusation', however, was a misnomer. The trials it conducted were summary trials, and on the hastily carpentered bench before which Ned was taken there were only three men, Rigault and Ferré whom he recognised, and an elderly member of the Committee of Public Safety called Felix Pyat, who like some of his comrades had spent half his life between prison and exile. All three were in paramilitary uniform, with red scarves and sashes and feathered hats, the hunchback, heir of 1793, being dressed to resemble as closely as possible his hero Danton.

Rigault himself took the part of the Public Prosecutor, reading the charge against Edouard Carey, *citoyen anglais*, and the name of his accuser, asking what the prisoner had to say in his own defence.

"All I have to say is that it's a tissue of lies from beginning to end. I administered British charities in aid of all the people of Paris after the Siege, and I'm working now in the Hertford Ambulance. I have had nothing to do with politics, either for or against Versailles."

"You made your opinions generally known, however."

"Is the Commune the enemy of free speech, monsieur?"

Rigault's face darkened. "The Commune has evidence of *your* enmity, citizen, and your association with the flunkeys of the jackal Thiers. Listen to this." He took from the pile of papers before him a sheet coloured pale grey and embossed with a coronet, which Ned recognised as Elvire de Grimont's last letter, written over a month ago and foolishly kept in his own wallet.

" 'Our Paris home, where we have often welcomed you with pleasure, will be closed until the defeat of the vile Commune, which I know you desire as ardently as we do.' Could anything be more convincing?" He turned to Pyat and Ferré. "This is written in a woman's hand, but it is signed 'E. and H. de Grimont' – H. standing for Hubert of that name, the so-called Minister of Justice in the Versailles cabal. Have either of you anything to ask the prisoner?"

Felix Pyat shook his head, feigning disgust, but Theophile Ferré, his eyes gleaming behind his pince-nez, spoke to Ned directly.

"Where is your friend Madame de Grimont now, young man?"

"I have no idea."

The hunchback was convulsed by a gale of silent mirth.

238

"Good answer, eh Rigault? Good answer!" he said when he could speak, but the Procureur, as if his dignity had been impaired, shook his head and ignored the merriment.

"Prisoner at the bar," he said, "the verdict of the Jury of Accusation is unanimous. Found guilty of complicity with Versailles, and ordered to be transferred to the prison of La Roquette." The feathered hats moved close together, like cockerels in a ritual dance, and to another whoop of mirth from the Prefect of Police, Carey was taken out to the courtyard, where a waggon of the guilty was already waiting.

There were armed guards with the prisoners, and the heavy fetters were not judged necessary where a pair of handcuffs would do. A blacksmith was found to strike the irons off Ned Carey's wrists. He looked like a capable artisan and had a decent face. While he worked he muttered to Carey out of the side of his mouth, "Where you bound for, comrade?"

"La Roquette."

"Tough luck."

"Why? What have they got at La Roquette that's any worse than Mazas?"

"The condemned cells."

A more distinguished victim of the Commune than the young man from Manchester had already been taken from Mazas to a condemned cell at La Roquette. This was Archbishop Darboy, for whom Thiers steadfastly refused to exchange Blanqui unless against the unconditional surrender of the Commune. The Papal Nuncio had appealed again and again to Mr Washburne, the highest ranking diplomat still available, to use his influence on the archbishop's behalf, but the best he could do was get Rigault's permission to visit the prison, and take Monsignor Darboy a bottle of wine. On 19 May, the third day Ned Carey was in La Roquette, in an overcrowded cell different only from the Mazas cell because three of the inmates were insane, his friend David Meade passed down another corridor in the prison labyrinth in attendance on his minister, carrying the bottle of Madeira and a bundle of newspapers. They had been allowed to visit the archbishop once before, and David saw that his condition had deteriorated through the weeks of confinement. At least in La Roquette he had a very small cell to himself where the *curé* of the Madeleine joined him from time to time to say the Office, and though he was feeble and emaciated he bore his imprisonment with Christian fortitude.

"Can't you leave us alone with His Eminence for half an hour?" Mr Washburne asked the jailer.

"Half an hour, citizen? It's as much as my job's worth – maybe as my life's worth too! The chief warder's very steady on his rounds, you see, but for a consideration I might let you have ten minutes..."

"I don't want to get you into trouble, Leblanc," said the prisoner, and David Meade had an inspiration.

"If it's all right with you, sir," he said, "I could go into the corridor with this man, and we could pretend to have some sort of conversation about the prison rules, or anything else praising the Commune, and you could have your talk in peace."

"Only ten minutes, mind," pleaded the jailer named Leblanc, and in the stony corridor, where the very walls held the prison stench, he asked David the time twice in the stipulated ten minutes, glancing so nervously to left and right that he hardly ever met the American's eyes. But he talked: about the patience of the 'priest' as he called the archbishop, about the courage of his own son Didier, serving with the 66th Belleville National Guard at the Gate of the Point du Jour, and David was too tense himself to recollect that Didier Leblanc was the husband of Babette's sister. But he took note of the man thoroughly, with his watery eyes, his balding blond head, his nervous mouth and above all the rapacious hand which came out when he said, "Now, citizen!" and seized the five franc piece which David gave him. There's a Red who'll take a bribe, thought the young man, and forgot the jailer as he and Mr Washburne stood with bent heads for the blessing of a priest who knew his days on earth were numbered.

The days of the Commune's supremacy were also numbered; they were reduced to two. One of these was a fine Saturday, passed of course in legislation, a decree on secular education being accompanied by a decree on legitimacy, very near to the heart of Louise Michel. "What a fool you are about bastardy, Louise!" said pretty Elisaveta Dmitrieva. "I'm illegitimate myself, and you never hear *me* whining about it!" This productive Saturday was followed by an equally fine Sunday, 21 May, for which an enormous open-air concert in the Tuileries gardens had been planned. Fifteen hundred musicians delighted the people of the slums who had walked nearly to the Place de la Concorde, and climbed on the railings and the barricades to get a better view. A favourite, because the highest, barricade was that at the foot of the Rue St Florentin where the remains of Elvire de Grimont and her three fellow victims of Ferré's cruelty were buried in their quicklime grave.

And then the breakthrough took place. It happened

without a cannonade, although for days the government's artillery barrage had pounded the weak point of the Point du Jour Gate. There was no need to open fire when it was discovered that the gate was no longer defended, that the 66th Belleville had copied the earlier runaways, and beaten their retreat into Paris. General Douay, one of Thiers's most experienced officers, had been waiting for days for such a breach in the ramparts. Long before sunset his troops were marching into Paris through suburbs devastated by two months of close conflict, and when the news reached the Hôtel de Ville, where the Commune was in its last session, the terrible sound of the tocsin echoed again from all the church steeples of the capital.

By dawn MacMahon had 70,000 troops inside Paris, advancing in the textbook formation of a central column heading for the Place de l'Etoile and the Arc de Triomphe, on top of which, heavily sandbagged and armed, the Tricolore was raised. On the right flank General Cissey crossed the Pont de Grenelle to the Left Bank of the Seine, and on the left, after a right wheel, General Clinchant attacked Montmartre, where the civil war had begun. It was the triple movement known to some strategists as 'the Caudine toasting-fork', greatly assisted by Haussmann's layout of broad avenues and oblique intersections, giving the fields of fire and the opportunities to manoeuvre cavalry which he had anticipated as necessary in just such a civil war as this.

Clausewitz would have concurred, and the government generals had been taught the doctrines of Clausewitz at St Cyr, but Clausewitz had been dead for nearly forty years, and as many more were to pass before military theorists got beyond tactics and logistics to examine the psychology of the soldier. For MacMahon his men were 'effectives' merely. For Delescluze, the Commune's Minister of War who knew nothing about war whatever,

242

they were champions of freedom. Neither leader realised that when it came to hand to hand fighting a huge wave of hatred would be released: that MacMahon's men were out to avenge defeat and German imprisonment, while the Federals were fighting, not for an abstract 'freedom' but to avenge the poverty of their lives and the squalor of their homes.

In the capital there were many men of military age and over who were uncertain where their duty lay. If they went into the streets they would be forced to carry paving stones for the second line of barricades which should have been erected long before, thus giving assistance to the Commune. If they tried, as ex-soldiers, to join the government troops at one of the several strong points established on the first full day of fighting, they stood a good chance of being caught in the cross-fire or, in civilian clothes, shot as spies. If they hid in their own homes, what were they? Cowards?

Marc Vallon thought he was a coward. That Monday, 22 May, was a noisy day in Montmartre, as the government generals took their revenge for the murder of Lecomte and Thomas by firing into the totally undefended fortress of the Butte. The cannon dragged so painfully up to the Champ Polonais, and there defended with such far-reaching consequences, had been neglected from that day forward and were not fit for action. The yelling of orders, the hunting for side-armour and breech-blocks, even for spades to dig out the gun trails, were heard in the Rue des Rosiers, where the Red Flag flew once more, and Marc Vallon, who had forsworn war for ever, argued with Babette about the need to fight again.

"Is that why you kept your uniform?" she said in a flash of perception.

"My uniform?"

"Yes, your tunic and breeches. We found them in that

trunk in the *cagibi*."

"Oh – I shoved them in there when I came back from Pontarlier, just to get them out of the way."

"No, they weren't shoved away. I saw, they'd been sponged and brushed and folded, ready to be worn again. Marc darling, why?"

He broke down then and told her that he'd been afraid since the civil war began of a Prussian intervention. It would be just in the style of Manteuffel or von Moltke to take advantage of the French impulse to self-destruction to invade again – they were still on the eastern perimeter of the city – and this time never stop until the whole of France was a German province. And if the invasion came he, Marc Vallon, would take up arms once more ... He was as shaken, as badly disturbed as on the March night when he had come back to Babette at the Old Farm.

She calmed him at last, and they ate a little, slept a little, listened to the guns until morning came. The Commune was fighting back as it had never fought before, and resistance in the Place de la Concorde was strong enough to keep the central forces of the government massed round the Arc de Triomphe. But on the flanks the turning tactics of the Versailles officers put them in possession of key points like the Parc Monceau, the St Lazare railway station and the Left Bank station at Montparnasse. The net was closing, and the Federals had instituted a house search to comb out every able-bodied man for combat or a prison sentence.

This last piece of news was brought to Marc and Babette by Adrien Jaloux, shortly before noon on Tuesday 23 May, just after Marc had announced that there was no food left in the house, and he refused to hide there any longer like a frightened beast. Adrien's message gave him the perfect excuse to go out and buy whatever food was obtainable, because it was a plea from Madame Verlet that

244

Marc would come at once to the Old Farm. The Russians were leaving and were arguing with the concierge, who said they were liable for six months' rent whether they completed their lease or not.

"Looks as if they've had enough," said Babette elliptically to Marc. "Adrien, are they all going away?"

"No, not the servant, not today I mean. He's going to pack up and follow them at the end of the week."

"Back to London?"

"I don't know, but the woman Michel's there, and she spoke as if they were going to Germany."

"What did I tell you?" Marc glanced at Babette. "*T'es un brave gars*, Adrien, to be in the streets today. You're big enough to be taken for a man; cut along home and don't fall into the hands of the Red recruiters." The boy, flushing with pleasure, said, "Shall I tell Madame Verlet you'll come, then? She said she couldn't handle that lot by herself."

"Tell her I'm on my way ... Now Babette!" as the boy hurried off, "don't start crying and don't try to stop me. I can't let poor Tante Lise down, and what do you expect the Russians to do? Dowse me with petrol?"

"It's not the Russians, it's Louise Michel."

"Don't be silly, darling," he said bracingly, and with a quick kiss he snatched up his corduroy jacket and beret and left her. She watched him go up the street, where the Reds at Number Six watched him too. And all the time Marc was gone Babette remembered how Louise Michel had threatened her on the day the 'wine' was delivered at the Vine House:

"Any more of your impertinence and I'll make sure that lover of yours is up before a conscription tribunal!"

But the time for tribunals was past. The Reds beginning their house to house search in the Rue des Rosiers had no need to force their way past Madame Camille, wielding a

245

defensive broom, into the building where Marc Vallon lived. They had a horse and cart across the width of the narrow street when he came back from the Old Farm, and they took him at his own gate after a struggle and bundled him into the vehicle. The terrified girl, crouching on the sofa and listening through the open window, heard the order shouted to the driver. "To the prison of La Roquette!"

When she was able to think, to plan, to walk, Babette opened the table drawer and loaded the American derringer.

18

Babette had handled the weapon so often by stealth during the time when she carried it in her bag that it felt familiar, and the grip shaped like a bird's head fitted comfortably into the palm of her hand. The short-barrelled pistol fitted equally well into the pocket of her alpaca working dress, and with a kerchief knotted under her chin and her purse and keys in a string shopping bag she looked exactly like a young housewife setting out to buy groceries on a warm May day in a world at peace. But when she got to the foot of the stairs the concierge came out of her *loge* and tearfully begged her to go back to the studio and stay there.

"Oh dear, dear, poor little Madame Babette, and did you see it happen? A gentleman like Monsieur Marc, a hero who fought for his country, to be arrested by those villains, and for what? Where are you going, my dear? You don't think you can go after him, do you? They would rape you or shoot you as they shot the generals without thinking twice about it, those rascals across the street..." So the stream of lamentations ran, until Babette said quietly:

"I know I can't follow him to prison, Madame Camille. But I must try to buy some food, to be ready for him when the Versaillais come in and set him free, and there's nothing to eat in the house."

"I made some soup at noon, let me heat a bowl of soup for you," coaxed Madame Camille. "Take time before you rush away and don't run into danger—"

"I think the danger's past, madame. Those men have gone away from the house across the street."

"But they're fighting all along the Butte, Madame Babette, it's not safe to go out!"

"I have to go to the Old Farm, too, because they're in some sort of trouble there—"

"Drink your soup."

The bowl of hastily heated soup was a real boon to Babette. It gave her nourishment, and also time to consider her plan of action. She had no intention of going to the Old Farm and listening to more lamentations from Tante Lise and Fanny; she was going to find Louise Michel, who she was convinced had egged on the Reds to arrest her lover. The mistake she made was in supposing that Louise was still in the Vine House with her Russian friends, but the pause in the *loge* also gave Babette time to sample what might be part of their activities. A strong smell of burning took Madame Camille and the girl to the front door. Mounting flames and clouds of smoke from behind the short cut to the boulevard where David Meade had made his proposition caused them both to think that the Reine Margot was on fire.

"Arson," said Babette tersely.

"Who would want to set fire to a restaurant?"

"For a rehearsal, perhaps? Don't keep me back, Madame Camille. I know I'm wanted at the Old Farm."

"But you can't go in that thin dress, without a coat or a

248

shawl."

"The things I have are too bright, and my cloak's too heavy."

It was with an old grey shawl of Madame Camille's wrapped round her that Babette went off, taking the familiar 'long way round' by the Rue St Vincent and boldly opening the gate to the front garden of the Vine House like an invited guest. The sound of sporadic firing was going on, but it seemed more distant than in the morning, and she was not afraid of gunfire in the distance, her baptism of fire having taken place long ago. But she was afraid when she knocked at the door of the Vine House, afraid of who might open, more afraid still when no one opened at all and a suppressed laugh made her turn to see the Russian manservant watching her from a clump of laurel.

"What do you want?" he asked.

"I want to see Madame Louise Michel."

"What makes you think she's here? Comrade Louise is in the streets, fighting the Versaillais with her Women's Battalion. If you don't believe me, look inside."

With a beating heart Babette followed him indoors. She knew the layout of the Vine House, and all seemed normal on the lower ground floor: the stone-flagged kitchen and pantries on one side and the wine-cellar with its empty racks on the other. Up a stone stair with an iron railing they came to two small sitting rooms, also empty, with Monsieur Renard's furniture tidily arranged round the walls.

"All correct according to the inventory," said Mitya/ Ivan. "The woman in the Old Farm was kicking up a fuss about that this morning, but your friend Vallon made her see that Monsieur Egorov was acting within his rights — breaking the lease, paying the rent, checking the furniture like an ideal tenant. Shall I tell the Egorovs of your interest, when I join them in Switzerland?"

"Was Louise Michel here when Monsieur Vallon came to help?"

"She was. She doesn't like 'Monsieur' Vallon very much, and she doesn't like you, little sister."

With a swift movement, surprising for a man of his heavy, stocky build, the Russian seized Babette by the wrist, flung open the front door and dragged her through the overgrown shrubs into the tool shed, where the last carboy of petrol had been removed from the shelves he made.

"Nobody here, you see."

"The place reeks of petrol," said Babette.

"And that's what you really came to look for, isn't it? I saw you spying on us, the day the stuff came in."

Her hand was in the pocket of her skirt, and her finger was on the safety catch of the American derringer. She said,

"Was it you who set fire to the Reine Margot?"

The man looked as nearly startled as his wooden features would allow. "It was a French girl," he said. "Beginner's luck, and she did well. But we have more important targets than a capitalist restaurant. Now, little sister spy, you know too much. Come here and let me give you a quick lesson in love before you die."

He took her into a bear's hug, forcing her down on one of the broad empty shelves, pushing her shawl aside and biting at the neck of her dress with a bear's fangs. Babette shot him through the pocket of her skirt, so that he fell away from her, wounded in the side but growling, shaking his massive head in disbelief. Crouching on the far side of the shelf she dragged the pistol clear and fired again. Like the girl who threw the petrol bomb she had beginner's luck, and Babette's second shot drilled the Russian through the brain.

She ran out in horror from the shed with the spattered walls, crawled through the shrubs (if Fanny looked out from their old bedroom window she might see her sister) and back to the basement of the Vine House. She sponged her skirt with water from the stone sink, and drank from the tap, waiting for many minutes for the sound of a hue and cry. Nothing stirred but the wild beating of her heart, for the barrage had started up again loud enough to drown two pistol shots. She walked back to the Rue St Vincent, trying to be calm, and only began to run when she reached the empty streets which led to the *maquis*.

There was a strange old building, between the village horse pond and a mill whose sails had once turned in the middle of a vineyard, known in Montmartre as the Castle of the Mists. Twenty years back little villas had been built in the grounds, all empty in 1871, and since the war a small colony of artists, beggars and gipsies had taken over the vegetable gardens as a small *maquis* of their own, simpler and less dangerous than the desperate *maquis* where the Malavals of Montmartre hid from the gendarmerie. In one of the empty hovels of the *maquis* Babette took refuge, barring the door but leaving the window ajar to let the sweet scent of appleblossom drive out the smell of blood which seemed to be everywhere, in her clothes and hair and on her hands. Her next aim was to find David Meade, who had promised to help her if Marc were conscripted, but could he help a man imprisoned by the Commune? Was Meade in Paris or at Versailles? And could she cross Paris to reach him, since Paris was now a battlefield?

Mikhail Alekseievich Saranov, anarchist, deceased, had not been wrong when he told Babette that Louise Michel was fighting in the streets of Montmartre with her Women's Battalion. Armed with her rifle and bayonet she had gone into action within half an hour of giving orders for the arrest of Marc Vallon, being able to recruit only twenty-five women from her squad, but twenty-five who showed more courage than any other of the defenders of the Butte Montmartre. Ten of them died in the long fight from barricade to barricade between Clichy and Pigalle, without their leader being able to execute the orders she had from Rigault and the Egorovs to blow up the whole of the Butte Montmartre with all the women and children in it. She waited in vain for Mitya/Ivan, otherwise Saranov, to meet her in the Place Blanche with the nitroglycerine capsules required for the explosion. Her confederate had died at the hands of a girl she despised, and while she waited, the cannon she had fought to save in March were recaptured by General Clinchant and his Chasseurs, who hoisted the Tricolore on the heights where the Red Flag had waved for weeks.

Babette in her hiding-place knew nothing of this, and she was spared one devastating sight in the Rue des Rosiers. With Montmartre in their hands, the soldiers of General Clinchant rode roughshod over the repetition of Thiers's orders for complete expiation according to the law. There was little legality in the arrest of forty-nine or fifty citizens, including women and children, and marching them to the courtyard where the two generals had been murdered on 18 March. There the unfortunates were made to kneel down in front of the wall against which the generals had faced the firing squad, and there, as an act of expiation, they met the same death.

It was about the same time, in another part of Paris, that a nondescript man, for whom the battle had no terrors, made his way through Clinchant's forces closing in on the barricades round the new Opéra and reported at Maître Gaucher's law offices on the Rue d'Antin. He passed the dead bodies of several children on the way, for the fighting in that quarter had been intense, but he found 'young' Gaucher in his *étude*, seeking professional peace after the misery of watching his house in the Parc Monceau partly destroyed during Clinchant's advance. Thank heaven he had sent his wife and children to the country weeks before.

"Well," he said to the visitor, whose code name was Perle, "have you got Madame de Grimont safely on her way?"

"That's just it, sir." The man twisted his shabby hat in his hands. "I can't find the lady anywhere. She never turned up in the Rue de Lille."

"*What?*"

"Mind you, she was smart to stay away, for the Rue de Lille's just a heap of rubble now. The Reds are making it one of their key points on the Left Bank, and the old prince and his lady cut and ran on Sunday. But their porter's still in his *loge*, and he swore the lady I described to him had never been seen at the house since last New Year's day."

"The devil!" swore Maître Gaucher. "When my man went to her house to put the servants on board wages they told him she'd left to pay calls one day and hadn't returned, which was just how I told her to go—"

"The servants didn't worry," said Perle. "Saving your presence, sir, I went to the Rue St Florentin on my way here, just in case she might have changed her mind and gone back home after all. Very hot spot today, the Rue St Florentin. Didn't want to linger too long there! Her maid spoke through a shutter in the gate, said Madame was very capricious and could be anywhere. Doesn't look too promising, if you ask me."

"Well, I've done all I can, and so have you, Perle. You'd better lie low for a day or two until the fighting's over, and then check with me again. Everything all serene at the Porte d'Italie?"

"All serene, but not much traffic since the Versaillais came in ... Oh, but there's one thing, monsieur. Word came from Orléans that the Duc de la Treille travelled north with his servants after he got your message. Wants to escort his sister to Hyères himself. I suppose when she don't show up he'll come on into Paris when the coast's clear?"

"Very likely," said Maître Gaucher, nodding dismissal to the *passeur*. And hold me responsible for whatever went wrong with the wretched woman's escape, he thought. Or else have a squaring-up of accounts with Hubert de Grimont. That's something I would dearly like to see.

As Perle had said, the Federals were fighting tenaciously on the Left Bank, and not only their left flank on the Rue de Lille but their right on the Rue Vavin, the street of Vallon's birth, was being speedily reduced to rubble. They were hard pressed in their central stronghold, the Place de la Concorde, and Marine sharpshooters on the Rue Royale and round the Opéra were taking their toll of the defenders on the Red barricades. One of the Red leaders had no compunction in setting fire to any houses on the Rue Royale which sheltered the Marines. If Elisaveta Dmitrieva's girl pupil had beginner's luck in throwing her first petrol bomb, there was no such thing as beginner's luck on the Rue Royale. With the soldierly precision which they had lacked so long, the fighters of the Commune applied their combustibles and torches to the great houses and the famous shops. From the Concorde to the Madeleine, one of the noblest streets in Paris was soon a sea of flame.

This was precisely what Raoul Rigault had advocated to the Committee of Public Safety as soon as it was apparent that the government troops had invaded in overwhelming strength. Make the old Ile de la Cité, where Paris began, the last bastion of the Commune, a redoubt for the defenders, and if need be, burn down the capital street by street on the heads of the 'Versaillais'.

To the saner of his colleagues the only choice now appeared to be between death and flight. Others were ready to take Rigault at his word. About ten o'clock a Communard named Jules Bergeret, who had (following the usual practice) been imprisoned for losing the battle in the first counter-attack of April and was free again, organised the burning of the Tuileries palace. While Douay's men and civilian volunteers fought alongside as many firemen as could be summoned to save the priceless treasures of the adjacent Louvre, the magnificent palace which was part of the history of France was gutted by the flames of hatred. Before the blazing night was over an imitative crime was threatened. A squad of National Guards entered the cathedral of Notre Dame and began piling up chairs, stools, confessionals, choir stalls and whatever movable wood they could find to kindle a fire which should make the Tuileries look like a candle flame. Notre Dame de Paris, with her Child on her arm, looked down in mild surprise at the vandals. One of the most famous churches in Christendom was spared at the last moment by order of the Committee of Public Safety, not for any religious reason but because of the danger of the fire spreading to a hospital full of their own wounded. So the night wore on for the sleepless men in the Hôtel de Ville, itself now full of wounded; for the regulars in their bivouacs; for Babette Mercier, creeping out of her hiding-place in the Castle of the Mists.

As St Pierre de Montmartre tolled the evening hours, she became more and more afraid for herself, more and more anxious to start her search for David Meade. The fighting had rolled away from the Butte, and if Louise Michel had not fallen at the head of her precious Women's Battalion, might she not go along to the Vine House to plan more devilry with Mitya? And find him dead? And start the hunt for his killer, beginning at the Old Farm? To go was easy for a girl who knew every lane and *raccourci* in Montmartre, but how would she fare in the unknown streets of Paris? She had seen so little of the capital apart from the Champ de Mars, site of the Great Exhibition, the Tuileries garden and palace, the Place de la Concorde, and the Elysée where Louis Napoleon Bonaparte had lived before the coup d'état which made him emperor. She only knew that she must make for the river, and the Seine (she was light-headed from hunger and fear by now) would lead her to the American Legation.

The blaze from the burning palace lit up the eastern sky, but it was dark enough in her own village for Babette to slide from staircase to alley like a prowling cat, checked by nothing until she came to the Place Blanche, where the Women's Battalion had made their last stand earlier in the day. Of the ten dead five had been removed by their families, but there were still five corpses lying in the square, with limbs distorted in their last agonies, and such trinkets as they wore stripped from their hands and ears by the harpies who were the first to shout 'Kill, burn, destroy' and snatch at the trumpery rewards. Babette sidled round the square and went on downhill, taking a side alley whenever she saw the fire of a soldiers' bivouac or the camps where the regulars were snatching an hour of sleep. After many turnings she had the good luck to come on the Rue de Miromesnil, long, dark and silent, which after she had sat for a time to rest on a doorstep led her to the Elysée and gave her her bearings. She knew now where the river was, where she had first seen light on water, the light which turned to gold for Renoir, and she went on down a wide avenue where all the trees had been cut down until she came to an avenue also treeless but more splendid and recognised the Champs Elysées.

Dawn was breaking, and all over Paris the troops were standing to. Babette heard the bugle calls and saw far up the avenue the soldiers moving about their strong point at the Arc de Triomphe, where above sandbags and light artillery the Tricolore hung motionless in the warm and windless air. It was the first time in her life that her country's flag had ever struck a responsive note in Babette's heart, and with the pride and pity came the dread of crossing that wide thoroughfare in the direct line of battle. She ran then, with all her remaining strength, and on the other side, outside one of the shuttered houses, she came on a concierge sweeping her area of the pavement clear of broken glass.

"Please, madame, can you direct me to the Rue de Chaillot?" Babette hardly recognised her own voice, and the woman said with rough kindness, "What's your mother about, to let a kid like you out alone on a day like this?"

"I'm not a child, madame."

"No, I see you're not. You're a woman, eh, and looking for your sweetheart, I'll be bound! So you want the Rue de Chaillot, it's not far away, but you'd best come into my *loge* and drink a *petit noir* first, else he's going to think you've risen from the dead."

The doorkeeper at the American Legation, himself a Frenchman, looked as if he would like to refuse admittance to this urchin with her shawl and torn skirt, a string bag clutched in her dirty hands and a face the colour of ashes. But she spoke so firmly when she asked if Monsieur David Meade were in Paris that he grudgingly said yes, what did she want with Monsieur Meade? and she answered, "Please to announce Mademoiselle Elisabeth Mercier." He found himself ushering her into a small waiting room where at least there was nothing that such a waif of the streets could steal.

"Babette!" David Meade, like every other member of the Legation staff (they had all, except the Minister and his secretary, followed MacMahon into Paris), had been up all night. He was in his shirt and trousers, without a cravat, and he hadn't stopped even to pull a jacket on when he heard who was asking for him. She began trembling when she saw him, and he realised that she was speechless.

"Darling, what is it? Try to tell me!" He dared not embrace her until the trembling stopped. "Is it Marc? Has he been conscripted? Worse? Not – not killed?"

"They took him to La Roquette prison."

"Oh my God!" Reports of Rigault's summary executions had been coming in all night. A prisoner in La Roquette – it was as good as killed, Meade knew.

"Darling, we'll do everything we can for you . . ."

"David, there's more. That Russian – Mitya, I told you about him. He was giving petrol to the Reds. You know, with Louise Michel and the Egorovs –"

"Yes?"

"I killed him. I – I shot him, David –"

"*What?*"

"With the gun you gave me."

19

He held her in his arms while she told her story, interrupting only once to ask her if she knew she might have shot herself when she fired through her pocket, the bullet could have lodged in her thigh and the Russian would have let her bleed to death. But there was the hole in her skirt with burned material all around it, and there in the pocket was the pistol which had put an end to the traffic in petrol at the Vine House. David Meade's mind was working quickly. Thank God the government now held Montmartre, where troops bent on 'expiation' had carried out so many punishments that agents in the pay of the American Legation should have little difficulty in adding one more corpse, and that one unrecognisable, to the piles of dead in the Rue des Rosiers. The rescue of Marc Vallon was almost impossible, but here was Babette, with her voice stronger and her body steadier every minute, suggesting something that could be done.

"David, Fanny's father-in-law, Didier Leblanc's father, is a jailer at La Roquette. Fanny always swore he took bribes from the prisoners. If he got a big enough bribe he might let Marc escape ..."

"Leblanc!" said David. "I know him! I talked to him for ten minutes, the day we had permission to visit the archbishop! A little man, blond growing bald, with a cringing manner and can't look you in the face? What a fool I am. He even mentioned his son Didier, and I didn't put two and two together! But Babette, darling, a jailer may take bribes to get his prisoners tobacco, or absinthe, or a smuggled letter, but to let a man escape from a conviction by Rigault would mean signing his own death warrant."

"Old Leblanc *likes* Marc," she said forlornly. "Maybe if I talked to him ... if *you* took me inside La Roquette –"

"You're not going anywhere till you've had food and sleep," said David firmly. "I'll fetch Emily March. You remember her, don't you?"

"Your Red Cross lady?"

"She's a very good nurse, and she'll look after you while I see what I can do for Marc." He kissed her, feeling like Judas. There was nothing he could do for Marc at that moment, nobody would be allowed to leave the Legation while the battle was raging with renewed fury; all he could do was get a message to the agents who would see to the disposal of the body in the Vine House. He found Emily March, who had come into the city with an ambulance on Monday, arguing with Mr Hoffmann, who had forbidden her to go out.

"I've brought you a new patient, Emily," David said. "Babette Mercier's here, lame from exhaustion. She – er – got away from the fighting in Montmartre and walked all the way across Paris through the night – little heroine that she is!"

He remembered that he must not explain the extent of Babette's heroism.

"But what brings her to the American Legation?" asked

260

Emily coolly. "What's so heroic about that?"

"She came to ask help for a friend in La Roquette. Will you please do what you can for her, Nurse March?"

"Certainly, Mr Meade."

In a very short time Babette was lying in a white bed in a clean bare room where there were three other empty beds, receiving a blanket bath at Emily's impersonal and competent hands before being put into a fresh nightgown. Then she was given a glass of hot milk, heavily sprinkled with sugar to cover the taste of a soporific, and saw Emily smile for the first time as she drained the glass.

"Is the American Legation a hospital now, mademoiselle?"

"Not yet," said Emily March. "This is one of the rooms fitted up for the German refugees Mr Washburne sheltered during the war. Luckily there are plenty of surplus clothes the American Ladies' Committee sent in for their use, so we can fit you out. You can't wear this dress again, that's for sure."

Babette relieved her feelings by putting out her tongue at the closing door. Now she was on a par with the destitute Germans for whom the United States had been the Protecting Power – she had quarrelled with David about that – and from the roof above her head the Stars and Stripes was flying. She was still lucid enough to see the irony of her situation, but when sleep came her only thought was of her lover; her prayer, that he was still alive.

Marc Vallon *was* alive, and after the first twenty-four hours were over had recovered from the shock of being behind bars, a prisoner. He had been defeated, wounded, sick while he was fighting the Prussians, now he had the humiliation of being thrown into jail by Frenchmen who hated all he stood for, as he hated them. His fear for Babette only exceeded his hatred of the Reds, and while she was making her nightmare journey across Paris her lover was praying that she was safe behind the bolted door of the studio which had been the setting of their love. Next morning he began to take courage. Their soldier guards, who had delighted in shouting out such news as the burning of the Tuileries and the defence of the Place de la Concorde, were sulky now and had stopped bawling insults at the captives. Any man with military experience could tell there had been news of a defeat.

Then, in the milling crowd of prisoners for whom there were no cells large enough, Marc had the good fortune to bump into Edward Carey – changed in appearance from the dandy English art student who had followed with such difficulty the language and the arguments of the painters gathered round the table at the Café Guerbois, but not changed at all in his massive self-assurance, now transformed into an entirely British optimism which did Vallon good. Asked how he came to be in La Roquette, Carey said he had been 'sold', as the French were fond of saying. *Vendu*, framed, any word you liked, but he knew who'd done it, and he'd settle accounts with the swine some day. Richard Wallace knew it too, in fact he'd given him a hint some time ago, and he was quite sure that when he didn't show up at the stables to go on duty the night the Vendôme column was destroyed, Mr Wallace had gone to work to find out what had happened, and enlist Lord Lyons's help to get him out.

"Monsieur Wallace and the British Ambassador should be a powerful combination," said Marc. "The question is, will they get to Rigault in time?"

"Perhaps the Versaillais will come in first."

"Don't deceive yourself, *mon vieux*! If the Versaillais were to reach the Rue de la Roquette, Rigault would give orders to have the lot of us mown down by machine-gun fire rather than see his hostages go free. You heard the execution squads in the yard last night? They were drawing lots for each batch of victims, while the Tuileries burned."

More than the Tuileries had burned by now. The calamity which had silenced the jeering guards at La Roquette was the burning of the Hôtel de Ville, the repository of three hundred years of Paris history and the scene of their own great triumph, by order of the Commune itself. They had adopted the scorched earth policy of Raoul Rigault, and through the Thursday of what was already being called *la semaine sanglante* – "Bloody Week" – the Palace of the Legion of Honour, the Palace of Justice, the Finance Ministry, the Council of State and other public buildings had been incendiarised. Paris was a sea of flame. "It's our red dawn!" exulted the Red Virgin, while the government troops, already out of hand, became uncontrollable in their desire for victory and the summary execution of the revolutionaries.

Raoul Rigault did not live to see the burning he had planned. The advancing Versaillais caught him in a cheap hotel in the Rue Gay-Lussac, where by coincidence the first German shells to fall inside Paris during the Siege had exploded in January. Bismarck had sworn to burn down Paris, and had failed. It took Frenchmen themselves to do that. On 24 May 1871 the leading arsonist, Rigault, was shot dead by a sergeant of the regular army and left in the gutter, where his body, partly covered by a cloak, was stripped by the loose women of the district and left to rot for two days – the end of a terrorist who had ceased to terrorise.

But if the dreaded Procureur lay like a dead rat in his

gutter, the even more terrible Prefect of Police was still alive, and had established himself in the *mairie* of the Eleventh Arrondissement, on the Boulevard Voltaire, close to Belleville and the heart of the Commune's resistance. It was in the hands of the 66th Belleville National Guard, which had failed to hold the Point du Jour Gate, but had fought fiercely before surrendering at the Opéra. Didier Leblanc, now an artilleryman of minimal experience, was one of the 66th who urged Theophile Ferré to proceed with the execution of the hostages in La Roquette, beginning with a batch of six unspecified prisoners. Ferré needed no encouragement. He wrote his order to Governor François: six hostages to be executed, 'and particularly the Archbishop.'

All the prisoners knew and were silent when Archbishop Darboy and five other priests were led into an alley inside the prison to face a firing squad chosen from volunteers of the 66th. The archbishop blessed each priest in turn and stood up to die with faith and courage. His executioners ripped open his body with their bayonets and carried it away. None of them noticed that one of the jailers who had led out the hostages, an elderly man called Leblanc, had difficulty in concealing his tears.

It was to the *mairie* on the Boulevard Voltaire, the headquarters of the Commune since the burning of the Hôtel de Ville, that David Meade drove with Babette in the Legation cab next morning, by a route of many detours to avoid the still burning buildings and the scraps of blackened paper with which the air was filled. Fighting was going on in the eastern area, chiefly round the barricades of the Bastille, where the Women's Battalion was in action again, the new casualties including the wounded Elisaveta Dmitrieva. David and Babette were

264

inured to the sounds of conflict, but silently hoped that the Stars and Stripes displayed on the cab would be a talisman against the virulence of Théophile Ferré.

As luck would have it, Ferré was at the Belleville *mairie*, the Twentieth, which was being used as a refuge for the new widows and orphans of the Federal side, and David's position at the American Legation entitled him to an interview with Delescluze, still the nominal leader of the Commune. The old man had been shaken by the murder of the archbishop – "What a war! What a war!" he kept repeating to the American – but in spite of Meade's eloquent plea for freedom for Marc Vallon, a veteran of the Prussian War, he refused to sign an order of release. He could not interfere with what he called without a blush the due process of law. But he granted Meade's second request, an order to see a jailer called Louis Leblanc, whose daughter-in-law, a Federal soldier's wife, was seriously ill.

"No luck," said Meade briefly, when he rejoined Babette in the cab, "and I hardly expected it. It all turns on Leblanc now, please God we don't meet his son en route. I saw some of those fellows at the *mairie* wearing the insignia of the 66th. Now listen, Babette! I'm going to make the cab wait about five hundred yards from the prison gates. You walk forward alone and wait until you see me come out. Then stand still and look up. Don't wave or signal, don't try to look for Marc, just wait till I come up to you to take you back to the Legation."

"David, dear, everyone has been wonderful to me at the Legation, but I'd rather not go back there. Every bed is needed for the wounded now."

"Why, where else can you go?"

"Home to the studio."

"Dangerous."

"You told me everything had been cleaned up at the

Vine House. And Marc would want to find me at home when he's set free."

"Oh my dear—"

"He *will* be freed, I know it, and then we'll be married, David—thanks to you."

"Don't thank me yet," the man said grimly, and they drove in silence away from the classic beauty of Paris, now reduced to smouldering ruins. He was only slightly more hopeful when he came face to face with Leblanc the jailer, who began by his usual whine that Meade's visit would get him into trouble, prison warders weren't expected to have visitors from foreign legations, but that stopped when the first few francs were slipped into his hand. Yes, he was sorry about Comrade Vallon, he was a nice fellow, and Fanny's sister was a nice little girl, but as to planning his escape, it was impossible . . . impossible . . . A thousand francs, did you say? Well, there might be half a chance, it all depended . . . How would the money be paid?

No, he wouldn't let Meade see Comrade Vallon, that would give the game away; but he would tell Vallon that M'selle Babette had gone to get help for him at the American Legation, and take him to the window above the great gate in ten minutes and let him stand there for five. Thank you, *mons*—citizen, as gold chinked again. And would the American diplomat speak up for him, if by any chance the government took over the prison of La Roquette? After all, he was a sworn servant of the French Republic, not of the Commune! Meade shook the jailer's hand, which was clammy, and heard his true thought revealed in his parting whisper: "It wasn't right, what they done to the archbishop. He was a good man."

Marc was taken to the window above the gate and watched the crowded Rue de la Roquette. He saw Meade come out and cross the street before he identified

Babette. She was wearing an unfamiliar dress, an ugly green plaid, and a round hat which didn't suit her, but she was there. Not a smile, not a wave, nothing that would make her conspicuous in that crowd of shrieking women and cursing men: the face he only knew as loving and laughing was pale and steadfast. He gazed until the jailer touched his arm. "Trust me," said Leblanc. "You'll see her again."

The next day was the day of the *pétroleuses*, the 1871 equivalent of the knitting women of the great Revolution, the *tricoteuses* who had sat beside the guillotines and marked the number of the executed into their knitting. There was nothing as simple as knitting in 1871: the *pétroleuses* were in the first place members of Elisaveta Dmitrieva's Union des Femmes who subscribed for the 'purchase of petrol and weapons for women prepared to fight'. The Egorovs had been the principal providers of petrol in Montmartre, but there were others like the Jaclard cell and French Communard groups who had procured petrol for the destruction of private property. Not everyone could aspire to burn down the Tuileries or the Hôtel de Ville, but any woman could carry petrol in a milk can with a long sulphur match attached to the neck. A match ignited, a spurt of flame, a milk can thrown through a cellar window, and there was a bourgeois house set on fire, and the fire travelling greedily up a street. "In war," wrote Karl Marx, "a fire is an arm as legitimate as any," and he asserted that "the Commune used fire strictly as a means of defence."

Les pétroleuses became another legend of the Commune. Thanks to Elisaveta Dmitrieva they were highly organised, and many of them paid for their incendiarism with their lives. The government troops, seeing Paris burning all around them, shot first in every case of suspected arson, and as the Federals were driven, like rabbits in a mown hayfield, into an ever narrowing circle, MacMahon's men rounded up their prisoners and sent them off in chains to prison at Versailles. The discovery of the archbishop's gutted body in an open ditch at the cemetery of Père Lachaise was the last straw. From then on no mercy was shown to the vanquished.

There was fighting all round La Roquette, but Governor François held the prison like a fortress. There were now so many hostages doomed to die that they were kept in the yard under armed guard, and taken out to be shot in batches. A group of priests were told they were free to go and were shot down one by one as soon as they were clear of the gates. On Friday fifty hostages were taken at the same time to the Rue Haxo and butchered in a courtyard there.

It was when the news of this atrocity was carried back to the prison by the jubilant executioners that Marc Vallon and Edward Carey began to lose hope. They had kept together in the yard, always watching the movements of Louis Leblanc, who was careful never to be seen watching them.

"I don't believe we've a hope in hell," said Carey on that Friday evening.

"Leblanc told me Babette went to the Americans for help," said Marc. "The Americans couldn't save the archbishop, I don't see why they should put themselves out for you and me."

"Leblanc told you to trust him, though."

"I never thought Leblanc was trustworthy."

Yet as darkness fell on that Friday evening, as one hundred and fifty hostages were crowded into the yard of La Roquette awaiting death, Leblanc sidled up to Marc and told him Governor François had given orders for their execution by twos, beginning in half an hour. "I'll let you back inside the prison," he whispered. "Barricade yourselves in, it's your only chance. The Versaillais are on their way."

The prisoners refused to believe him. Go *back* inside the prison — it was folly, it was another trick to gratify their torturers with a new way of death. It took the combined authority of Vallon and Carey to force the majority to go back through the door Leblanc had opened and tear up the floor boards for barricades. The return became a rush when it was seen that those who lost their heads and made a dash for freedom were instantly shot down. Bleeding hands tore at the flooring, the doors of the cells, the bars which were all they could use as weapons. They were soon attacked by the execution squads, which set fire to the horsehair mattresses and tried to smoke them out.

"We'll be burned alive!" Marc heard a youngster wail, and he shouted, "No, we won't! Throw that burning rubbish back on those devils and then attack! Give them 'Kill, burn, destroy' until they sicken! Follow the Englishman and me!"

It was a battle of men armed with bars and bare fists against men with rifles, but the riflemen were blinded by the smoke of their own fires and overwhelmed by prisoners driven mad by the fury of freedom. Amazingly, they began to retreat. Carey and Vallon encouraged their followers to hang on. They still had a chance, they were alive, and help was coming. Some of them were wounded, all blackened by smoke and dirt, none had food or drink through that long Saturday when they heard the sounds of a desperate battle in and around the cemetery of Père Lachaise. It raged until Whit Sunday morning, 28 May. Then the Marines of the government broke into La Roquette and set the prisoners free. Louis Leblanc was still alive, and still saying, "The archbishop would say I done right. He was a good man!"

At about the same time the very last bastion of the Commune, the heights of the Parc des Buttes Chaumont, surrendered, and, in the place where he had begun his courtship of Fanny Mercier, Didier Leblanc died in the last firing of his *mitrailleuse*.

It was only a few hours after that, while the long files of Federal prisoners were crawling west towards Versailles, prodded by bayonets, struck by the parasols of fine ladies, shot on suspicion of arson in the treeless wastes of the Bois de Boulogne, that Marc Vallon came home from the wars for the second time. He shook his head at Madame Camille when she came out of her *loge* with an offer of help. He had said goodbye to Edward Carey when the Englishman went off with the anxious Richard Wallace. He didn't need either of them this time, because he knew where help lay. It was in the arms of the girl who loved him, and when she opened the door of the place they called home he only said, "You saved me, Babette," and fell on his knees at her feet.

20

You saved me, my darling; you saved me, my brave girl. He said it again and again between the kisses which turned to passionate lovemaking, and only when their passion was sated did Babette, stroking Marc's dark hair and tracing his strong features with one hand, tell him it was not she who had saved him, but David Meade.

"That's not what *he* says."

"You've seen him?"

"He was at La Roquette when Governor François surrendered, along with Carey's Mr Wallace."

"Was *Carey* in La Roquette too? And did old Leblanc let you both go?"

He told her about the mass escape encouraged by the jailer who had never got over the murder of the archbishop.

"Meade offered him a thousand francs to let you go. Now you say over a hundred men escaped. At ten francs a head, David Meade got a bargain."

"But a thousand, darling! How'm I ever going to repay it?"

"Has he asked you for it?"

"Not yet. He was too busy telling me how you walked all the way across Paris, that night of all nights, to let him know what had happened to me and ask for help."

"Did he also tell you what happened at the Vine House?" asked Babette, and Marc tightened his grasp on her bare shoulders.

"Yes, he did."

"Do you care?"

"I've killed too many enemies to worry about one more."

"I thought it might disgust you with me."

"*Disgust* me! I love you more than ever – my little soldier!"

"I was really going after Louise Michel. I thought she turned you in . . ."

"Yes, she did, so Wallace said. But she turned herself in, this morning after the surrender, when she heard they were holding her mother hostage, and now she's on the long march to Versailles."

I hope they send her to the guillotine, thought Babette, but she did not say it aloud. She had seen dreadful things on her drives through the blazing streets of Paris with David, but she guessed that Marc had seen far worse, and words like 'guillotine', '*pétroleuse*' and 'firing squad' were to be avoided. In fact Marc had seen the beginning of the mass executions at the prison of La Roquette. Governor François had been formally arrested and later stood trial for his part in the murder of Archbishop Darboy, for which he was executed, but the massacre of the hostages in the Rue Haxo roused the government troops to such a frenzy of revenge that they herded their Commune prisoners into the yard of La Roquette and shot them there, to the total number of nineteen hundred. The stench of cordite and the reek of blood were still in his nostrils, and he allowed the subject of Louise Michel to drop.

What he wanted to say, and Babette wanted to hear, was that they must be married as soon as possible. "Ask me again when we're out of danger," she had said once, and now the danger or at least the civil war was over he would ask her every day if that would please her. He had been planning it all while he was in prison. They would be married at the *mairie*, where Théophile Ferré was no longer mayor, and then in church, and then they would get out of this nightmare city and start their life as painters in the country. Babette agreed to everything. The Rue des Rosiers had become a place of death, the Rue St Jean led to the Vine House and a terrible memory. She wanted to leave as much as Marc did, but she said her first 'No' when he proposed going to the Old Farm next day and telling Tante Lise and Fanny about their plans.

"Let's wait a day or two," she begged. "We don't know what happened to Didier, and you say you never saw his father again after the government troops came in. Maybe he was arrested, maybe he was shot. He might have been denounced as a spy. Madame Camille says everybody in Montmartre is denouncing his neighbour, and heaven knows Montmartre was Red enough in the beginning, though now you see the Tricolore hanging out of every window."

He agreed to wait, but not more than a couple of days. Marc, who had been a wounded man in a field hospital at Wörth, a hunted man in the snows of the Jura and finally a prisoner of the Commune, was longing to be free. He wanted to get away with his wife from the memories of their ordeal, he wanted with all his heart *to paint*.

As time went by, three hundred thousand written denunciations of those suspected of Red sympathies, sheltering Communards on the run after their defeat and, worst of all, throwing petrol in bottles, cans, soaked tow and fusees, were received in official quarters. One case which quickly came to light was the murder of Elvire de Grimont in the Rue de Rivoli. The spectators who recognised her had kept silent to save their own skins, but as soon as the First Arrondissement fell to Douay's troops the whispers and the rumours began. They reached Anne, Madame de Grimont's maid, in that vast sounding board, the St Honoré market. Horrified, she ran to Maître Gaucher's law office, and horrified he passed on the story to the all-powerful Richard Wallace.

"Ned, I've some bad news for you." The banality of the words made the story worse, and Edward Carey, who had come through the Mazas and La Roquette with his self-confidence unimpaired, broke down completely when Wallace told him that the woman he had loved, if lust were love, had been shot dead before a jeering crowd and buried in quicklime. He blamed himself, for being carried away by Elvire's charm, for compromising her, for believing her letter telling him she had gone to Versailles, for failing to go to the Rue St Florentin to make sure that she had really left Paris ... the storm of self-reproach went on while Mr Wallace listened in silence. He forbore to remind Carey that Elvire's husband had paid for his abduction on the night the Vendôme Column fell (that he had established beyond a doubt) and that Elvire's letter of dismissal, foolishly kept in Ned's wallet, had nearly caused his death.

For consolation he could only say that Elvire de Grimont was brave. She died trying to protect two helpless old people and their son, died taunting her murderer, died worthy of her name. "*Noblesse oblige!*" was a phrase Ned seemed to find comforting. His princess had died nobly, defending the poor. Presently he was controlled enough to hear what else Richard Wallace had to say. Yes, he was leaving Paris. He had given his word to his father to return to England in May, and this red May was nearly over. As to what he would do there ... He listened to Mr Wallace's proposal, and agreed to think about it. Meantime he would gladly take a message to Marc Vallon.

So it was Edward Carey who was the first visitor to the studio where he had once lived himself, and where Babette had spent most of the last day of May in screwing up her courage to go back to the Old Farm. Messages carried by the ever-useful Adrien Jaloux had assured her that Madame Verlet was safe and well, Fanny always improving; it was Fanny she was afraid to face, scared, she said, "to hear Didier's dead and and scared to hear he's still alive." Carey was made very welcome, and Carey in an English suit with a black cravat and a bowler hat with a narrow brim looked very unlike the prisoner of La Roquette.

"I've come to say goodbye," he told them. "I'm leaving tomorrow, by coach to Calais and then by the packet boat to Dover."

"Oh, Carey," exlaimed Babette, "don't you know we're getting married? Won't you stay for our wedding? You'd only have to wait a few days longer!"

"Have you set the date?"

"Saturday week, the eleventh of June," said Marc. "That was the earliest day they could guarantee a *maire-adjoint* to perform the civil ceremony."

"I wish I could be there, and I'll drink your health in England, but my parents are anxious to have me back. And Mr Wallace – but I'm starting to tell my story the wrong way round."

"I thought Monsieur Wallace was great on Sunday," said Marc.

"Greater than you know. He took it upon himself to pay

the jailer, old Leblanc, the thousand francs David Meade promised him if he connived at your escape. Said you couldn't afford to repay a thousand francs, and Meade wasn't a rich man, but he was ... and you know, Marc, a thousand francs to Richard Wallace is like two sous to you and me."

"He's very, very generous," said Babette. "How I wish I could meet him and thank him!"

"He wants to meet you both when he comes back from London. But meantime he thought you'd like to know that he's given old Leblanc a job at Bagatelle, supervising the gardeners who're going to get the rose garden back into shape. Said a man who set a hundred prisoners free was a hero in his own way, but hardly likely to keep his job as a jailer."

"I don't believe Leblanc knows a thing about gardening," said Babette, and laughed the light laugh which made him see her as cheeky Babette again, and not as strained and serious as she had been when he first came in. She'd been through the mill since the generals were shot across the street, and she must have been crazy while Vallon was in prison. She was cheerful enough now as she fetched brandy, water and glasses, and they all lit cigarettes.

"Mr Wallace had another job to offer," said Ned, after he had admired Study in White on the familiar easel. "For me this time."

"Something to bring you back to Paris?"

"No, something to keep me in London. You know Mr Wallace was related to the late Lord Hertford?"

"It's common knowledge," said Marc drily.

"He's going to go on living here, at Bagatelle, but he means to keep the great collection of paintings at Hertford House in London. And he's asked me to be the first curator. No, wait a minute! I'm sure Babette feels I know as much about painting as Leblanc knows about gardening, but he thinks I'm a pretty good organiser, and so he's offered me the job." What Mr Wallace had said was "You're a first-rate administrator, Ned, you proved that again and again in your work for the Charities Fund and the Ambulance."

"Living among great paintings – how splendid for you, Carey," said Babette. "What exactly will you have to do?"

"I don't know, because I'm not taking it on," said Ned. "I told Mr Wallace so this afternoon. I made a promise to my father, and this is one I'm going to keep."

He closed his eyes on their surprised faces, and behind his lids he saw his future. He saw the gates of a great textile mill in Lancashire, and above the gates in tall letters of gilt the name of Carey and Son.

The news about old Leblanc's good fortune decided them to go to the Old Farm next day. It was a glorious afternoon, the first of June, and the rose bushes in the Rue des Rosiers which had been trampled down when the generals were murdered had put out fresh shoots, and even a few blooms, and they talked about their wedding as they passed the spot where Marc was taken prisoner only a week before. It was discouraging to find that Fanny's father-in-law had been at the Old Farm before them, with news which had restored Fanny to her old position of tearful importance and complete inattention to anyone's concerns but her own. Didier was dead, had died a hero's death (said his widow) defending his machine-gun position in the Parc des Buttes Chaumont. His father had all the particulars from a Federal, now in hiding from the avenging regulars. "All his comrades said Didi was very brave," sobbed Fanny. "I know he had his faults, but it'll always be a comfort to me to know he died for what he believed in. And he's buried there in the park where we met, and were so happy, only two years ago! Oh Didi, Didi, who would have thought then that it would end like this!"

Who would have thought, that summer night in 1869, that the Parc des Buttes Chaumont would hold the funeral pyres of hundreds of Federals killed in action, or shot on the spot by the conquerors? In the Luxembourg gardens, where Federals or suspected arsonists were being shot in batches of six, the pyres were burning too, and continued to burn for days after the street fires and the ruined public buildings had ceased to smoulder. Those who collapsed on the death march to Versailles were given the *coup de grâce* as they dropped out and buried where they fell, sometimes before the breath had left their bodies, so that a hand or a foot could be seen feebly moving below the freshly turned earth. Babette knew nothing of this, but she had her own memories, and kept her eyes turned away from the Vine House when Madame Verlet followed them into the cobbled yard.

"I'm so happy for you both, my dears," Tante Lise whispered as she kissed them, "and so will Fanny be, when she's got over the shock the old man gave her. Come again soon." She never said to Babette, "Where were you, all through the Bloody Week? How did you live and what did you do?" Madame Verlet had her own ideas; she had watched the strange workmen who came with bags of tools and buckets of whitewash to the Vine House, but she stayed away from them and kept her ideas to herself. Babette and Marc were together again, and the war was over.

"I wonder if we're expected to join in the canonisation of Saint Didier," said Marc as they walked home, but Babette did not laugh.

"Fanny's right about one thing," she said. "Didier did die for what he believed in. The workers *ought* to have a living wage, and family allowances, and free medical care, and decent homes to live in instead of slums like the Impasse du Drapeau. Didier may only have been parroting off what he heard said by cleverer men, well, agitators if you like, but he did believe in these things, and they are the truth."

"I quite agree, but you can't come at family allowances and free medical care by murder and arson."

Babette giggled in her old irrepressible way. "Oh darling, I'm so glad we've had a rehearsal for marriage!"

"So am I, but why?"

"Because if I were a nervous young bride I'd probably burst into tears if you spoke to me like that. You do snub me sometimes – sweetheart."

"You've got a sharp little tongue of your own – and I adore you."

Postal and telegraph services were quickly restored, and next morning Marc received two letters, one from his mother and sister in Biarritz, which eased his mind about them, and the other, to his great delight, from Pierre Auguste Renoir. "He'll be in Paris today," Marc told Babette. "He suggests we meet at Drouot, if it hasn't been incendiarised, and find some bistro for lunch. You don't mind?"

"I think it's a great idea. I'll ask Madame Camille to come up and help me with my wedding dress."

"What can she do to help? What are you going to wear?"

"Ah-h! What are you?"

"That's the problem. And here's another, darling. What about the witnesses?"

"Fanny for me, I suppose. Only she'll weep at the *mairie*, and say it was there Dr Clemenceau married her

279

to her darling Didi."

"I'd like to ask Renoir to be my witness. What do you think?"

"I think it would be marvellous. Oh darling, do ask him!"

"Right, I will."

She thought it was eagerness to ask the people at Drouot, old Moïse particularly, about the picture auctions starting up again, that took him into the city so early, but Marc had another objective: he wanted to see what the war had done to the Rue Vavin, which he had heard was badly shelled. It was tragic to see Montparnasse laid waste, the *quartier* where he was born, went to school and church, won his scholarship to the Beaux Arts and joined the army, and the Rue Vavin was the worst hit of all. His parents' apartment, his father's prosperous little oil-and-colourman's shop had disappeared from the face of the earth. Marc walked back down the Boulevard Raspail, past the Croix Rouge where a pitched battle had been fought only a week before, and across the Seine. There were streaks of red in the river from all the blood shed in parks and barracks as 'expiation within the law' took its terrible course, and a straggle of women, suspected *pétroleuses*, were being herded up the Rue de Rivoli on the start of their twelve-mile tramp to imprisonment at Versailles.

The whole thing made him feel ashamed to be a Frenchman, but Renoir's genial company raised his spirits, and he was wildly elated when he returned to Babette.

"Yes, he'll do it. He'll be a witness to our marriage, both at the *mairie* and in church, and he says if we like he'll rent a little house for us near his mother's, where we can all paint together for a few weeks until you and I go to the coast. I told him we wanted to paint light on the sea as Monet did, and he said Monet's coming back from London

280

soon. The trains are running again and everybody's on the move."

Everybody's on the move. That was what jovial Dr Quimby said when he came with Emily March to say goodbye to the American diplomats at the temporary Legation at Versailles, which was about to close its doors.

"I'd no idea we were going to lose you so soon, Emily," said David Meade with formal politeness, aware that others were looking on.

"Nor had I, until Miss Barton's telegram arrived. She feels that my work here is done, and she needs me in London. I'm glad to be making the trip with Mr and Mrs Wallace."

"Glad to be leaving France?"

"Glad to be leaving Satory," she said with tightened lips. "It isn't a hospital any more, it's a prison camp! A place of execution where the condemned dig their own graves! Where I've seen twenty thousand human beings 'processed', as it's called, before they're sent in cattle trucks to the hulks at Brest and Cherbourg. No wonder France has shocked and horrified the world!"

"Pat Quimby isn't shocked or horrified," said Meade, looking across the room at the laughing doctor. "He seems to be enjoying this send-off."

"Dr Quimby is going home to Boston to be married; he'll have forgotten Satory two months from now."

"You're harsh in your judgments, Emily. By the way, did you know that Babette Mercier and Marc Vallon are being married on Saturday? I'm going to the wedding in Montmartre."

"Married!" she said, with a spark in her eyes. "Your little heroine! Shall you feel inclined to forbid the banns?"

"I'll kiss the bride and wish the bridegroom joy."

He bowed to her stiff curtsy. She tightened the strings of her nurse's bonnet, buttoned her uniform cape to the chin, and turned to speak to Mr Washburne. So that was that, and David Meade had made his decision. Perhaps it was the wrong one, perhaps Emily March *was* the right wife for him, and he had thrown away a new life for them both because he couldn't get over, and never would, a pair of brown eyes, a wave of brown hair, and the smile of Babette Mercier.

Hundreds of exhausted people were leaving Paris, hundreds more were coming back to see what they could salvage from the ruins of their homes and workplaces. Among the early arrivals was the Duc de la Treille. He had no house in Paris, his spendthrift father having sold the ancient *hôtel* de la Treille soon after Elvire's marriage and his duchess preferring life on the Riviera, so he was not well known in the capital. Maître Gaucher, on whom he called two days later, noted that at forty the duke was still a handsome man, a masculine version of his sister, and dressed in deep mourning.

He had arrived in time to be the chief mourner at the funeral of his mother, whose living death had ended at Versailles, and he first faced his brother-in-law, Hubert de Grimont, across the old duchess's grave. They did not shake hands, but neither did they quarrel publicly, and he told the lawyer why.

"When that man Perle brought me your letter at Orléans," he said, "and I learned that Grimont had stripped my sister of money and jewels and all the comforts of her home, I meant to pick a quarrel with him for some trifling reason and then challenge him to a duel."

"You used to be known as a dead shot, *monseigneur*."

"Thank you. But when I reached Paris and saw all the devastation, I had second thoughts. I went to the foot of the Rue St Florentin, where they told me the barricade was, and saw men repairing the roadway. They were pouring fresh cement at the corner of the Rue de Rivoli."

His voice shook. "When I realised that my sister, whatever remains of her, lies *down there*, I wondered what good the revenge I planned would do. Nothing will bring her back to life. And there has been too much killing, maître. I was told at the Jockey Club that more than twenty thousand Parisians died during the Bloody Week and after. A holocaust!"

"More than in the whole of the French Revolution."

"We have to think of the future now, as I told my wretched brother-in-law after the funeral. I thanked him for his care of my mother, and reminded him that a breath of scandal about Elvire's death would certainly cost him his position as the Minister of Justice. So, with that threat as blackmail, I got what I wanted from him."

"Which was?"

"The right to bring up his son with my own. Young Alain's a fine lad. He gets on splendidly with his cousins. He shares their schoolroom and their outdoor sports. Their tutors will give him a first-rate education until it's time to prepare him for St Cyr."

"You intend him to follow the profession of arms, then?"

The duke rose, and ended the interview with a little bow. "We are a military family, Maître Gaucher," he said.

"Quite so," said the lawyer, with a deeper bow. When the distinguished visitor had gone he sat at his desk wondering about the military future of Alain de Grimont, and if he would be a serving officer or a retired general when the next war with Germany began. Maître Gaucher was one of the thinking Frenchmen who believed like Marc Vallon that the surrender of Alsace and Lorraine was the certain prelude to a great war.

Not everybody thought of the lost provinces, for there was optimism in the air. Monsieur Thiers spoke of the convalescence of France, and pointed out that in the midst of civil war his government had achieved one astonishing success. The first instalment of the reparations France had agreed to pay to Germany was handed over almost immediately after the fall of the Commune, and two Departments had been cleared of the Army of Occupation. Delescluze walked out to die on the barricades. Ferré was shot at Satory and Louise Michel was transported to a penal settlement in the South Pacific, while Courbet, who had brought down the Vendôme Column, fled into perpetual exile in Switzerland to escape a prison sentence and an enormous fine. The terrible year was over.

St Pierre de Montmartre could claim to be the oldest church in Paris, once a place of worship of the Druids. The fabric, destroyed more than once by the accidents of war and time, was still surviving in June 1871, squat and heavy at the highest point of the Butte Montmartre. Inside it was very dark, and one side chapel next to the choir was lit only by two candles on the altar and the sunshine admitted through a narrow window in the thick stone wall. But to David Meade, standing next to Madame Verlet, all the radiance of the June world outside was embodied in the pretty bride, dressed in pink, on whose finger the tall and handsome bridegroom was slipping the wedding ring.

Like all hastily arranged weddings, theirs had been a triumph of confusion. There was red tape to be cut at the disorganised *mairie* of Montmartre, there was peace to be made with a Church only too well accustomed to hearing confessions of living in sin and the taking of human life, there was Fanny to coax into being Babette's witness ("nobody wants to see a poor widow at a wedding"), there was giving up the studio on their ill-omened street, and plans to be made for a new life at Le Havre. There was the problem of the wedding dress, for Babette had nothing to wear but last summer's pink muslin, laundered and pleated to perfection by Madame Camille. Fanny had fashioned a little wreath of pink silk appleblossoms for the bride's dark hair, at the same time making a decidedly attractive black veil for herself. There were the paintings to be packed and put in storage at the Old Farm, where new arrivals only added to the pleasant confusion. The two artists who had gone to Italy at the start of the war with Prussia came back and occupied their old studios, and even the Vine House had new tenants, for the astute Monsieur Renard had rented it as separate apartments to two business men and their families from the boulevard, where their homes had been destroyed by *pétroleuses* now regretting their activities in the hulks. There were children in both families, whose noise and laughter filled the garden and drove away the old sinister silence, and if anyone had had time to look at the vineyard they would have seen the tiny grapes of a new vintage among the broad green leaves.

But they were married at last by Church and State, and left the dark old sanctuary hand in hand, Babette and Marc, a tearful Fanny with Renoir, and David Meade supporting the stout form of Madame Verlet. After the rages they had known, it was pleasant to find smiling people in the Place du Tertre, all happy to shout "*Vive la mariée!*" as the little group walked across the cobbles to the Pichet restaurant, where Madame Jaloux and her two sons were waiting to join them in a luncheon of classic proportions. All the guests had sent flowers, so that the little private room was a bower of beauty, and Babette, according to Renoir, 'the loveliest flower of all'. It was sheer flattery, of course, but it was not flattery when he rose to propose the toast of the bride and groom and wished them all success in their career as painters. The women laughed, and the Jaloux boys laughed while they applauded (Roger, the returned prisoner of war, was flirting discreetly with Fanny) at the idea of Babette as a painter. But twenty years later, when the struggling Independents had become the great Impressionists, the name of Elisabeth Mercier was famous among them, the equal of Berthe Morisot and Mary Cassatt.

David Meade did not laugh at Renoir's prediction. After the healths were drunk he produced what he called a special present, a thick envelope addressed to Madame Marc Vallon. Babette broke the seal and exclaimed in surprise:

"A copy of the *Figaro*!"

"I didn't think you'd have time to read the paper this morning," smiled David, "so I brought it along. Turn to the back page."

And there it was, her old wish realised, Meade's sketch of Babette at the Fountain with her sabots and her pitcher, published in a Paris paper. Later on it was reproduced as a lithograph, but Meade on the road to celebrity was never more rewarded than when Babette herself threw her arms round his neck and kissed him with a whispered "*Merci!*" Marc and Renoir congratulated him heartily – Marc with his arm round his bride in a clasp which said to the artist:

"You may have the picture, *mon vieux*, but I've got the girl!"

Then Renoir began to tease Babette by saying he too had a present for her. No, it wasn't here, it wasn't at the Old Farm or even in Paris, but she would get it very soon and he hoped it would make her happy. She kissed him then, and there was a flurry of embracing as the time came to end the feast, and a hired *calèche* drove up to the door of Le Pichet. Among the cries of good luck and the cheers of the bystanders Babette thought she only fancied she heard Marc saying something about St Germain.

"Aren't we going straight to Louveciennes?" she asked him as they drove away.

"Louveciennes is for tomorrow, Madame Vallon," said her husband. "Tonight is Renoir's present. *Cocher*, drive to the station for the St Germain Railway."

She had an inkling, then, of what the present was, and when after twenty minutes in the train they got out at the station for the Ile de Chatou she knew that Renoir was giving them back the lovely past. They were going to La Grenouillère, where the proprietor, Monsieur Fournaise, was waiting with his family to welcome them. "We were delighted when Monsieur Renoir told us to expect you, and we hope you'll be comfortable, though we've never done much in the hotel line," he said. "It'll be great to have the painting gentlemen coming back to the restaurant, after all that mess in Paris. I've been doing some cleaning up this past week, and repairing the planks and the bridge at the bathing place. Maybe you'd like to stroll down and see it, before it begins to get dark?"

The bathing place was on the Ile de Croissy, and between the islands the Seine flowed softly, cleansed of the stain of blood and touched with the first gold light of sunset. The willows trailed in the water, the wild flowers starred the banks, and Marc drew Babette down to lie in his arms on the grass.

"This is our real beginning, darling," he murmured. "This is our wedding night."

"I'm so glad we're at La Grenouillère," she whispered. For both of them the river and the islands were almost sacred, evoking the images of the great paintings created there and the others which were to come. "It's too much happiness," said Babette. "Tonight, *here*, and tomorrow

287

our own little house at Louveciennes —"

"Then Le Havre, and learning to paint light on the sea," said Marc. "And if more of the country is free by Christmas, we can travel to Biarritz and see my mother while we're painting the Atlantic under the winter sun. Do you realise it, darling? We're free at last! We can go to L'Estaque and see Cézanne, we can paint what we like, go anywhere we like —"

"And when to Paris?" said his wife, kissing him.

"There's no reason to go back to Paris," said Marc Vallon. "The Paris we knew is dead."

"Yes, the Paris we knew is dead," said Babette. "But we must be there in time for the resurrection."